Stea's House

15

Betty's

Sam's Place

Last Chance

Embassy Club

Pool
Hall

to Newton

to Hickory
and Chunky

Thick & thin

A NOVEL IN
SEVEN STORIES

For my good friend John.

Preface

This book was written because of a friendly wager with my good friend John, on who would have a book in publication first. The theme of his book is some half-baked cookbook/mystery, while mine deals with life's larger issues, mainly growing up in small town USA. Thankfully, I won, because Lord knows we don't need another cookbook.

It goes without saying that this is a work of fiction; however, most of the places depicted were real. The cast of characters is strictly the result of my imagination, but since characters tend to be drawn from life experiences, I would like to take this opportunity to thank every individual I have ever known and who has known me, even those that mistook me for country music legend Don Williams. Since I grew up in Philadelphia and Decatur, that list is quite long, and my wish is that they not necessarily read the book, but at the very least, buy it.

Currently, I am working on my second Rango/Gimlet novel. If one of my books is ever picked to be sold in an airport gift shop, I will feel I have achieved success.

Don Williams
March, 2005

Contents

Introduction

It's not every day you find a friend like Theodore Thomas Anderson, Jr. To most everyone in the small town of Decatur, Mississippi, he was 'Gimlet'. He was my best bud through thick and thin. And while some people opted to call him Doughboy, Blimp Butt, or Lard Ass, I paid no attention to the exterior. Gimlet usually took offense to these unflattering comments and often ended up sporting a purple eye or swollen nose as a result of the altercations that ensued. He found no solace at home. When he complained to his mother, Miss Hortense, she would placate him with "it's a glandular condition" and the old standard, "it's what's on the inside that counts." During the times when Miss Hortense had had too much to drink, she would just smother Gimlet in a massive hug and call him her "lil' butterball." Gim had three older sisters, Tammy, Tootsie, and Tyrone. They once told me that Gim had actually been skinny up until he was about five years old, and that his mother had even given him worm treatments cause he wasn't filling out right. I guess they must have worked, because back then Ol' Gim could have

missed two or three days of eating, and nobody would have been the wiser. Of course, he never did miss two or three meals ever. Gim could make a platter of fried chicken or greasy pork chops disappear faster than croton oil thru a widder woman.

'Glandular condition', my ass.

In addition to being "pleasingly plump" Gimlet had an affinity for, what I would call, snug clothes, usually two or three sizes too snug. The combination of the tight threads on the usually bruised, ample body made for quite an interesting scene. Although he was my best friend, I hated the thought of walking down the street with him, especially if there was a chance we'd run into one of the local honeys.

Our friendship got off to an inauspicious start, as it's not everyday you make friends with someone you catch trying to steal your bike. But

never the types to hold grudges, we duked it out right then and there and have been close ever since.

As for me, Sidney "Durango" Spears, compared to my ace pal, I was just your average, hormone-driven teenager. I went by the nickname "Drango" 'cause the Drango Kid was always my favorite cowboy. Me and my buddies would ride our Western Flyers to the Saturday matinee and for one thin dime could see two cartoons and a double-feature western. We would argue for hours on the best cowboy: a mix that included Hop-a-Long Cassidy, Johnny Mack Brown, Lash LaRue, Roy Rogers, of course, and Ol' Durango. I liked all of 'em, but to me the name "Durango" seemed to fit the name of a real cowboy. After a while, all my friends, and even some of my teachers had shortened it to Rango. It had a nice ring to it. I spent a lot of time in high school imagining myself hearing the announcer at Tiger Stadium in Baton Rouge. "Rango Spears fades back to pass…he spots Crawfish Jones open in the end zone… Touchdown!"

In 1958 the population of Decatur, Mississippi, totaled fourteen-hundred, give or take a few. It was mostly filled with friendly, church-going, conservative Yellow Dog Democrats, who tended to work hard and believed in the "Early To Rise" creed. The town had two small groceries, a clothing store, a bank, a drug store, an appliance and hardware store, a movie theater that was only open Thursdays through Saturdays, and three cafes. The economy of the small town was held together by small farms, a shirt factory and the local junior college. Decatur was the county seat of Newton County, located right between two larger towns, Jackson and Meridian. Being the county seat, Decatur boasted a fine old county courthouse with the town square built around it. There were a bunch of magnolia trees on the grounds of the town square; in fact, we spent much of our formative years wasting time sitting in the shade.

On Saturdays the town square came alive when all the country folk came in to shop. Merchants would have drawings for cash prizes every week. It really took on the feel of a carnival. Around election time the rhetoric of lying political hopefuls would echo off the walls of the closely placed stores situated around the court square. Gimlet would often comment that, "If you could gather all the bull manure they put out, nobody'd need to buy fertilizer anymore."

Decatur, like any small southern town, had its allotted share of eccentrics. One of our favorites was Mr. Rufus A. Thomas, who usually showed up Saturday at Merchants Day 'bout half shit-faced and minding everybody's business but his own. When the political season was ripe, Mr. Rufus was in his element. He had a comment for every slick candidate, showing no favorites. During public debates, candidates often found themselves toe-to-toe with someone as silver-tongued as themselves. In fact, as Mr. Rufus' reputation grew, candidates began to refuse to speak, passing entirely to their opposition. Many would-be political careers in Newton County were over before they got started.

In addition to being best buds, Gimlet and I lived right next door to each other, which made it kinda nice when we needed to discuss the weightier problems of the world. Our houses were of middle class status, typical for the town of Decatur, with white frame houses and huge front porches in front and several big rockers in place. We were both raised by single mothers who worked at the shirt factory, my mom in production and Gim's, Miz Hortense, in some type of executive position. My father had died a couple of years after I was born, so we got a little Social Security check each month to help us make ends meet. Gim has never told me about his dad, but since Miz Hortense always had late meetings at the factory, she had a live-in housekeeper to cook, clean and pretty much make life miserable for Gim.

We called her Auntie Maw. She was part housekeeper, part caretaker, and full-time warden. A large black woman of indeterminate age, she ruled the Anderson household like Attila the Hun. She came from the colored section of town on the other side of the tracks and had a houseful of kids that pretty much fended for themselves. There were thirteen in all, twelve girls and one boy. She told me all their names one time, and I only remember the cool ones, Vagina, Clorox, Formica and Fetus. After that, I'd say the rest were kinda ordinary. I think there were two Bettys -- Betty I and Betty II. And an only son, Too Sweet. He was our age and was making a name for himself in the colored football community. There was talk several of the northern colleges were recruiting him pretty heavy going into our senior year.

Anyway, Auntie Maw and I had a good relationship for several reasons. For starters, I didn't live under her roof. Secondly, she could cook up some of the best groceries in the free world, and I had a standing invitation to put my Brogans under her table any time. My fondness for Auntie Maw also stemmed from the fact that she could get off some of the best zingers I'd ever heard, and they were almost always directed at Gim. I would always take her side, all in good fun. It might have stirred his pot every now and again, but I figured, what the hell, that's what best friends are for.

Thick and Thin

Early Rue and the Indians

Gimlet blew in his fist, making a shrill whistling sound that alerted me; he was calling another one of his all-important meetings. "What's up, Kemosabe?" I inquired of my pudgy friend, as we took our anointed seats on Gim's front porch.

"I wanted to talk 'bout football practice Monday. I'm thinking 'bout not going out this year."

"Not going out, Gim? Hell, you might have a chance to play a little this year and next year, prob'ly be a starter."

"Naw, Rango, I ain't sure it's worth it. I played tackling dummy last year, and ol' Bugger Barnes usually ended up knocking my jock strap in my hip pocket."

"Last year was last year, Gim. I hear Bugger's up in Parchman Prison raising turnip greens. You'd prob'ly have ol' Joe Don Watson try'n out for yo' position, and you know he's a candy ass. Only made first team cause his daddy's the school shyster."

"I don't think Coach Dick likes me, Rango. You 'member last year, when he had the manager put the red hot balm in my jock, and I blistered my jewels?"

"The manager swears that's bullshit, Gimme. Told me somebody thought your strap was a clean up rag and wiped the jar clean, that's all. What then? You gonna be one of those band homos and play yo' little skin flute at halftime, or you gonna be a real man and play a man's game. Besides that, you know the band homos get all the skanks, and football players get the real tang bush. Why, you might even have a shot at Betty Sue Mullins if you had that letter jacket."

"You not just saying that, are ya', Rango? You really think Betty Sue might go out with me?"

"If I'm lying, I'm dying. I kinda think she was a little sweet on ya last year, 'specially after you got to play in that last game of our freshman year and got in on that tackle."

One thing I liked about Gimlet; I could stretch the truth, embellish a little, or just flat out lie to him time after time, and it was like the next hour, the previous fib had been forgotten. The boy trusted me implicitly, which made me feel a little bad sometimes, but I always rose up and overcame that. Anyhow, Gimlet was a sucker for the old "girl likes him" story, and I must admit I had used it more times than I can remember.

"'Sides, Gim', you know we always get more to eat in cafeteria during the season."

That was the coup de grace, the straw and the nail. Gim looked at me, and I knew I had him.

"Ok, Rango, I'll go out this year, but I'm telling you, this might be my last time."

"An' Gim, we'll soon be seniors; the big dogs, the team leaders, and the poon' will be flocking to us. We'll have to fight 'em off with a stick."

"Aw, crap, Rango."

"Anyhow, what you wanna do tomorrow; you know this is our last weekend 'fore practice."

"You want to hitchhike over to Chunky and check out the forty-fives?"

"You got it, my man. Meet you here 'bout nine in the morning. Night, Gim."

"Night, Rango."

Just after nine the next morning, Gimlet and I went out on Highway 15, thumbing to Chunky to check out the used records store. It wasn't really a record store; the ol' dude owned a bunch of jukeboxes, and these were old used records he changed out. If you were real lucky, you could find some real classics. Last trip we took there, I found "Do You Remember?" by L. C. Cook and "Calling All Cows" by the Blues Rockers. I was still looking for "Pledging My Love" by Johnny Ace; this might be my lucky day. The fact that the records were, for the most part, old and worn out, mattered not one iota to us. We figured for a nickel a record it was hard to go wrong.

Anyhow, Gim and I were out on the road in the hot sun, trying to look presentable so a kind motorist would pick us up. Chunky was only ten miles away but was definitely too far to walk. A dozen or so cars had passed us by; most of them barely glanced at us, so we figured it might be a long day. I looked over at Gim; he had on his tight, tight black pants and equally tight Decatur High School t-shirt. Every time a car came by, old Gim would show all his ivories and look friendly. But to no avail.

"Gim, what you think, ol dude, we gonna be out here tomorrow morning at this rate. You wanna save it for another day? The natives ain't too friendly today."

"Nah, you give up too easy, Rango. I got a plan."

"Not another of yo' half-ass-get-us-in-big-trouble-havin'-us-clean-up-the-whole-courthouse-for-a-month type plan, I hope."

"Nah, nothing like that. This one's jam up and jelly tight."

"Let's hear it, big boy."

"All right, I'll lay down beside the road like I'm overcome with heat exhaustion; you be fanning me trying to cool me down, and somebody's got to stop to check us out, and you tell them that I have a diabetic condition, and you need to get me to Dr. Moore in Chunky."

"What's wrong with Dr. Kennedy here in Decatur?"

"Tell 'em Dr. Kennedy's out of town. Who's gonna know the difference?"

Against every instinct I had, I said, "Ok, let's do it, Gim."

"All right, Rango, see if you can find me some ditch water or something to sprinkle over me, so it'll look like I overheated."

"You always look overheated; you're sweating like a whore in church right now. Besides, it ain't rained around here in weeks."

"All right, forget the water. Lemme find a clean spot to lay down, and this plan's a done deal."

I'll bet, I thought to myself.

Gimlet lay down beside the road. I squatted down next to him with a piece of newspaper I found and commenced to get ready to fan at the first appearance of a vehicle. Twenty-minutes later this big black three-hole Buick, hauling major ass, came into view. The big roadster must of been doing 80, if it was doing ten. Gimlet did his best to look pathetic, which wasn't hard seeing how he could already pass for a beached whale, and I went into my windmill act with the paper. You could hear brakes squealing, as the big Buick's driver stood on the brakes for what seemed a full minute. A lot of tire rubber was left on old Highway 15 that day. The Buick went a good half-mile before it was fully stopped. The driver then commenced to back up to me and Gimlet at damn near the same speed as he was going forward. When the black angel finally stopped and rolled down the window, we saw then that the fates were going to get their jollies at our expense. For in fact the driver of this magnificent chariot was Early Rue Jones, a local entrepreneur and philanthropist, but mainly known as the town drunk extraordinaire, who puts Rufus A. Thomas to shame. Early Rue was a black man in his early 50s; he looked exactly the same as the first time I saw him some ten years ago. His skin was the color of coal and looked like somebody had greased his face with lard. Early Rue probably weighed in the neighborhood of 300 pounds, and his face was always lit up with a permanent smile highlighted with a mouthful of gold teeth. Everybody said Early was always happy 'cause he was always drunk. Anyhow, Early Rue kicked open the door of his black beauty and went sprawling right out in the middle of Highway 15. I hoped to hell another car didn't come along 'cause no way could we get that blimp butt off the road. Early Rue shook his head, looked around to get his bearings, patted his pockets to make sure his shine was still intact, and slowly focused his one good eye on me.

"Hey, white boy, what's hap'n?" Early Rue then spotted Gimlet laid out beside the road. "That fat

boy dead?" asked Early Rue, smiling ear to ear. The glare off his gold teeth blinded me instantly. Didn't matter if he was talking bout a funeral or a bottle of shine, Early always had the same go to hell expression. Well, 'bout that time, Gimlet knew that the game was up.

"Who you calling fat boy, fat boy?"

"That you, Gimlet Ass? How come you laying out by the road?"

"Had a little heat stroke, that's all. Thought I might need to go see Dr. Moore over to Chunky."

"Headed right that way; you white boys jump in and let's ride. You look like yo' need to see a doctor. Look like you might have a touch of 'iritus."

Now my friend Gimlet was commonly known as a hypochondriac. If there was a new disease to be had, cultivated, nurtured and played for all it was worth, ol' Gim was the perfect candidate.

"Well, I have been feeling a little crappy lately. Appetites' been off, and I feel like I'm losing a littl' weight. What's this 'iritus disease, anyhow, Early Rue?"

"Well, I'll tell you, boy. It's when yo' eye muscle and yo' ass muscle get crossed and you have a shitty outlook on life."

With that, ol' Early Rue fell across the hood of that three-hole Buick, sucking in great gulps of air between spasms of giggles. His black face got even darker, and tears were sliding down his greasy face faster that he could wipe them off. I've never seen a man — black, white or red — laugh like that. I thought for a time or two, Early was going to buy the farm. His whole body looked like one giant spasm as giggle after giggle shook that blubbery frame. Gimlet, of course, was not pleased.

"Early Rue, you ol' drunk, why don't you get yo black ass in that tank and get the hell out of here."

Well, that exchange made Early Rue really lose it then, and the belly spasms started all over again.

"Come on, white boy, just one of ol' Early's little jokes. You and yo' friend get in Early's love mobile, and I'll take you boys right to downtown Chunky."

"Thanks, anyways, Early, I guess we better be getting home," I says, backing away, as if Early was going to throw me in that Buick and take me to Chunky against my will.

"Come on, Gimlet, hadn't yo' ma got some chores for you to do?"

"Now hold on, Durango, ol' Early is going right to Chunky. We want to go to Chunky and sounds like a deal to me."

I looked at Gim to see if he was pullin' my leg or something. I thought maybe he was trying to make me sweat a little after that 'iritus joke that I rather enjoyed. But ol' Gim was just about as serious as I had ever seen him; either that, or he was using his best poker face.

"Huddle, Gim, I'm calling a huddle." If Gim and I wanted to talk things over and didn't want anybody to eavesdrop, one of us would call a huddle. That way we figured we could be cool and not hurt anybody's feelings. It was our inner circle. Population, two.

"Huddle it is, my man," said Gimlet, making his way down the road out of Early's hearing. "Early, we'll be right back to you. Have a little swig and unlax."

My blood was just about at 212 degrees when Gim finally made his way into the huddle.

"Are you crazy? I ain't riding with that drunk son of a bitch. He drives like a bat outta Decatur. He'll get us all killed. Actually, just you and me – the booze will keep his drunk-ass preserved."

"Cool it, Rango, ol' Early has had a little to drink, but have you ever known him to have a wreck? 'Side's that, Chunky's only ten miles; hell, we'll be there in fifteen minutes tops. What could possibly happen? Plus, I got a feeling yo' Johnny Ace records gonna be there. Hate for ya to miss that little classic."

"Gim, Early's drunk as ten Choctaws. He couldn't piss on the side of a barn he's so drunk, and you want to get my virgin, lily white ass in that… that… hearse?"

"Tell you what, we take the ride with Early, and I'll buy you a double chocolate malt over at Pearl's."

Now I liked a chocolate malt good as the next man, but I liked my unscarred butt even better. Gim could see I might be getting a little weak, so he threw in the dealmaker.

"And, I'll spring for an order of fries and gravy."

Damn.

Now ol' Gim had me just about over a barrel. A double chocolate malt and an order of gravy and fries. "That a full order or half order of fries, Gim?"

"Why, a full order of course. Only the best for my ace boon coon."

Shit. I just knew in my heart of hearts that I was getting screwed on the deal and that the malt and fries were somehow not going to be worth it. But, what the hell, I was sixteen years old, indestructible, looked, felt and smelled like a million bucks, and somehow, we'd work it out.

"All right, let's go, Gim, but let's try to be home by six."

"Done and done my man, let's move."

We walked back to the car to find ol' Early even more lit than before. His huge black shiny moon face, replete with a full rack of gold teeth, was beaming with the anticipation of sharing his car with two dumb ass white boys. Or maybe, he was thinking about Big Jack, the biggest bootlegger in the county, located right in the big city of Chunky, our destination.

"You all right, Early?"

"Damn straight, boy, let's roll," he said as he completely missed the door handle, lost his balance, and went sprawling against the car. "Jus' gettin' my sea legs, boy. Get in the car , and le's rock and roll."

"Front or back, Gimlet?"

"Front seat, then."

"Suits me."

"You two candy asses get in, iffin we's gonna get there by dark."

The first coupla miles went ok. Ol' Early was driving straight and true, the white road stripe never wavering. Only eight miles to go, I thought. This is gonna be all right. Little did I know.

Early was watching his speed, dipping between sixty and sixty-fiv, and driving like a champ. Even Gimlet relaxed a little. However, just ahead, was the thing that would spoil our perfect day. It was an old farm truck, rusted all over, about as much bondo as metal and smoking like a chimney. Inside, there appeared to be two Choctaws, one driving, one riding shotgun. The truck was piled to the brim with watermelons.

Well, there was one thing that was well known around Decatur. Choctaws and coloreds didn't mix, like oil and water, like croton oil and widder' women, like the Yankees and Dodgers. I chanced a quick sideways glance at ol' Early, who was already squinting and trying to focus on the vehicle now just ahead.

"Ain't that some damn' wahoos in that piece of shit truck?" Early roared.

"Cool it, Early, just some Choctaws taking a load of melons. Look, they not bothering anybody," I reasoned.

"Like hell they ain't. They's blocking my way."

"Early, they just moseying along on their own side of the road. They ain't doing nuthin'. Just pass 'em by. We 'bout to Chunky, anyhow."

"I'm gonna teach those damn injuns a lesson."

For the next mile or so, our drunk chauffeur decided he would drive within an inch of Tonto's ass.

"Sons of bitches, all they do is stay drunk all the time. Stole my daddy's land." And with that, Early goosed the old Buick up another thirty miles an hour and shot by the truck like it was standing still. As soon as Early cleared the truck, he slammed on the brakes and slowed to a crawl, enough so that the bondo truck had to slow down or run smack ass into Early's car, and, truth be known, several of the Choctaws were known to imbibe from time to time, so my money was on getting rear-ended by a truckload of watermelons. Luckily, though, the Choctaws were either teetotalers or needing to sell some seeds before they could friendly up to ol' demon rum; the bootlegger was a cash only dude. Anyhow, their truck slowed down and tried to keep a respectable distance behind the ol' Buick.

"See, Early, they minding their business. Stop the car, and me'n Gimlet'll walk on into town. Only 'bout two miles to go, anyhow." It was like I was talking to a cowpile or something. No response at all from the mega drunk. He just stared straight ahead, and speaking of Gimlet, my number one honcho had been quiet, much too quiet our entire ride.

"Gimlet, Gim, let's get the hell out of Dodge and walk on into town. Exercise'll do you good. Ya ready?"

Silence returned from the backseat. I turned around to check things out. Lo and behold, my ace buddy had a shit eatin' grin smeared all over his face, an empty pint bottle of Mad Dog 20-20 clutched tightly in his sweaty little hand.

Oh, hell, Gimlet, you stupid jack ass, I thought to myself.

I now had two drunks on my hands and a truck full of probably harmless native Americans and watermelons on my hip pocket.

"Ok, Early, Gim looks like he's gonna puke. Don' wanna mess up yo' nice vinyl now. Stop and we'll be on our way." My invitation to Early went by like a fart in a whirlwind. 'Bout that time the Choctaws, probably thinking bout some good shine, decided to pass the creeping black beauty and press on to Chunky and sell some produce. For some reason, this simple act of motoring didn't set too well with Early.

"Ya see them sum' bitches. Gave me the finger when they passed."

"I didn't see nuthin', Early. All they did was pass."

"Booo shit, I's gonna teach them red asses a lesson."

"Just let us out, Early. Don' told you Gim's 'bout to blow lunch." No reply came from Early, who now seemed oblivious to everything but the melon truck and red skins. Dropping the pedal, he shot by the melon truck like a cannon. My initial thought was that Early was gonna do another of his pass and slow games, but it was short lived. Not this lush. Early passed the truck, missing it by no more than a foot and slammed on brakes. How the old truck missed Early's rear end, I still don't know, but at that point I was grateful for any small favors. The truck screeched on the brakes, swerved to the left, swayed a few times, and came back in the right lane.

Now the Choctaws were ready to rumble. They were shaking their fists and shooting the bird to Early, as they pulled over to the side of the road to plot their strategy. Early did likewise. After a few minutes of hand gesturing and animated talk, the one riding shotgun jumped out and got in the back of the melon truck as the truck slowly pulled back on the road. Why we did we not jump out when Early pulled over to the side of the road, I'll never know. Anyhow, Early pulled right in behind the now rapidly accelerating truck

"Damn thing must be souped up to be moving that fas'," Early muttered under his breath.

Our caravan of two was now prob'ly pushing 70. The Choctaw war strategy was also becoming clear, for just at that moment

the point man reached down, picked up the largest melon he could lift, and tossed it right at Early's speeding car. The melon hit smack on the front radiator and burst into a million pieces. Two seconds later, another and another. Melons were making direct hits on Early's car and the windshield. Soon we were flying blind. Well, 'bout that time the Choctaws decided they were gonna' play Early's former game and slow down. Bad mistake. Early, by now, couldn't even see the centerline, much less the old truck stopped in the road. The Choctaws made up for that big mistake by abandoning ship, for the ol' black beauty was on a collision course with the truck. Two seconds later we were crashing into the back of the abandoned produce wagon. My one regret was that I wasn't outside to see the explosion of red and green. The whole deal, from the first sound of the crunching metal to the final hiss of the busted radiator, could've only been a few seconds, but to me it seemed like at least five minutes. They say that some melodramatic shit happens before you buy the farm, like your life passing before your eyes, but strangely enough I had enjoyed the hell out of this wild ride. After the thrill subsided, my first thought, other than checking to see if my ass was still in one piece, was Gim.

"Gim, Gim, you ok?' No reply.

Finally, I spotted Gimlet's grinning face through all the watermelon debris.

"You all right, Gim? I'm gonna whip yo ass for getting me in this crap."

Suddenly, a breakthrough.

"Right as rain, dude. How's Early?"

I had forgotten Early, the source of all our problems.

"Early, Early, you ok?"

Then came the spasm of giggling, and the whole car was shaking from Early's gutted laughter.

"Ain't funny worth a dam', Early. 'Bout bought the farm."

"Funny to me, white bread. Nothing like a nice Saturday ride."

"Ya'll both cut the shit. That sounds like a siren to me. Let me do the talking. Ya'll both so drunk you couldn't hit a bull in the ass with a bass fiddle."

That got Early's attention. Not the siren or the fact that the sheriff was on his way, but that Gimlet could have, must have, surely did drink som'a his Mad Dog.

"You little shit, you been in my good liquor."

"Shut the hell up, Early, the sheriff's pulling up. I told you, let me do the talking."

"You owe me two dollars for that bottle," Early hissed to Gim.

"Shut up, both of you."

"Anybody in there?" The booming voice of Sheriff Kincaid resounded through the car.

"Here, Sheriff. It's Sidney Spears. Gimlet, and ol' Early."

"You ok, Sidney?"

"Fine, Sheriff. Gimlet and Early just got the breath knocked out of them, and can't talk, but everybody's ok."

"Ya'll get out all right, Sidney, or you needing some help?"

"We coming, Sheriff, if we can get these melons out the way." Gim, ol' Early, and I probably looked like the north end of a south bound mule, but what the heck, we were alive to fight another day, and if I could keep ol' Early quiet, we might just laugh this off as just another fucked-up adventure.

"Hey, Shur'f Kincaid, how dey hanging?" Early yelled out as he staggered out of the car.

"Thought you couldn't talk, Early. You ain't been drinking, have you, boy?"

"Naw suh, you know I's quit drinking bout a year ago," lied Early, as he struggled to gain his equilibrium, slipping and sliding all over the busted melons.

"You smell like a damn brewery, Early. Don't tell me that's the watermelons."

"Naw suh, Shurff, I had a half full bottle under the seat ol' Early plum forgot bout. Crash musta broke it; that's all. If I lying, I dying, Shurff Kin–."

One of the good guys, Sheriff Kincaid's face broke into a wide grin. "I'm gonna take you back to town, Early, but you ain't getting back in your car til you sober up and that won't be 'til tomorrow. Get yo black ass in the trunk. Don't want you up front with all that booze and piss on you."

"Ain't piss, Shurff, that's… that's, uh… watermelon."

"Whatever, Early, in the trunk. I'm gonna' go real slow. If you try and jump out, I'm gonna put your ass on the work detail at the county farm."

"Naw suh Sheriff, I be good. Ol' Early done had a change of heart."

With that, Early crawled in the open trunk, sprawled out and was out like a light, both legs dangling over the side of the car.

"Now, boys, what the hell you doing riding 'round with that ol' drunk. Ya'll been drinking, too?"

"No, sir," I jumped in the game. "We's going over to Chunky to the record store."

"Well, get in the back of the car. I oughta put ya'll back there with the nigger, but ya'lls candy asses probably fall out, and I'd have to clean up the mess."

"Yes, suh," we both yelled in unison and jumped in the back of the squad car 'fore Sheriff could change his mind.

Kincaid turned the patrol car around, heading back towards Decatur. "Oughta put you boys on work detail 'bout a month; that way you wouldn't have all that spare time."

"Aw, Sheriff, we start football Monday, and school after that. We ain't gonna have no extra time."

"All right, boys, but if I e'vr hear 'bout you starting any hassle, I'm gonna be all over you like stink on shit."

The eight mile ride back home took an eternity, mainly because the high sheriff wasn't going over 20 miles an hour to allow for the fragile baggage in the trunk and partly, I think, to teach me and Gimlet a little lesson. First of all, Brother Thames, pastor of the local Baptist church, came poking by. I thought he'd break his neck when he spotted the spectacle in the constabulary car. Gimlet and I tried to hide as best we could, but at 20 miles an hour, it was tough. I think most of the populace of Decatur had been or were going to Chunky on that fine fall day — school teachers, neighbors, potential honeys, teammates, school mates, you name it. We were the number one attraction of the day. With all the hoopla and pointing and laughing, it was almost enough to drive a man to drink even more. At least, Early was oblivious to it all. Blubber Butt Brown even had the nerve to moon us out of his buddy's car. The sheriff, seeing Blubber Butt, just laughed and waved. But the humiliation of humiliations came to pass when the absolute finest white woman in Newton County, the prom and homecoming queen, head cheerleader, sixteen-year-old Jennie May Twildey appeared by the side of the squad car in her Ford T-Bird. I had the hots for her, and she knew it. Jennie May looked me right in the eye and kept looking as she desperately tried to take in this whole sorry spectacle, from the open trunk with the legs sticking, out to me and Gim, flushed red from everything from embarrassment to watermelon juice to Mad Dog. After looking back to front, front to back, she smiled her killer smile and waved to me. I, trying to look cool, smiled and waved back, feeling the whole time lower than whale shit. Finally, Sheriff Kincaid made it to Decatur, but instead of going straight to his office, which was just on the edge of town, went instead right into downtown, the court square, where the rest of the population that hadn't already seen us out on the highway awaited. The sheriff, always the gentleman and looking out for our education and welfare, made us roll our windows down. This enabled us to hear all the smart-ass comments from our friends and neighbors, now seemingly gathered in mass on the court square.

"Told you boys stay out them whore houses."

"You boys playing Indians and niggers?"

"Ol' Early is the brains behind that gang, Sheriff."

"Hang'em up Sheriff. Looks like a bad bunch to me."

After another ten minutes, the sheriff decided we'd had enough and delivered us to his office in a saner part of town.

"You boys learned your lesson?"

"Godalmighty, yes, Sheriff. Whatever we did, we'll never do again. You can count on it."

"Just don't want you boys going around getting killed. Be careful who you go getting in the car with."

"Yes, sir. We learned our lesson. We'll never ever get in the car with a drunk again." To my knowledge, except for three times after that, we never did.

"You boys get on home and get cleaned up. But first I need you for one more thing."

"Anything at all, Sheriff."

"Move Early Rue inside the jail. Let him sleep this off, and I'll let him go in the morning."

After that odious task was finally completed and we were making our way home, Gimlet looked at me and smiled that same shit eatin' grin. "Not a bad way to end the summer, huh?"

I felt like cold cockin' him, but upon reflection decided, "Yeah, not too bad considering what little reputation we had and any chance of dating some major leaguers is now all shot to sh–."

Just then, Gimlet hunched over and got sick.

"Nope, not bad at all," I mused.

Booker T.

Booker T. Washington was the local colored school. It was located on the outskirts of town in what was commonly called the quarters. Where that name, Negro quarters, came from, I never heard, but that was what everybody called it. The Booker T. Washington Hornets was one of the powerhouse black football teams of the state, usually winning their conference and playing in the annual black championship game held in Jackson in December. Of course, we couldn't play them or go to school with 'em, but we had heard of them all right. They always played their games on Friday afternoons, 'cause their football field didn't have lights. We always played nights, 'cause ours did. Well, as fate would have it, Booker T. had a Friday afternoon game; we had an open date, and so the stage was set. Since we had won our first four games, we – being most of the football team – felt like we owed it to ourselves to cut Friday afternoon classes and go see this football juggernaut. Might be, we'd pick up a few pointers. Besides that, we wanted to get a gander at "Too Sweet", Auntie Maw's prize son and star running back of the Hornets.

"How we gonna do this, guys? Coach Dick's gonna be suspicious as hell if we all take off sick Friday afternoon."

Booger Scales, in his usual brilliant fashion, blurted out, "Screw him, he ain't gonna suspend the whole damn football team."

Tommy Munn, starting left tackle and good ole' boy, interjected, "He may not suspend us all, but we'll damn sure wish we were before we get our asses out of the bullpen."

The bullpen was one of Coach Dick's favorite training tools, motivators and molders of young men. One player called the Bull got inside the middle of a circle of other players who were then assigned a number, usually from one to ten. When Coach Dick yelled out a player's number, that player rushed the "Bull" at full speed and cold cocked him. The big problem was that Dick or "Dick Head" called out numbers seconds apart, so that the result was usually six or seven players rushing the Bull simultaneously, usually resulting in a full-scale collision of the Bull and the other players. So, Bull or Circle, didn't really matter, cause the results were the same. Everybody ended up hitting, getting pissed off, fighting, all the things that Coach Dick lived for.

"I still say we go," said Booger. "He can't take a chance on the whole team getting hurt in a bullring."

I, always the voice of reason and sanity for once, agreed with Booger. Big mistake.

"Yeah, Coach will probably be watching game film and never miss us. I say we go."

Since I was the starting quarterback and spiritual leader of the team, everyone agreed it was an excellent idea.

Tommy said, "Why don't we all slip away one by one and meet down by the "Toot N Tell It," a local drive-in and home of the semi-famous Buster Burger.

"Done and done, my man; let's say one-thirty. Game starts at two, it'll give us time to walk over and get good seats."

The plot was set.

At precisely 1:30 PM, the eight of us, all starting players, made our way from the hallowed halls of Decatur High, home of the fighting Warriors, to the Toot 'n Tell It. Each of us prepared an excuse:

Me: "I'm sick on my stomach."

Booger: "I got the shits."

Tommy: "Doctor appointment."

Erkine Brown: "Jock itch."

Al Newman: "Iritis."

Blubber Butt: "Piles."

Gimlet: "Mumble, mumble."

Freddie Flash: "Blue balls."

"You told Miz Campbell you had the shits, Booger. Bull hockey."

Booger, looking a tad hurt, "Aw, you know Miz Campbell can't hear a fart in a quonset hut. She just told me to go on."

"Good job, men. Let's proceed to Booker T. post haste."

It was an absolutely beautiful fall day, perfect for football, band, cheerleading, and other all American stuff.

We could hear the noise when we rounded the corner and set foot on the dirt road leading to the stadium, still a good mile away. Yep, Booker T. was at a fever pitch, especially since they were playing their old rivals, the Conehatta Curs, and both were undefeated.

"What the hell's a cur?" asked Gimlet.

"Like a cur dog, you idiot dingle berry," said Booger.

"Wonder how much it costs to get in the game," Tommy asked. "I only got 50 cents."

"Let me do the talking, guys." Being their leader, I kinda figured it was up to me to look out for their welfare.

As we got closer and closer to the stadium, you could almost feel the bass beat of the band vibrating through your body. It looked like all of colored town had turned out for this epic showdown of unbeatens. The purple and red of Booker T. stood out against the all black uniforms of the Curs.

As we got in the long line at the ticket booth, many of the black folks knew us and vice versa, but most of them made it a point not to acknowledge us in any way. After all, this was their turf.

Finally, I was at the ticket window.

"Twenty-five cents, boys. Student rate," said the old black man selling tickets.

"We's on a field trip for Coach Dick, mister. Wonder if we can get in free so's we can do this assignment for him."

"Har, har, Coach Dick ain't sent you boys nowhere. Matter of fact, y'all pro'bly cuttin' class right now. I bet if I call Coach Dick, yo' white ass be in plenty trouble. I let you all in for three dollars."

"Pay it, Rango," yelled Gimlet. "Sounds like a good deal."

"Gimlet, you peckerhead, that's more'n twenty-five cents each. Thought you said twenty-five cents each, mister. That'd be two dollars for eight of us."

"Other dollar's so I forget I seen you and to make sure don't nobody call Coach Dick."

You'd have thought the whole damn extortion thing was my idea, from the ranting and hell raising my comrades in arms provided. After all, I figured an extra dollar was a small price to pay for us to enjoy the game in peace.

"Rango, you pile of shit. Leave it to me, leave it to me. I'll take care of it," Blubber Butt mocked in his best falsetto.

That's something I never could get. Anytime Blubber Butt got enraged, which was often, his voice, already almost a soprano, rose a few octaves higher.

"You dumb skid mark, leave it to me, leave it to me."

"Shut the hell up, Blubber, we in. Let's watch some ball," someone remarked.

We had all been bickering and bitching at each other, so we really hadn't paid any attention once we got into the stadium. But upon reaching the bleachers, we all looked around, and I think, collectively, our mouths dropped open. I had heard of school spirit, but this was tops. On the home side, there was purple and red clothing on every warm body. On the visitors, likewise, all black.

The purple and red was colorful as hell, but the all black on black folds made it almost spooky. All you could see was white eyes and white teeth. Looked like something out of the twilight zone. Of course, wasn't over 2,000 people at best, but for a small school like Booker T., it was very impressive.

"Where we gonna sit, guys? Looks like the stands are full."

"Hell, let's walk the sidelines. That way, if we have to make a quick getaway, we can."

We all milled around the 20-yard line, waiting on the Curs and the Hornets to make their grand entrance. Meanwhile, the noise was deafening, each band and cheerleader corps trying to outdo the other.

"Beat 'em up, beat 'em up, we don't care. We got a hospital right over there!"

"Exlax, Exlax, open up 'dat hole!'"

"Too Sweet, Too Sweet, he our man. If he can't do it, Tyrone can. Tyrone, Tyrone, he our man. If he can't do it, Leroy can!"

"Beans, beans, good for yo' soul. Booker T., Booker T., all assholes!"

Booger and BB were in their element. Unless they were naked, the majorettes and cheerleaders had on the skimpiest possible outfits. The Booker T. cheerleaders' outfits barely covered their butt cheeks, and the tiny thong in front looked like a piece of string. The all black outfits of the Curs, looked like body suits. The game hadn't even started, but, needless to say, we were already pulling for the Hornets.

"Hot damn, look at that," exclaimed Booger. "That barely covers the poontang. Wish our cheerleaders dressed like that."

Then a mighty roar erupted as the Conehata Curs, resplendent in all black, stormed out of the locker room through the goal posts. The Cur cheerleaders, looking fine in their all black outfits, led the way. The Hornet cheerleaders offered their welcome:

"Kick 'em in the knee, kick 'em in de butt, Cur cheerleaders be ho's and sluts!"

An even greater crescendo exploded as the mighty Booker T. Hornets came storming out onto the field. The Hornet band erupted into a funky rendition of Soul Man; the cheerleaders and majorettes, clad in little more than abbreviated jock straps, shook their butts in time to the beat.

"Damn, look at that action. Looks like pigs fighting in a crocker sack," exclaimed Booger.

"Which one's Too Sweet?" asked Tommy, always a student of the game.

"No. 22," I said, as we watched the Hornets go through their pre-game drills.

Watching them warm up, a couple of distinctive things about the Curs' and the Hornets' team uniforms occurred to me. First of all, since the Curs were wearing all black, no way in hell you could tell who anybody was, since black on black numbers didn't show, and secondly, the Hornets' uniforms looked like, well, hornets. Leastwise, the stripes were supposed to look like hornets, but alternating purple and red reminded one of, truth be told, clown outfits. It was a simple observation at the time, but one that would prove rather prophetic just a short while later.

Kickoff, finally. Booker T., winning the coin toss, elected to receive. The Cur kicker approached the teed-up ball, drew back with his right foot, and hit nothing but grass. The whole Cur team by then was 20 yards downfield, looking for the ball and somebody to tackle. The Hornet team was prepared, looking for somebody to block. The end result was a Chinese Fire Drill, since the ball was still firmly ensconced on the kicking tee.

I thought I was going to have to give mouth to mouth to Booger. No way in hell. He was laughing so hard, snot and tears were running down his beet red face, and he was trying to get his breath between massive spasms of what could loosely pass for laughter. The rest of the gang was in similar stages of mirth.

Then, out of nowhere, No. 22, Too Sweet, ran up, grabbed the ball off the kicking tee, and ran like the wind for the opposing end zone. One referee signaled touchdown as Too Sweet crossed the goal line; one threw his penalty flag, and the other was giving arm and hand signals that I have never seen before.

I asked the resident expert and brain Eskine Brown, "What the hell kinda signal is that ref giving?"

Now Eskine knew all the ref type signals, since he once took a mini course at summer camp.

"Looks like he signaling roughing the kicker and illegal receiver down field."

Meanwhile, the other ref was still signaling touchdown, and, in fact, the scoreboard showed Hornets 6, Visitors 0.

The opposing coach, a former tackle for the New York Giants and a monster of a man, went running out on the field when he spotted the erroneous scoreboard. I really thought that would be the end of the game right there, with a probable free for all, possibly involving the cream of the Decatur High football team, whose only transgression was to play hooky on a fine fall afternoon to give support to our fine colored football squad.

"Hold on dere, coach," yelled one of the take-charge refs.

"Wad't no touchdown! De ball got to go ten yards fo' it's in play. Re-kick, five yard penalty on de black team"

That got Booger back in a spasm of belly laughing, "Which one?"

Finally, the refs got the teams lined back up; the kicker actually kicked the ball, and the game was underway.

Both teams swapped the ball back and forth; three downs and a punt turned into a regular routine.

"Boring game, huh, Gimlet?"

"I dunno, I see some things we can use next game we play."

"Such as what?"

"Well, when the team breaks huddle and gets up to the line, and you yell out, 'Ready, Gang', and the rest of the team yells back, 'We's ready' and then turns a somersault, I think we ought to try that."

"Coach Dick'll have us running wind sprints 'til our jocks fall off, not to mention the bullpen, plus probably benching our sorry asses."

"I'm talking last game of the season; we ahead. What's he gonna do then, Rango?"

I must admit I couldn't see any flaw in that argument. "Ok, Gim, last game; if we ahead, we'll go for it."

"Not much of a game, huh, guys," Tommy said.

"Well, Too Sweet has made some good runs. Maybe the halftime show'll be good." And it was.

Well, what we saw of it, anyway. With thirty seconds left in the second quarter, the rest of the team slipped off to who knows where when our fine fall day came to an abrupt end.

"Oh, shit. Gimlet, is that who I think it is?"

"Where?"

"There, butt breath. Coach, fucking, Dick."

Too scared to notice, the humorous nature of those last two words escaped me.

"Oh, shit, oh, shit. I begged you not to bring me here; I wanted to go to class and study today. We'll be suspended for sure. There goes my damn scholarship."

"Cool it, Rango. Gotta be a way outta here other than the front gate. Where'd the other turkeys go?"

"Bet they in the shithouse. Too late now. Dick'll see us for sure if we try to go there. Cut across that way."

"Plan, Rango. We both wearing black shirts. We'll go sit on the Curs' bench until Coach leaves. He'll never look there."

"Let's do it, Gimlet. We'll run right across the field to the Curs' side. Maybe with the bands and cheerleaders out for halftime, we'll be invisible."

Across the field and half-sneaking around the sidelines, we finally made our way over to the Curs' bench. I must admit that all the night maneuvers that Gimlet and I had done finally paid off. We got with this group of cheerleaders and that band group, that group of majorettes, standing out all the while like a whore in church. But luck was on our side, naturally. Turned out, Coach was looking for us in the spectator group and not in the participants. Now, the Cur team must have had some kind of ritual or mojo with their helmets, because when we got to the bench, all 30 or so helmets were lined up in a neat row, awaiting their owners at the start of the second half. Fate? Maybe. Anyhow, Gimlet and I, recognized that something of a divine nature had to intervene before we got our honky butts out of this annoying jam. Looking at each other briefly, we both knew what we had to do.

My helmet fit perfectly. Problem was, Gimlet choose one so big, he could almost turn his head around inside of it. Now Gim had a large head, but this helmet must belong to the son of Bigfoot. No time to waste, though. Gim and I sat down on the end of the bench, all the while keeping a watchful eye out for our tenacious coach.

Meanwhile, the halftime festivities drug on and on. Normally, this would have been a hell of a show, but in our fearful state, every minute seemed like an hour. I must admit, with our black shirts and confiscated black helmets on, we almost blended in. Meanwhile, the bands were playing their hearts out, rocking and shakin' their booties to "Midnight Hour," etc.

"Aw, hell, Rang, Dickhead's coming this way."

"Shit, shit, he spotted us yet?" I asked. "Oh, crap. Keep your head down. The Cur team's coming back on the field." A mighty roar signaled just such a happening.

The Cur team was pretty decent about the whole thing, seeing how we were sitting on their bench wearing their helmets. Matter of fact, they seemed to be downright amused, thinking that maybe we were part of the halftime show and just hadn't made our way off yet.

"Yo, bro," called Gim to one of the friendlier looking natives, trying to sound colored.

"What is it, man?"

"You be lookin' good, kickin' the hell outa Booker T."

'Bout that time, the Cur coach, still looking like he could play in the NFL, was makin' his way to our end of the bench. We tried to look cool, nonchalant, and invisible. Didn't work, cause, truth be known, you couldn't drive a seven penny nail up our asses, we were so scared.

"What the hell you white boys think ya doing sitting on my bench? We's 'bout to play a game."

Again, since I was the spiritual and emotional leader, I felt the huge burden of saving our butts fall on my now frozen shoulders.

"Coach, we's here to show support for yo' team, that's all. We's fellow players ourselves, and we thought we could pick up some tips from a fine coach like yourself. We heard you one of the best in the state, black or white, plus my friend Gimlet here got a picture of you on his bedroom wall. When you was in the pro's, you his favorite player," I said, lapsing into a little colorese and gilding the lilly a tad. Well, at those noble words, a slight grin creased the coal black face.

"Don't you be trying to bullshit me, boy. You boys cuttin' school, ain't you? Matter of fact I played a little ball. I see Coach Dick right over there on the sideline. Might just call him over and see if'n he knows you boys."

"God Almighty, Coach, don't do that. Jes' let us set here 'til Coach Dick leaves."

"All right, boys, but when Dick leaves, y'all gonna have to be water boys. My manager done quit on me at halftime."

"Anythin', anythin' at all, Coach, we'll do it."

"All right, set yo butts down. Some of you hard butts sit down by the white boys til their coach leaves; then I'm gonna put 'em to work."

When we were safely hidden from Coach Dick's eyes, the big black coach strolled over, "What position you boys play?"

"Quarterback. And Gim here's our starting left tackle."

Coach went on, "You boys got a game tonight; did any of the locals see you come over here?"

"Naw, sir, we's open this week, and I don't think nobody saw us. They's too busy watching the band."

"Hmm," said our new found coach. You could pretty well see his brain cells kick into overdrive. "Got me a little idea here. Cyrano, how much of da eye black we got?"

Cyrano, obviously did more managing than playing, just by looking at his small size and clean uniform. "Bout two and a half jars, coach."

"Hmm," said the coach out loud. "Hmm."

Oh, shit, what was going on, and was the coach thinking what I was thinking? Surely not. After all, even tho' this was not our team, this was our town, and a town pulled together, did it not? We root for the black Decatur team; they root for the white Decatur team. Simple. Besides, some of the Booker T. fans were sure to recognize us. After all, everybody in Decatur knew everybody in Decatur.

"Hmm," said the big black coach again. "Boys, I done changed my mind. I'm gonna need you for another project. Y'all don't need to carry water after all. And, if you boys ain't wantin' to help Ol' Coach out, why, I can always yell over to my good friend Coach Dick and tell him how you refused. Maybe he'd be proud of you for trying to learn some new plays."

Somehow, I didn't think Coach Dick was gonna be too proud of us, playing hooky, sitting on the Curs' bench with our oversized headgear on, right in the middle of–

"What you got in mind, Coach?" even tho' the sinking feeling in my gut had told me already.

"Boys, I got a secret play in mind that I might be forced to use if don't nobody score. You just hang loose. Don't go nowhere."

Right, like we could.

Meanwhile, the second half kickoff got underway with a long end over end kick to Booker T. that Too Sweet gathered in on the fifteen yard line. A juke here, a juke there, and Too Sweet was downed on the thirty. From there, it was the same ol', same ol'. Five yards here, a fumble there, a pass, an interception, and most disconcerting – no score.

Meanwhile, me and Gimlet were sitting there praying that one or the other team'd take a big lead, so's there's no danger of what began to look more inevitable with each passing quarter.

"Gimlet, what's gonna be worse, us getting suspended by Coach Dickhead if we surrender now or us getting found out if we try and play for the Curs. You know damn well the conference will make Coach kick us off the team. That'll be the end of your football career and scholarship."

"Yeah, but if we go to Coach Dick now, we's caught. There's still a chance we won't even get in this game, and if we do, we might just get away with it."

End of the third. No score. Not even close.

"Cyrano," came the command from the coach. "Y'all form a little huddle 'round them honkies so's the fans can't see what's happening. I want you to make 'em look like ebony warriors. Make 'em black as the ace of spades."

With that, ten or so of the Cur players formed a two deep circle around us, while Cyrano proceeded to blacken our faces and hands. Even though I was shitting bricks, I must admit the transformation of my ol' bud Gim was nothing short of amazing, and I had to chuckle when he grinned that snaggled toothed smile, set in one of the blackest faces I had ever seen. Don't think that eye black would'a been cool in a minstrel show.

My obvious amusement tended to further piss off my boy Gimlet. Somehow, I knew he felt this whole damn thing was my fault. I admit it might have been my idea to play hooky and come to the gam, and maybe even to hide from Coach Dick on the Curs' bench, but I think it's a stretch to blame me for absolutely everything. After all, I never took all the credit when things were all hunky dory. Besides, who knew the Curs had such a scheming, conniving coach?

With the last smear, we absolutely, positively knew one of us would affect the outcome of the game.

Two minutes left in the game. No score.

Finally, the call came that we both dreaded, yet somehow we were relieved when it did. I'd been up and I'd been down. Roll the dice. Chips fall where they may. It's not whether you win or lose but how you play the game. Or in this case, by how much.

"Fresh meat," yelled out the sadistic Cur coach, obviously referring to me and the Gim. "Here de plan. Been working on it all week. You, Mr. QB, get back in de single wing, four yards behind the center. Yo fat ass friend, he gonna drop back as a running back. Marcel here gonna center de ball back way over yo' head. Tyree, he gonna run straight down de field. You run de ball down and throw far as you can down the field. Ol' Tyree here'll catch it, I guarantee. And you fat boy, you don't let nobody get their hands on Mr. Hollywood heah 'fore he chunks the ball."

"But, Coach, what if de ball don't bounce up; what if I overthrow Tyree?" It had major fuck-up written all over it.

"Listen, boy, you just get yo' white ass in there. Ain't no score, anyhow. Nuttin' to lose. Tyree here run a ten flat hundred. Throw the ball high; Tyree run under it. We score. You unsung hero. And Coach Dick, he none the wiser."

Couldn't argue with that logic. But somehow, I had a feelin', just a feelin'....

Here's the situation. My new team had the ball on our own forty. Nothin' to nothin'. First down and 60 yards to go. Had to score. A minute and a half to go.

With that, me and Gim and our new teammates, Tyree and Marcel, went racing onto the field and into the Cur huddle.

"Who the hell these guys, Tyree?" The players on the field hadn't seen mine and Gim's amazing transformation from lily white to midnight black.

"Coach sent us in with a secret play. Just do what the QB say. Tyrone, Leroy, Edsel, Flash, you's out of the game. Let's go."

"All right, men, here's the play." I tried to sound as authoritative as I could under the circumstances and despite my misgivings. "I gonna line up five yards behind Marcel. Marcel gonna center the ball way over my head. Gimlet here gonna drop back to block for me. Tyree gonna run straight down the field. When I run de ball down, I gonna race back and throw far as I can. Tyree gonna run under de ball. Touchdown."

Most of the Cur players, a pretty well disciplined team as you could imagine, especially since they were playing for Coach Attila the Hun, didn't say squat. But, you could tell by the rolling of their eyes and their disdainful grunts just what they thought of some honky ball player coming in to lose the game for them.

"All right, guys, ball over the head, down field pass on count of three," I said, already putting my jet black game face on. "Break huddle."

With that, the mighty Cur team broke huddle. Me and Gim got five or six yards behind the center; Tyree split out wide to the right side. The show was set.

I noticed then that the team lined up 'bout three yards behind the line of scrimmage. "Gimlet, what the hell they doing? We gonna get penalized if we aint' on the line."

"Hell, Rango, didn't you see none of the game? You got to call out, 'Ready gang'."

"Oh, yeah. Damn near forgot. Ready, Gang," I yelled out, trying to sound as colored as possible.

The team slowly turned and yelled, "Ready," turned a somersault and took their positions on the line of scrimmage.

"Well, let's go, then. Hut one, hut two, hut three," I counted cadence. On the count of three, like a shot out of a cannon, the ball flew five yards over my head. I turned and ran like hell to chase it, my heart pounding brotime, cause I knew that if I didn't catch up to the errant pigskin, it could result in a score for Booker T. Damn, Marcel really put the juice on the snap. The ball was a good fifteen yards away and still rolling. Oh, please, please, let me get to the ball; please, please let me pick it up, and please, please, let me find Tyree down field. That's all. Nothing more.

I kept running, trying to get a good hop on the bouncing football so I could field it cleanly and at least pass it incomplete. Almost there. Gotcha. Scooping the ball up and feeling like I was moving in slow motion, I turned back down field, and just as I turned to throw the possible game winning pass, I got creamed. Oh, shit, where the hell was my perfection, my ace, my partner in crime, the sorry ass Gimlet, who was not supposed to let this happen. I looked down, and the creamer, the one who had in fact cleaned my clock, was none other than Gimlet. There was not a purple and red jersey within 20 yards of us.

"What the hell, Gim, what happened?"

"You know we ain't got no cleats on. I must have tripped and fell into you, while running back to block."

Now, a normal person would have said, that's it. Game over. No more. No mas. But that's a normal person.

"Time out, Mr. Ref," I yelled. Still time to pull this baby out of the fire. The coach liked sand lot ball, did he? Well, he'll see that Rango Sidney Spears is the master.

"Huddle here, men. Let's go!"

I think the Cur players were resigned to a scoreless tie at best and dejectedly made their way into the huddle.

"All right, here's the play. Gimlet here is gonna play center. I'm gonna line up under his butt and this is what we gonna do."

Twenty seconds later, the Cur players, however disciplined, were almost in revolt.

"No way dat fuckin' play gonna work. We gonna lose the game with that kinda bullshit." And other comments not quite so nice.

"Look, boys, yo' coach got us right in the middle, and by God, me and Gimlet gonna help you win this game. 'Sides, worst that can happen is you lose, and yo' coach have you running wind sprints 'til your jocks fall off. Let's go, snap on two. Break huddle," I said, not believing any of it. Besides, we had gone too far to turn back now.

Out of the corner of my eye, I could see my new coach frantically trying to get my attention. I ignored him. Served his ass right. Make it or break it. Sink or swim. No prisoners. No timeouts left. Not a damn thing he could do. The game was in my very capable hands, and he knew it.

Thirty seconds left. Curs to the line. "Ready, gang."

"Ready." Somersault. I calmly stepped up to the line, and stuck my hands under Gimlet's massive butt. "Well, let's go. Hut one, hut two."

Gimlet snapped the ball perfectly into my waiting hands. The line exploded off the mark; receivers took off down field. Meanwhile, in one smooth move, I put the ball on the ground right under Gimlet, spun out of center, and faked to the full back, running like hell, like I was going back to throw a last minute desperation pass. Meanwhile, Gimlet, cool as a cucumber, grabbed up the ball and, still bent over, placed it in his ample gut. By then, I was back a good ten yards, my ace boon coon was a good twenty yards downfield under a full head of steam and looking good. None of the fans, the Booker team, or the refs knew where the ball was. They could see by now I didn't have it; the full back didn't. Finally, a mighty roar erupted when my man Gim, still striding high, was spotted way down the field. No way nobody was gonna catch him now.

"Run, Gim, run."

Just as I thought it was all over but the shouting, out of nowhere came No. 22, star halfback, Too Sweet, favorite son of Auntie Maw, rapidly closing the once insurmountable distance. Not knowing what else to do, I hitched my non-spiked shoes and took off down the field after either triumph or tragedy. By now, Gimlet, never priding himself on his stamina and endurance, looked like he was moving in slow motion. Too Sweet was closing fast. Now, Gim and I sorta had a telepathy or call it a mood thing in that oft times as not, we had a feel for what the other was doing and, I swear, sometimes, thinking. Anyhow, Gim, knowing his long ride was rapidly coming to an end, maybe, kinda, sensed I was gonna be backing him up. Just as Too Sweet went into his tackling mode, Gim threw the ball straight up in the air and body slammed ol' No. 22 into next week. Now, when I tell you that Gim could knock yo' jock strap off, believe it. And where did the ball land but in the capable hands of the QB, who high kicked into the end zone just as the final gun was fired. Of course, with the Curs 6, Booker T 0, pandemonium erupted: the Cur bench, cheerleaders, players, coaches, and fans made a beeline with the intent of giving me and the Gim our rightly deserved accolades.

"Kick 'em in de knee, kick 'em in de nuts; Booker T. Hornets be's pimps and sluts."

The only problem left was easing off into the sunset before some of the Curs fans started wondering who these magnificent strangers were who had won the game almost single-handedly.

Just as I tossed the game ball to the ref, most of the Cur players and fans were on me and Gimlet like white on rice pounding me on the back, high fiving me and each other, bumping butts and generally behaving in the way most football fans do everywhere. Some of the Cur players put me up on their shoulders and gave me a victory ride. Others tried to do the same with Gim, but after several futile attempts to hoist him, decided against it. Gim and I finally got within shouting distance of each other.

"Way to go, Ol' Dude," I yelled to the rightfully proud Gim. "Just the way I drew it up."

"Bullshit," retorted Gim, "but it worked, anyhow."

Meanwhile, I caught a few comments from our newfound team and fans.

"Who de hell dees boys, anyhow?"

"Must be some uh L. C.'s boys. Dees black as a coal miner's ass."

"Coach musta just put 'em on de team. Don't recall seein' 'em 'round Conehatta."

"Dat fat boy might be one uh Lolith's boys. Dey all big."

'Bout that time, our new coach, surveying the situation and knowing that all our good work could go to shit in a New York minute, intervened. "You two heroes, come on wid' me. Scout from Jackson State wants to talk to ya," he lied smooth as could be.

"Coming, Coach," me and Gim said in unison and took off in a jog behind him.

Well, to get to the Cur locker room, we had to pass right through the middle of the Booker T. contingency, still somewhat stunned by the sudden turn of events and somewhat pissed that their star player, No. 22, Too Sweet, had to be helped off the field after Gimlet unloaded his 250 pounds of fury on him.

"What kinda dam play that be?"

"Damn sho' ain't legal!"

"Ref shoulda called dat back!!"

However, these comments were like water off a duck's butt. My main concern at the moment was standing squarely in front of us, looking from my midnight black face to Gimlet's. She had an expression on her face of utter disbelief. She just knew it was us, but then again, it was incomprehensible that it really could be. I mean we had pulled all sorts a what some might describe as hair brained schemes. Like the time we sat on the porch naked one Sunday morning while people were walking by on their way to church, exchanging good mornings, as if sitting outside naked was the kosher thing to do, or walking downtown with jock straps on our heads. Dancing and singing at the colored church revival. Even doing a little preaching when the spirit moved us. But even for us, this was a stretch.

Before Auntie Maw could really focus on us and start asking questions, Coach had us through the opposing hoard and into the friendly confines of the locker room.

"Damn good job, boys. Ol' Coach might get a little raise next year beating der butts like that. What a stupid ass play. But it worked. Say, boys, you wouldn't consider coming back and playing with the

Curs again, would you? Jus' need you for couple plays a game."

"We'll sho nuff think about it, Coach," I said, lying through my teeth. If we could get outta here in one piece, I'd be happy.

"Well, anyway, let me help you get that black offen yo' faces. Why don't you come over and eat the victory dinner wif us? You boys deserve it."

Now, I've never known Gimlet to turn down a meal of any sort, much less a free one.

"What yall having, Coach?" asked Gimlet.

The coach, eyes twinkling, replied, "Pro'bly start with some of dem pigs feets fo' horsedivers, den some possum, chitlings, sweet potatoes, biscuits and such."

Gimlet's face sorta sagged, torn between gracefully declining or accepting the unappetizing, but free, invitation.

"I's bullshitting you, boy. We's having steaks and all de trimmings, plus some fresh coconut and potato pie to finish."

"Hot damn, count us in, Coach," said Gim without even consulting me.

"Whoa, Coach and Gimlet, where's this dinner gonna be, and won't yo' real players be suspicious, having two white boys at their party?"

"Leave de other players to me. Six o'clock down to Moonbeam Café. You's be welcome."

"Thanks, Coach, we'll try to be there. But, first, help us get away from here. I saw some people we recognized out there. Gimlet's mom's maid, for one."

"Follow me, boys," Coach said, as he removed the last of the grease paint from our faces. "Know a back way out."

Coach led us out through a little used back entrance and made sure we were safely off the Booker T. grounds. Before going back to his real team, the ol' coach embraced both of us in a bear hug.

"Ol' coach just might win the conference now," he said, slyly rubbing away a small tear. "You white boys aw-ight. Y'all come to de dinner, now."

"Thanks, Coach," we said, hugging him back. This was a pretty emotional moment for all of us. After all, how many white boys had even played for a colored team, much less single-handedly won the game. Yeah, this was a big deal. No doubt about it. The only bad thing was we couldn't tell a single soul. Couldn't brag about it, couldn't talk about it, and worst of all, embellish it.

Halloween Party

Auntie Maw was Miz Hortense's maid and second in command of Gim's household. Auntie Maw probably spent more time there than Miz Hortense did, and she ran it just like it was her home, I'm sure.

I liked Auntie Maw. She allowed Gimlet no quarter, and if properly pissed, went out of her way to make life miserable for him. One thing we both learned about Auntie Maw is that she was always singing or humming a few lines from some song, and her mood usually reflected what she was singing. Happy song, good mood. Sad song, bad mood. Then, there were some songs we couldn't classify and steered clear of her just to be safe.

Oh, and Auntie Maw liked the taste of the adult beverage. Demon rum, shine, beer. Didn't make no never mind to her. She didn't cull any. We really never saw her completely bombed or commode hugging drunk, but she liked to stay in a perpetual state of, let's say, blissful awareness. And in the off chance that she ran out of her cocktail du jour, look out. It'd be better if you'd just taken a bone from a yard dog. It goes without saying that Gim and I laid low on those rare occasions, usually even skipping Auntie Maw's bountiful groaning board of a table. As good and as tempting as her vittles were, we reluctantly took the coward's way out and got the hell out of Dodge. This was one of those days.

"Better lay low, Rango, Auntie Maw's got a cob up her butt. Heard her singing, 'Since You're Gone' (an old classic by Ferlin Husky). Bad sign."

We slinked off to our favorite hiding and chewing place up in the chinaberry tree.

"Gimlet, I gotta plan. Give me your undivided. Mis Hortense is out of town all week, right?"

"Right."

"Her three-hole Buick is sitting out in the drive way gathering dust, right? And we got th' big Halloween party Friday night, right? And you've got the hots for Becky Sue Gibbs, correct?"

"Do I ever."

"With her fine butt sitting in the back of a fine machine like that and those big bazookas in that tight black sweater, I'd dare say you've got an excellent chance to get to at least second base."

As I lied through my teeth, I could see I now had Gimlet's undivided attention.

"Becky Sue, huh. You really think so, Rango? You not just saying that?"

"Gim," I replied, trying to look hurt, "have you ever known me to lie to you?"

Of course, lying is a relative term. Maybe I stretched the truth here and there, quite possibly have skirted the truth a touch, but an out and out real lie, I don't think so. As my ol' friend, Booger Scales, amateur philosopher, says, "There is a little truth in the biggest lie." So, taken in that context, I was home free.

"Rango, that ain't a way in hell Auntie Maw's gonna let us take that car, and I damn sho' ain't gonna take it unless she says we can. So you can forget that plan. Maybe Becky Sue's mama'll take us to the party."

"Oh, my, yes, Gimlet, that'll be a lot of fun. Let's see, me, you, Becky Sue, my baby Pamela Sue, and Miz Gibbs. Hmm, maybe we can get Auntie Maw to ride with us. While we're at it, why don't we get Booger and Early Rue to come, too. We can have an orgy."

Gimlet looked offended. "You got the bright idea, Rango. You get the damn car."

"Ok, I got it. We got to get Auntie Maw to let us have the car. Her weakness is demon rum and rhythm and blues, right? What we got to do is get her into a record contest with me, kinda like 'Name That Tune.' It'll be a contest of wits. She wins, we give her a bottle of shine; I win, we get the car Friday night."

"Rango, you gonna match Maw on naming tunes? Man, she'll whip yo' ass. You know that ol' fat lady knows every R and B song ever recorded."

"Ain't gonna be just rhythm and blues, Gim. Any song. And not the name of the song, but the singer."

"Maw ain't that crazy. She ain't gonna get in a contest with you on no Lawrence Welk cake eating crap or any shit kickin' country."

"Well, I think you wrong, Gim. Maw sings more country songs than blues. All right, what we'll do is limit it to blues and country. 'Side's that, we'll make sure she has plenty of shine on hand to keep her happy."

"About as much chance as a fart in a whirlwind, Rango, but what we got to lose 'cept a bottle of shine; And I think I can get Blubber Butt to steal us a bottle from his daddy's stash. So let's go for it."

"But we can't rush this, Rango. The party's two weeks away, right? We got to soften up Auntie Maw. Can't just challenge her to a contest cold like that. Booger Scales always says, 'A contest is only as good as its participants.' So, I don't want you sulling up every time Maw burns yo' ass. Lighten up. Laugh at her jokes."

"Gim, we are going for the kill, here. Think about Becky Sue's fine butt sinking down in that vinyl. Think about puttin' yo' hand on that hard nip."

I knew my best friend like a book. The one thing I could always count on was that any mention of the female anatomy got his full attention, and my bidding was now his command.

"Ok, Rango, what's the plan?"

Now if I have any major flaws, I would say that I am much too modest. But I have to admit, when it came to records, singers, record labels, and flip sides, I blushfully have to say that I, to my knowledge, had no equal. Now Auntie Maw was good, damn good. Damn, damn good. But as Booger says, "It's far better to be good in one thing than an expert in two." If Maw didn't trip me up or if I didn't choke in the clutch, I could just envision us in that three-hole Buick some two weeks hence. But a man that didn't choke as quarterback of the Caledonia Curs, I would say was damn near choke proof. We'd see.

Part of the plan was that me and Gim would start hanging out more and more around the house and, of course, Auntie Maw. Not enough she'd get suspicious, but without the ol' song contest on the agenda, our brilliant plan was down the toilet.

"You boys ain't got nothin' better to do but hang yo' sorry asses round the house, gettin' Ol' Maw's way?"

"Well, me and Rango been wondering if you had any ideas for the Halloween party," said Gim, doin' his best to butter up the old woman.

"Well, boy, I do. You could stick out yo' tongue and go as a hemorrhoid. Perfect match," choked out Auntie Maw, tears rolling down her dark cheeks. "And yo' friend there, he could get him a fake beard and put ketchup on it and go as a period."

With that, Auntie Maw lost all control. The whooping and hollering went on longer than usual this time, seeing how she zinged Gim and me at the same time. Good sign. Good mood. Good joke. I glanced over at Gim. I could tell he was getting bent out of shape.

"Uh, Gim, not a bad costume idea, huh," I said, giggling a little. "Me as a period and you as a hemorrhoid." Gim said nothing.

As Auntie Maw turned to cleaning and singing , I looked at Gim and held out my hands, cupped toward my chest to simulate big boobs – reminding him of our mission. In an instant , Gim's mood lightened.

Then Maw began to sing.

"When the Lawd made me, he made a simple man, not much money and not much land. He didn't make me no banker or legal charmer. When the Lord made me, he made a black land farmer."

"Good sign or no, Gim?"

"Real good; that's one of her happy songs. She's in a choice mood."

"Time to hit her with the contest?"

"Tell you what, Rango, a little more of the ol' fire water, then maybe."

But it was not to be that day. Maw seemed to be in a fine mood, but somehow the opportunity never came. Now, when you been around the circuit as long as I have, you kinda sensed these things. Or as Scarlett said, "Tomorrow's another day."

Tuesday afternoon. Nine days and counting…

As I approached Gim's house, I whistled on my fist, the standard way of calling Gim out. Moments later he appeared.

"What's up, Rango?"

"Same ol', same ol'. How's Maw?"

"Don't know. She hadn't started singing yet. C'mon in."

As we made our way across the old front porch, the sound of Auntie Maw's whiskey soaked voice rang out.

"You must have thought that I was sleeping, and I wish that I had been, cause it's best to get to know you and the way your heart can sin. I thought we belonged together, thought our hearts beat fulla love, but I was wrong 'cause I was watching from the window up above."

"Oh, shit, not a good sign, Rango. That's Maw's screwed, blued, and tattooed song. The worst."

Well, even I knew when to retreat. No need to push our meager luck today. As my bud Booger Scales always says, "Never kick a fresh turd on a hot day."

"Let's go down to Wheeler's, Gim. I'll buy you a cherry Coke, and we'll talk strategy."

Now Wheeler's was the way a drug store was always meant to be, none of this selling everything from hammers to hammocks. It was an ol' fashioned drug store with a real soda fountain and a real pharmacist in the rear. In the back there was the waiting room for Doc Kennedy's office, and it was usually full. You came in, saw the Doc, got yo' medicine and maybe a double malted or a fountain Coke. Like something out of a Norman Rockwell painting, Wheeler's even smelled like a real drug store, with that slight medicine taint, and its aisles crammed with everything from Hadacol to hemorrhoid medicine, a real marble floor, the smiling pill pusher, and the fresh scrubbed face of newest soda jerk.

"Let's sit in a booth, Gim. Whaddya want, a cherry Coke?"

"Double chocolate malt with a egg, Rango."

"Two double chocolate malts, both with an egg."

Lester, the newest soda sap, was sorta in our grade. He took some classes with us but mainly kinda showed up when he deemed it appropriate. As he often showed, he was definitely not the sharpest knife in the drawer.

"How ya make that, Rango. Do ya boil the egg first or what?"

"Just put the damn egg in the malt and blend it up like normal."

"Well, how you gonna get the shell out when it's ground up like that?"

"Lester, you just put the ice cream, milk and malt in, blend it up real good, and give me two raw eggs. I'll handle the rest. Okay?" Yep, not too sharp indeed.

So Lester handled this small chore, put two stainless steel containers full of the priceless elixir on the counter, along with two raw eggs, and moved down the counter to take his next order.

"Here's yo malt, Gim, and egg. By the hardest."

"What's wrong with ol Lester there? Got to be one a the dumbest white boys in the entire county."

"Aw, Lester's all right, Gim. When he was young, heard his daddy used to lock him up in the hog pen when he went out chasing road whores. That's got to affect yo mental state, wallowing around in all that pig shit."

I lazily stared out the window.

"Well, looky here, Becky Sue and Pamela Sue are headin' our way and lookin' fine. Wanna see if they'll join us?"

Now, I could almost hear Gimlet's butthole pucker up when he heard Becky Sue's name. Gim was pretty cool in a whole lot of things, but the fairer sex was definitely not one of 'em. The color started to rise in Gim's face, and he looked a whole lot like one of our Choctaw neighbors.

"Come on, Gim, I thought you wanted to ask her to the Halloween party. Ain't but two weeks off. Time's awasting."

He sat in silence, so I took matters into my own hands. I couldn't have Gimlet living his whole life a damn virgin.

"Yo, Becky Sue, Pamela Sue, come on and join us. Buy you a cherry Coke?"

The two lovelies squeezed in beside us, me and Pamela Sue on one side and Becky Sue and stiff-as-a-board on the other. I motioned to Lester.

"Two cherry Cokes, on my tab."

"So, what you ladies been up to?" I ventured, trying to break the ice. "Ol' Gim and I was just talking about the big Halloween party. Y'all are going, I hope."

"We's looking forward to it. Trying to decide what costume to wear and all," said Becky Sue, in her high pitched nasal whine.

Now Becky Sue had all the right body parts, and they were put together in a most enchanting way, but, and there was no nice way to put this, her voice sucked. It was as annoying as fingernails on a blackboard or a dripping faucet on a tin pot.

"What you boys going as?" asked Becky Sue, as she looked my crimson partner right in the face.

Big chance, Gim. Don't blow it. Be cool, and we'll have these two foxes in our love machine.

Gimlet, gathering courage from some unknown source, stammered out, "Rango's going as a period, and I'm going as a hem..."

"Whoa, Gim, don't be giving away all our secrets. Beside we don't wanna spoil the surprise!" I yelled out before Gim totally and irrevocably screwed up, not only with Becky and Pamela Sue, but every split tail in town. "Sides, we hadn't fully decided on our costumes."

Pamela Sue, current love of my life, sweetly asked, "What, you was thinking about going as a period? I think that's cute. Me and Becky Sue could go as commas or colons," obviously thinking about different kind of periods, praise Jesus. Colons. Ha. I giggled to myself.

"And Gimlet's going as what?"

"A Himalayan," I said, thinking fast, trying to get us out of this mess, "but that's just talk right now. Probably won't decide 'til next week."

I looked over to Gimlet, giving him my double-barreled evil eye. Gimlet sheepishly returned my gaze, knowing that he had damned near called the dogs on our meager social life. I could tell that he'd try to be cool.

"Speaking of the big party, ladies, why don't you be mine and Gimlet's dates? We's thinking about taking Miz Hortense's Buick, and we'll arrive in style," I said, going out on a short limb, but I didn't say, definitely.

"I didn't know yall had yo driver's license yet."

"Well, learner permits, but I heard if you stay in town, it's all right," I lied.

"Well, let me and Becky Sue go powder our noses, and we'll be right back," said Pamela Sue.

After they were safely inside the confines of the pissory, I exploded. "Gimlet, you dumb ass, idiot, imbecile, crazy, bastard!"

I could see all my wonderfully laid plans going to hell. Sure, we didn't have the car yet; we didn't even have dates yet, but that was a minor annoyance that could easily be overcome with trust, justice, and the American way.

"Stuff it, Rango."

Maybe there was a spary to Ol Gim after all. The boy was standing up to his superior and all, even mouthing me a little bit.

"By God, Gim we're gonna make this thing work."

As my ol bud, Booger Scales, always says, "You can't measure a man's character by the depth of his well."

Finally, the two Sues, Becky and Pamela, looking all bright and radiant, returned , and somehow I just knew that we had us dates for the big party.

"Boys," they said, sliding into the booth next to us, "we'd love to go. Y'all can pick us up 'bout seven. We're looking forward to it."

With that, they each gave us a quick peck on the cheek and were gone. "See you later."

Gim was absolutely stunned. He had never ever been kissed by any female, cept Miz Hortense and his aunts. Gim's crimson face had just turned candy apple. In fact, his whole face put me in mind of Rudolph's nose.

"Rango, I'm in love. Becky Sue's the only one for me now."

"Yeah, yeah, I know, Gim, but we got important stuff on our agenda now, mainly getting Miz Hortense's car."

"We gonna get it, Rango. The gods are smiling on us."

As Booger always says, "Show me a man that takes a chance, and I'll show you a man."

"Let's ease back over to yo house, Gim. We got to get working on Auntie Maw, or our whole plan's gonna be dog crap."

"We'll get it done, Rango. I got something to live for now."

I guess Gim was talking bout Becky Sue. He tended to be overdramatic, either on a super high or a whale shit low. But that was what I loved about the lad. Predictable.

As we cut down the alley between Hawkins Grocery and Jordan's Western Auto, we formulated our plan.

"We got to make somethin' happen soon, Gim. Time's getting short."

"I got a feelin' we fixin' to put this thing to bed, Rango. A real gut feeling."

As we approached Gimlet's front porch, we could hear the raspy sounds of Auntie Maw's singing.

"Won't you let me take you on a sea cruise; oh, wee, oh, wee, baby. Won't you let me take you on a sea cruise?"

"What the hell, Gim. 'Sea Cruise?' What's it mean?"

"What we been waiting for. Maw's favorite song. Now's the time."

Hard to believe that Maw, a true blue rhythm and blues expert of the highest order, a real fan of Bessie Smith to the Flamingos, would even listen to a piece of shit like 'Sea Cruise,' much less have it as her favorite song, but as the famous Platters' song said, "To each his own."

As we expectantly made our way through Gim's house back to the spacious kitchen, we knew we would find Auntie Maw well on her way to getting sauced. Today it was Thunderbird wine.

"What's de woad, Thunderbird. What's de price, a dollar twice!"

Yep, sauced.

"Hey, Auntie Maw, how ya doing? Good sound. One of my all time favorites." I said lying like a rug.

Auntie Maw fired back, "I always said you had good taste, boy."

It hurt. Hurt me bad, but me and Gim joined in a chorus or two of "Sea Cruise." Anything for the cause, right?

"Uh, Maw," I began hesitantly, as if the idea had just occurred to me. "You a big R&B fan, know most of the sounds and singers, know most of the country sounds, too. How would it be if we, maybe, had some kind of contest on seeing who could name the singers on some of these songs? Be kinda fun, and if you wanted to, we could even have a little friendly wager, just to make things interesting."

It's funny how a whiskey soaked body can suddenly snap to attention at the simple word wager.

"What you got in mind, boy? What kinda contest? What kinda bet?"

"Well, we could each name, say, five or ten songs, and the other has to name the singer. One that gets the most right wins."

Now I could almost hear the bells and whistles going off in Auntie Maw's brain. She was good, real good, probably knew more songs and singers than anybody alive, except my modest self, and I had to be lucky and hope the pressure didn't get to me.

"A bet, boy. You said something 'bout a bet."

Now for the clincher.

I rubbed my chin as if deep in thought and hesitated a minute or so. "Say two bottles Thunderbird, you win. I win, me and Gim get to take Miz Hortense's car to a Halloween party next week."

Now, it was Auntie Maw's turn to ponder. "Make it three bottles, and y'all have the car in by eleven-thirty. Either one of you boys got a license?"

"Yes, ma'm. I got a learner's permit. Legal in town." I repeated the familiar lie.

Auntie Maw, now sober as a judge, carefully recited the rules of the contest. Amazing. Two minutes ago, she couldn't find her ass with both hands.

"Write this down, Gimlet ass. These be the rules. Number one. We has a panel of five jurors that be the final word. I gets to pick two, you pick two, and we pick one extra to be the supreme judge, who only votes in case of a tie and whose vote be's the clincher. Number two. We's pick a total of five songs each, no cake eatin' shit, either blues or country. One who gets the most out of five, wins. If it's a tie after five songs, we pick til you miss."

"Whatcha' mean, me miss, Maw? I'm gonna beat you like a drum," I half-heartedly boasted.

Maw ignored the challenge. In fact, she could already taste the booze.

"Number three. If de judges rule against you, dat decision final unless you can find the tune in question and play it on de record player we'll have set up. Any questions?"

"Sounds good, Maw. I'll pick Gimlet and Booger Scales to sit on the panel."

"All right, I'm gonna pick Nushawn Johnson and Rufus Bass."

Now Nushawn was all right, but Rufus Bass never sobered up long enough to judge anything.

"Ol Rufus, Maw. He's usually in jail, and if not, he's so drunk, he'll never even find the contest."

"Dat's my choices, any how. And for the Super Judge, I nominate Early Rue Jones."

Judge Early Rue. I had to admit, it had a nice ring to it. This was going to be good.

"All right, Maw, Early Rue it is, but any dispute and you got to produce the record to be played. Now where we gonna have this contest?"

"Tomorrow five o'clock right here. Since Miz Hortense out of town, dis be a perfect place. I'll get some 'freshments for the Judges. You bring yo' ol forty-five player over, and we be set."

Somehow, this was all going a little too smoothly, and somehow I felt like all was not necessarily going to go according to Hoyle. But, it was the only chance we had to get the love mobile, and I for one wasn't gonna look a gift horse in the butt.

"Five o'clock it is, Maw. May the best man win."

"Oh, she will, honky, she will," Maw chuckled heartily.

Maw could be a real bitch at times, but I needed to stay on her good side 'till I had the car keys in my sweaty little hand.

"Gimlet, I got to have me a egg milkshake and soon." Some people took to whiskey for a crutch. Me, I had my milkshakes. So we made our way to Wheeler's Drugstore to talk this thing over.

"You nervous, Rango? You know Maw's gonna be loaded for bear tomorrow, and why the hell you let her pick Early Rue as the supreme judge? You know he'll be knee walking drunk."

"Don't make a rat's ass, Gim. I'm gonna have the proof on my forty-fives, so when Maw misses, I'll whip out the vinyl as proof."

"All right, Rango, you been thinking 'bout the tunes you gonna name?"

"Well, the way I figure this thing, it's gonna come down to the wire. Only I got to pick one song that I got on forty-five that Maw ain't heard of. I figure one record gonna win it."

"You know that old woman heard most tunes ever made. It damn sho' better be a good one."

"And it will be, my man. You just leave everything to one of the most magnificent white men alive. As Booger always says, "Show me who ain't got a song in his heart, and I'll show you a tight ass.""

"All I know is you better damn well be ready. Maw wants that Thunderbird and the chance to be the big nigger."

"She's a big nigger already, Gimlet. I, on the other hand, am the coolest honky around, and I will win this contest handily," I said with a bluster and conviction that I really didn't feel.

"What's yo' choice, Rango? I'm buying in honor of your big win tomorrow."

"Gotta keep my strength up. Better make it a double chocolate malted with two eggs. I've got a tough night ahead of me."

"Yo' thought about what songs you gonna put on Maw, Rango? I gotta gut feeling there gonna be some hanky panky on her side. You know, with Early Rue as the final judge, yo' ass is fried 'fore we even start."

"Well, first thing I'm gonna try and get a good night's sleep and go through my whole forty-five collection and see if I can't surprise Maw."

As Gimlet and I walked out of Wheeler's Drugstore onto the main square, it seemed like half the town had already heard about the big contest. As we slowly made our way home, several words of encouragement were forthcoming from my many friends and classmates.

"She gonna whip yo' ass, Rango."

"You dumb shit, picking tunes against Auntie Maw."

"What's the word? Thunderbird. What's the price? A dollar twice."

Yup, they were behind me all right.

"Don't pay them any attention, Rango. Wait 'til they see us drive up in the big three hole with our two virgin beauties. It'll be our turn to gloat."

As we made our way home, I decided I had some work to do.

"Gim, I must take leave of you, my man. If you'll do me the favor of calling Booger and making sure his sorry ass shows up on time tomorrow, I must prepare myself for the contest of the century."

"Done and done, Rango. One question. Do we allow spectators at the contest? We don't want a house full of drunk spooks around."

"Ah, what the hell, Gim. Maybe all the spectators'll make Maw nervous. Why not? Besides who's gonna waste time coming to something like this?"

I had spoken too soon...

Sleep did not come easy that evening. I tossed and turned, trying to come up with some good stumpers. I remember thinking that if I just let my mind wander, all kinds of magic thoughts would invade my gray cells, and I'd hit that Eureka!, my "Elementary, my dear Watson." I had some good tunes in mind, but I needed one real pearl if I was going to take this contest. I fell asleep going through my musical repertoire. "The Wayward Wind" by Gogi Grant. Nah, Maw would say that was cake eating. "Gossip Wheel" by the Clovers. She had to know that one. Perhaps my best strategy was to find four easy ones and hit her hard on the last one?

Finally, like a bolt out of the blue, a magic, wonderful old country tune came to mind. Who the hell sung it? George Jones? Ferlon Husky? Aw well, it'd come to me. I fell into a deep satisfying sleep while visions of Pamela Sue danced in my head.

I slept 'til eight o'clock the next morning. After a big breakfast, eggs, bacon, sausage, grits, biscuits, and two glasses of milk, I headed to Gim's house. A quick whistle later, my best bud and I were reunited for what could be one of our finest hours.

"You been downtown yet, Rango?"

"Naw, what's up?"

"Auntie Maw's got signs plastered all over town about the contest. Charging fifty-cents for admission. Even got a name for it. The Black Pearl versus The Squirrel."

Whoa! Maw has damn well gone too far this time. No way.

"As my right hand man, Gimlet, approach Maw about a fifty-fifty split of the money post haste, so the battle of wits can proceed."

"Aw, Rango, she'll have my ass for lunch, if I go in demanding anything. You know how she gets when she's on a roll."

"Nevertheless, my good man, fair is fair, and I must secure my financial position before proceeding with what might be the biggest day in the history of the metropolis of Decatur," I replied.

Maw's response was less than accommodating.

"Bullshit, boy, my idea, my contest, my money!"

"Now, Maw," I snapped back, "we got to do this thing fairly. What about winner takes all the money?" I could see Maw's heavily poisoned mind slowly reacting.

"All de money plus the Thunder...er, medicine, you say. Ha, you on, honky. Ol' Maw gonna knock yo' jock strap clean off."

I knew I couldn't zing Maw too much until after the contest, since I sure as heck didn't want her changing her mind.

I humbly replied, "We'll see, Maw."

"Meanwhile, Gim, I am in dire need of some liquid sustenance down at Wheeler's. Shall we proceed posthaste?" I said in my best James Bond imitation.

"Better go get you 'nother pair jeans, boy. When ol' Maw get through tearing up yo' ass, you gonna need a size smaller," said Maw cackling viciously.

Gim and I, tails tucked between our legs, proceeded down to Wheeler's Drugstore, and were greeted with more encouragement and salutations.

"Dumb shit."

"Black hope vs. de dope."

"Rango, the people's champion," said Gimlet sarcastically.

"The town can eat me, Gim. After today, I'll have the last laugh," I replied halfheartedly. I just wanted to score some wheels, go to a party with my date, maybe get my finger wet, and do all the other things that red blooded American boys do. Seems the good citizens of Decatur had already forgotten that it was me who almost single handedly took the football team to an undefeated season and the conference championship. And now I was in danger of being an object of ridicule, scorn and derision? I figure, when the going gets tough, the tough get going. As Booger Scales always says, "It's easy to second guess a moron."

"How you feel, Rango? Nervous?" asked my solicitous friend Gimlet.

"As a whore in church. Why in hell did I let you talk me into this half assed contest, anyhow?" I fumed.

Gim kept his peace. He was used to my little outbursts, and besides, what were friends for but to console you before and after major fuckups?

"A double egg chocolate shake'll make you feel better. I'm buying."

Ol' Gim always came through.

"Lester, two chocolate malts and two whole raw eggs, please."

"You want the eggs floating in the malts, guys?" asked Lester in his most professional soda jerk manner.

"Naw, Lester, just bring the eggs on a plate on the side."

So Lester did, also bringing us each a fork and knife to, I guess, eat the eggs.

"Well, Lester, you a good man. Wasting your time here at Wheeler's, though. With your epicurean skills, you should be slinging hash at the Toot'n Tell It."

Excitedly and quite pathetically, he replied, "Thanks, Rango. I try."

Lester made his way back behind the soda counter, no doubt thinking deep, deep thoughts about the meaning of life.

"Well, Rango, almost kickoff time. Two o'clock now. Three hours 'til D-Day. Time to suck it up.

Root hog or die. Win one for the Gipper. Tippacanoe and Tyler, too, and all that horseshit."

"Thanks, Gimlet, I guess. I'm ready as I'll ever be." It's funny how fast three hours can fly by when you really, really dread something. Now three hours 'til supper; that's an eternity.

Gimlet and I slowly made our way to Miz Hortense's to enjoy either the thrill of victory or to endure the agony of defeat. As we drew closer to the house, the crowd grew larger, and as people spotted me, the cheers and chants grew into a virtual crescendo until Gimlet and I could hardly hear ourselves talk.

"Five dollars on Maw."

"Seven dollars on Maw."

"Dumbshit."

As Booger Scales always says, "Don't do no good to kick a dead horse."

It looked like the whole populace of Decatur had turned out. The inside of the house was crammed pack and then some, white bodies, black bodies, even a few red bodies. The people that couldn't get in milled around outside like vultures.

"Coming through, coming through, let the winner in so this contest can begin," I bravely shouted out. With that, the crowd slowly parted as me and my right hand man triumphantly entered.

Well, the contest room, as Maw called it, was cleared of observers, except for the main players. The crowd was peeking in the windows and doors hoping to catch some of the excitement. Maw, to her credit, had two big Booker T. football players as security, so nobody could get in or out of the main room.

On Maw's side were her two able assistants, Nushawn Johnson and Rufus Bass. Rufus, as usual, was listing to the side and, if he didn't have the wall to lean on, would have been laying on the floor. Another small giveaway to Rufus' condition was the smell, a mixture of booze and body odor. A goat's ass would smell better and in the enclosed room, an olfactory treat it wadn't.

"Damn, Rufus, you shit yo' pants?" asked Booger in his usual tactful way. "Crack some windows 'fore I puke."

Ol' Rufus, never one to be ruffled unduly, just smiled his usual shiteating grin and nodded, "Yes sah, yas sah." Rufus was as useless as a boar's tit.

Nushawn, at least, was approaching this like the serious contest it was, wearing his Sunday best. Looked like he'd even bathed.

My second was Booger Scales. You could have got the finest tailor in London and gone to the finest haberdashery to outfit Booger, and he still looked like shit. The boy just had no couth, no savoir-faire.

As Booger often said, "You can't make a silk purse out of mountain oysters."

Auntie Maw, my worthy opponent, like her aide Nushawn Johnson, was also dressed in her Sunday best. Maw, in her large loose fitting muumuu looked like a field of pink flowers. To top off her ensemble, she had a veiled hat with orange fruit all over the top. She was the picture of sartorial splendor. Now there are some people that can have one drink and be affected. Maw was definitely not one of these. Out of the corner of my eye, I studied Maw for any sign of weakness, any advantage I could exploit. I could detect nothing.

Last, but certainly not least, was the judge. Early Rue - what can I say? Early had "borrowed" a choir robe from Anointed Sacred Sacraments Church. The initials A.S.S. were in bold print on the right pocket. No way was Booger gonna let that go unexploited.

"Looked like they done spelled yo' name right, Early Rue."

Early Rue, never at a loss for words, yelled out, "Odah, odah, while we's in session, I be the Judge Early Rue to you. Any contempt of court and da judge gonna fine yo' honky ass five dollas."

"Bullshit, Early Rue, you ain't no real judge."

"Dat's yo' first warning, honky. One mo' and it be thirty days or five dollas."

It was time for cooler heads to intervene. I quickly interjected, "Just cool it, Booger." I shot him a look that let him know I wasn't in the mood for his shit. The black choir robe with the purple stitching and the A.S.S. imprinted on the right pocket seemed to convey just the right amount of ludicrousness to the contest, especially when set off by Early Rue's mortar board graduation hat with the gold tassel hanging down in front. You talk about sartorial splendor! His costume was complete with a handmade gavel, a piece of block nailed to a sawed off hoe handle. The whole effect was somewhat spoiled by the fact that Early and Rufus had obviously stopped by the Moonbeam Café or some other fine establishment and partook of some of their fine grape. The overall effect was that neither one was standing exactly straight. Maybe, that would work to my advantage, but even I had my doubts.

Bam!

"Ordah in de court, order in de court. De honorable Early Rue Jones in command. Let me lay out da rules fo this heah contest." Ol' Rufus jumped like he'd been shocked.

"Where?! What?!" screamed Rufus holding his hand over his heart.

"Sit down, Rufus, da judge giving his final instructions," intoned the honorable Early Rue.

"Yas, suh, yas, suh."

"Number one. No smoking, chewing, cussin', spitting, fartin', or talkin'. Number two. Each contestant, Maw, and da honky-er, Rango, take turns naming five songs. De judges rule on de answer the answeree gives. In case dey's a tie, de honorable Early Rue be's the final judge. However, Honorable Early Rue can be overruled only if de song in question be played on the record playah. You got five minutes to play the record iffen you don't agree with the judge. De one got the most right answers be da winner. If there be's a tie after de ten songs named, it be name 'til yo' shamed first one misses got de biggest asshole; he's de loser."

Now, I was impressed. Early Rue was damn near coherent and almost seemed to understand the contest. Maybe this thing was going to be all right. But, was it better to have Early Rue commode hugging drunk or lucid? Time would tell.

Maw, I noticed, had her huge stack of forty-five's lined up neatly over on her side of the room. Likewise, did I. I only hoped all my record labeling would pay off.

Slam went the gavel, scarring the hell out of Miz Hortense's fine dining table, I'm sure.

"Any questions, Maw?"

"Naw, Judge."

"Any questions, hon…er, Rango?"

"Objection, yo' honor, calling my boy a honky. We playing under protest," shouted Gimlet.

"Protest this, monkey ass," said Early, bending over directing a gigantic passage of wind in Gimlet's direction.

"Gimlet, you idiot, shut the hell up. I want to use yo' mama's car on our big date. Keep jacking around, and we screwed."

Now things were getting down to the level of the illustrious Booger Scales, one of the few white men I knew that could break wind on command. And, my sidekick Gimlet was an extremely close second. As soon as "Judge" Early let loose, the twin guns cranked into overdrive. Braaaack, Braaaaack salvoed the meaty butts of my two seconds. Again, Rufus awoke with a start.

"Shoot low, Paw, he ridin' a Shetland," he commented on the mini-barrage taking place all over the room.

Finally, Early decided to restore order, "Ordah, ordah, in dis heah court. Anymo' outbursts like dat be's a five dolla fine."

"Hell, you started it, Early, er, Judge Early," protested Gimlet.

"Dat right, and I's gonna end it," and with that Early bent over and let loose with such a gigantic fart bomb it made me wish I'd had a stopwatch. Ten seconds, at least.

"Now, ordah, ordah, let's get dis contest started. We flip a coin; winner go first. Yo' call, Maw. Call it in de air," said Early, as he flipped a quarter.

"Heads."

"Heads it is. Call the first song, Maw."

Now I was trying to calculate before the contest if there would be any odds in going first or second, and I came to the conclusion that in the great scheme of things, it probably didn't make a rat's ass.

I always liked Maw, always got a kick out of her humor and mirth, but when I looked across the table, I could tell that humor and jolliness were out the window. Maw had her game face on, and I could tell she wanted this contest as badly as we did. Good; I wouldn't have it any other way.

"Blueberry Hill," said Maw.

"Fats Domino," I said right back.

Maw was obviously going to throw me some soft balls and go for the kill on the tiebreaker. Not a bad strategy. Not bad, indeed.

"Correct," said the Judge. "Any bitch?"

Silence. Actually, Rufus was cutting Z's now, so he was useless anyway.

"Yo song, Rango."

"Young Love."

"Sonny James," snapped Maw.

"Correct. Any problem? Ok, dat's one song. Maw, number two?"

"Lavender Blue."

Too easy. She was settin' me up for sure. "Sammy Turner."

"Correct. Any issues?" A pause. "Yo' song, Rango."

"I Only Have Eyes For You."

Maw sneered as she answered, "De Flamingos."

"Correct. Any argument?" Pause. "Dat's two. Maw, song three."

"Then I Didn't Care."

I grinned and answered, "The Inkspots."

"Correct. Any trouble?" A pause. "Rango."

"Turn Me Loose."

"Knew you'd have to throw in some cake eatin' shit, Rango. But de answer be Fabian."

"Correct. Any bullshit?" A pause. "Dat's three. Maw, song number four."

"Pledging My Love," said Maw.

"Johnny Ace," I retorted.

"Correct. Any gripe?" A pause. "Rango."

"Do You Remember?"

"Dat's good, Rango. L. C. Cook."

"Correct. Any fuss?" A pause. "Dat's four songs. Number five coming up and tiebreaker 'til you miss. Let's take a short recess 'fore we continue." Bang, went Early Rue's gavel. "Fifteen minutes."

So far, I was very impressed with Early Rue. He appeared sober and, except for the cheese cutting incident, almost competent. Also, I seriously doubt that Early Rue knew any of the songs that were named but was taking his cue from Maw. When she protested, then I'd better produce the proof. I just hope I had the record on hand to back me up.

Gimlet, Booger, and I made our way outside through the near mob now gathered around Miz Hortense's house.

"You gonna win, Gimlet?" queried one fan.

"Does a fat baby poot?" answered back Gimlet in his own inimitable style.

"What'cha think, Rango?" asked Gimlet.

"So far, so good. I kinda figured the first four songs would be easy. Gonna get nasty now. You guys just be ready to pull out the records. Remember, we got five minutes to put up or shut up."

"You know ol Early Rue gonna be 'sidin' with Maw on every song. We got our work cut out for us."

It was about time for Booger to come out with one of his choice quotes, and he did, "Remember, a song not sung is just as pretty."

"All right, guys, almost time. The next songs will tell the tale, either driving to the party like white men or slinking in disgrace."

A little melodramatic, but then again I was like that. And we slowly made our way back to the contest.

Judge Early Rue was in serious discussion with Maw. Rufus was still in never, never land. Nushawn was, well, just Nushawn. Early Rue spotted us coming in.

"You boys ready?"

"Yes, yo' honor," might as well try and humor "Judge" Early Rue.

"Let de games begin, den. Maw, yo' honor."

"Callin' All Cows," said Maw in a confident voice.

Uh, I might be in trouble. Better stall for time.

"Good one, Maw. Very good, but not good enough. You really think you could stump me with that ol' ditty. I bet even Rufus knows that one," I emphasized Rufus's name to see if he would stir. Sure enough, he did.

"Where we at? Nother break, barkeep. Where de shithouse?"

"Ordah, ordah," boomed the Judge. "Rufus, pipe down, and you, Rango, you got five minutes."

I knew that song. Think I even had it in my vast collection. What the hell? Think, Rango, think.

Callin' all cows down on the farm…

Callin' all cows up to the barn…

We gonna get a little milk and cream…

We gonna get a little margarine…

Might as well sing a little to liven things up and just possibly fake Maw and da Judge off.

As my soft, well modulated singing voice effortlessly and with perfect pitch, I might add, sang the so meaningful words to "Callin' All Cows," I could see a look of confusion pass over Early Rue's face. He looked to Maw for guidance.

"Knowin' de words ain't gonna help, Monkey Ass. Got to be the singer. Judge, he got 'bout two minutes by my watch."

The Something Rockets? The Blast Rockets? Nah. The Booming Rockets? Um… oh, I had it.

"The Blues Rockers," I slowly enunciated each work as if it were a savory morsel of an open-faced steak sandwich (with gravy and fries) from Betty's Kitchen.

"Damn, damn," said Maw. "Thought I had his lily butt on that one."

Early Rue looked to Maw for instructions. Maw nodded.

"Correct. Any bitch?" Pause. "Rango, yo' turn."

Now this is what I imagined it would come down to. My song was good, but was it good enough to stump Maw? The ol' woman was maybe, I hated to admit, as good as me. Well, here goes.

"Shanghaied."

Maw burst out laughing. "Dat de best yo' can do? Thought you might give ol Maw a fight. I can taste dat Thunderbird now."

At the mention of Thunderbird, Rufus, in a semi-conscious state came alive. "What's de price? A dollar twice?"

"Ordah, ordah," said the Judge, banging down his gavel on Miz Hortense's dining table.

"Well, Maw, you still ain't answered and, even if you right, still just a tie. If you wrong, I win," I hoped to put a little pressure on Maw.

"I played around in China Town, passing the time of day,
BlackJack Red hit me on the head, and when I woke up next day
I was a thousand miles away.
I was shanghaied on an ocean freighter
I was shanghaied eating beans and taters
I was shanghaied for the rest of my life
I was shanghaied; I had a pretty little wife
and I'm never going home no more!"

Maw sang in her gravelly, bluesy voice, looking yours truly straight in the eye. She was loving this.

"The singer, Maw, the singer?" I asked.

I thought Maw looked a tad uncertain. Kinda like me on "Calling Cows." Knew the words; singer's a little tougher.

A little sheen of sweat popped up on Maw's upper lip. Was it possible she didn't know?

"Two minutes by my watch, Maw," acting like I was gazing at a pocket watch. In truth, I didn't even have a watch, but they didn't know that.

"The singer, my little honkey friend, is none other than the great…."

If Maw got this one, this thing could go on all night. I knew she had given me her best shot with the Blues Rockers and this was the best I could come up with.

"Ferlin Husky."

Ferlin Husky, Ferlin Husky. Had the great Auntie Maw said Ferlin Husky? The Giant chariot was mine, all mine. Who knew what pleasures awaited me and Gimlet in that magnificent machine?

"Correct. Next song, Maw," said Early Rue, trying to skip ahead.

"Whoa, Judge, we protest. Ferlin Husky didn't sing that song," I yelled.

By now, my two sidekicks were coming alive. "We protest this travesty of justice," Gimlet shouted.

"Do what?" asked Early Rue, looking to Maw for directions. Maw nodded.

Early Rue, intoned in his most serious tone, "De Judge done ruled. My word final."

"Yo word final if...if we ain't got the song on a forty-five, and we got five minutes to look for it," said Gimlet.

Early Rue, in his choir robe and mortarboard hat, again looked to Maw.

"Dat's the rules, Judge. Written down right here," again Gimlet.

Early Rue reluctantly said, "All right, five minutes; clock start now."

With that, Booger carefully pulled up his T-shirt to reveal the magic forty-five plastered against his ample belly.

Then, with a deep breath, I began.

"Ladies and gentlemen of the jury, I give you the evidence. Said song was not sung by one Ferlon Husky, but was in fact sung by one Webb Pierce. Therefore, by the rules and regulations of this court, presided over by the Honorable Judge Early Rue Jones, I hereby claim this noble victory over a most worthy opponent, the one and only Auntie Maw, who even in crushing and total defeat, is, I'm sure, in her heart of hearts, wishing me the best, and knowing that while I am driving the magnificent motor car to the Halloween party, I will also have nothing but admiration for the brave way she handled herself in the most humiliating defeat of possibly all time. I thank you, Judge, Auntie Maw, other distinguished members of the panel."

"Cram it up yo ass sideways, white boy, and not so fast. De Judge ain't seen that record up close, and how we know you ain't had that label special made for dis contest. We wants to hear it on the record player to make damn sure it ain't Ferlin."

"Booger, my good man, the proof, if you please," I said. Booger peeled the 45 away from his belly and started to hand it to the Judge. Luckily, we had wrapped it in wax paper, since Booger tended to sweat a little.

"Whoa, white boy, I ain't handling that nasty ass record. You hold on to it, and I'll look at it."

"A record can be looked at, but it's beauty never dies," Booger said seriously.

"Do what?"

"Show him the record, Gimlet. Booger, hand it carefully to him."

Gimlet handled the record as if it were a piece of fine china. On my instructions Gimlet did not let the record out of his gamey little hands but held it at arm's length from Early Rue.

I guess Early could read. Anyhow, he stared at the record label like he could.

"It say Webb Pierce, Maw," Early sheepishly looked at Maw.

Case closed. Piss on the fire and call the dogs. The good guys had won.

"Hold on heah, now, Rango. How Maw know you didn't switch record labels and put the Webb Pierce where the Ferlin Husky name belongs to go. Dat's damn sho' what it looks like, don't it, Judge?" she browbeat Early Rue.

She glared at Early, and Early, being the impartial judge, naturally agreed with Maw.

"Well now, on de second harder look and reflecting on de whole situation, does appear there was a little mojo work here. It entirely possible the whole thing a hoax. Fact, I gonna have to rule for Maw 'til we get dis matter straightened out."

My two second went ape shit. "What da hell you mean, you crazy ol bastard. The label is the label. How anybody gonna change the name on a record label."

"Ordah, ordah," yelled the judge. With that he slammed his gavel down on Miz Hortense's table, breaking the piece of block off the end of the broom handle. Unerringly, the block sailed across the room, cold-cocking Nushawn Johnson in the process. Nushawn, not a lightweight, by any means, went down with a crash, breaking two of Miz Hortense's lamps in the process.

"Now, you've done it, Early Rue, breaking Mama's two best lamps. Yo' sorry ass gonna pay for this," cried Gimlet.

"Just hold on now, Gimlet, honey child," said Maw in her sweetest con voice. "Maw gonna take care of everything. There two lamps in the attic look better 'n them ol' things anyhow. Maw clean up the mess and everything."

She continued, "Anyhow, boys, looks like we done reached a small stalemate, an out and out tie. Here's what let's do. Ol Maw clean up this heah mess, replace the lamps, and I won't tell Miz Hoetense you boys had yo' little party in de house while she gone." Smell mate is right. I jumped up to protest. "Now just hold on, boys. Let ol Maw get through. Ain't she always been fair with you?"

Right.

"Now we call dis a tie. You gets to use de car. And, boys, you know Maw bends over backwards to do the right thing with my two favorite mens. You just buy Maw one bottle of her medicine as a token. We split the admission money; we's shake hands, and ol Maw make you one o' her famous apple pies."

Gimlet perked up, "With cream, Maw?"

"With cream."

"Huddle outside, guys," called Gimlet.

We made our way back out through the crowd, trying graciously to acknowledge the "well-wishers", headed for our favorite tree, and I exploded, "We won fair and square, troops. Ol bitch trying to shaft us."

"Now, hold on, Rango. We gonna get the car. Maw baking us a pie. All we gotta do is buy Maw a bottle of wine, and our share of the admission money can spring for dinner over at Betty's."

"Yeah, but it's the principle, Gimlet. We the winners; we ought to be crowned de winners."

"You might be a major winner Friday night with Pamela Sue, Rango. Ever thought of that?" Gimlet was using a little of my own psychology on me.

It worked.

"Ok, let's go for it. What do you think, Booger?"

"A tie is like pooting in the bathroom by yourself."

I replied, "Let me guess, either way you win?"

"Right."

We triumphantly made our way back inside the contest room. Rufus was passed out cold. Nushawn was out. Judge Early Rue and Maw had uncapped a bottle and were laughing uproariously over a joke Maw had just finished telling.

Maw knew she had brought victory back from defeat, and she was feeling good.

"All right, Maw. We get to use the car, but til twelve midnight, and we buy you one bottle of er...medicine," I offered.

"Dat fair, dat's sho nuff fair. You boys got you a date with some nice gals, or y'all gonna ride round and lope yo mule til midnight." She laughed hysterically.

Early Rue threw in his two cents. "Iffen you boys get desperate, I got a stump broke mule out in my pasture."

He and Maw were by now laying on the floor, laughing helplessly, tears streaming down their faces.

Where was the justice? We had won a contest fair and square. It should be a time for mirth and celebration on our side. Instead, we were scorned and ridiculed at every turn.

"Let's go, guys," I said. "Oh, and Maw? Yours and Early Rue's asses can suck swamp water."

And with as much dignity as we could muster, we left.

The Big Date

"Gimlet, whacha gonna go to the party as?"

"Well, you know, Rango, last year I went as a clown. I wanna change up a little bit. Thinking about going as a Roman. All I need is a sheet and some shower shoes. I can put some gold beads round my arms, make me a head wreath outa some crosscut vines, and I be set."

"Not bad, Gimlet. Whacha gonna wear under the sheet, yo' jockstrap?"

"Nah, I'll probably just wear some underwear. I'll get Maw to drape me in the sheet and put a few stitches in it, and I'll be set."

"What about you, Rango? The Durango Kid again?"

"Naw, I'm gonna change up, too. Might go as a baseball player. Already got the uniform. 'Sides, I don't fool with no mask. I'm planning on playing some suck face with Pamela Sue."

"Lay out the plan for me, Rango."

Gimlet liked for me to tell him my plans for the big night, even though realistically, I think he knew that if we got to play a little smacky mouth with our two vestal virgins, the night would be a huge success.

"Well, Gim, this is how I see it. You and I might just have us a wee taste of Maw's fine elixir 'fore we go pick up our dates. We'll put on a little foofoo water to drive the women wild, pick 'em up 'bout six in our freshly washed and waxed wheels, head over to Betty's Kitchen, and have us a fatburger and malt. Then we'll ride around afterwards, talk, break the ice a little, and make our triumphant entry 'bout eightish. Then we'll dance the night away, take our leave about ten-thirty, drive out to the ol fire tower. Me and Pamela climb to the top; you and Becky Sue stay in the car. Then, every man to his self. Who knows, with all that T-Bird around, Maw won't know if we stay out all night."

"You think we might, Rango, I mean, stay out all night? Maybe get us a motel over to Newton with the two honeys?"

Yeah, sure, Gimlet, 'bout as much chance as Booger Scales winning the Miss Mississippi contest.

"Well, you know, Gimlet, I'd think that is a real possibility. As Booger always says, 'You get a poon tang and a pecker together and may the best man win.'"

"You think we oughta go ahead and book a room? Weekend and all, everything might be full."

"Naw, lets wait, Gimlet. Besides, Becky Sue might get so hot, she'll can't wait…might take you right on the back seat of the car," I teased.

"You really think so, Rango? Damn, damn, I can't wait!"

Now this kind of talk could go on for days with Gimlet. You could call Gimlet naive, gullible, eternally optimistic , but mostly you could call him horny. I would have to say that was all probably true. But, by God, he was my boy, and I felt partially responsible for his welfare and his introduction to the sexual delights that might await him. Now, you ask what makes me such as expert, such a cocksman, and I would modestly reply, "'cause."

"Enough of this poon talk, Gimlet. We have many things to do before our anointed time, mainly getting the car ready. I want that sucker shining when we pull into Pamela's driveway. How much money did we get from Maw for the contest?"

Seven dollars and twenty cents. Had to buy Maw some wine, 'bout two bucks. I got five dollars saved from my allowance."

"Damn, Gim, we gonna have 'bout twenty, enough to fornicate and fix a flat. We're in good shape."

"Think we oughta buy the girls a corsage or some shit?"

"Naw, that's for proms and stuff. Some of my massive manhood be enough present," I replied.

"You lying, Rango. Only time yo' manhood's gonna be out is to take a piss."

"We shall see, Gimlet, we shall see."

The next few days went by like molasses, with me and the Gim just hanging out, trying to keep Maw on an even keel so that somehow she and Gim wouldn't get crosswise and blow our big date.

Finally, the big day arrived; I eased over to Gim's house hoping that Maw had her usual big breakfast laid out. Wouldn't hurt to shower Maw with compliments. Come too far to blow our deal now. As Booger always says, "Don't pee in the pool unless you're getting out."

"I guess I'll drown in my own tears," soulfully crooned Maw with the ol Ray Charles tune.

"Great song, Maw, a master singin' the master," I said as I walked in.

"Ah, go on now, Rango. Dat song always puts me in the best mood. I did me some slow belly rubbing with ol Early Rue down to de Moonbeam last night dancing to dat tune."

Early Rue? Early Rue? Now I never really knew Maw's taste in men, but damn, Early Rue?

"A fine gentleman, Maw, a man whose talents are always appreciated."

Now, if Early Rue had any talents other than drinking and farting, it was news to me, but it never hurt to gild the lily. After all, our big date was now less than ten hours away.

"Where's my ol' Gim, Maw?"

"Boy's probably in the bathroom playin' with his self. Never saw a boy so 'cited 'bout a date. Better not bend over in the shower, Rango, or you might have you a new best buddy," giggled Maw.

"Boy's excited, that's all, Maw. His first real date, less you count the time he took Tammy Sue Jones to that church picnic."

Maw guffawed. "That the time out to Brown's Farm, dat big bull got after Gim's butt, and he had to stay in a tree all day?"

She had me there. Gim was not a major success in the dating scenario, but with my expert guidance and compassionate cool countenance, I felt his luck was just about to change.

"Stayed in the tree and got poison ivy on his gonads," I answered in the mirthful mode with Maw. At this point I decide there's no need to ruffle the water. Well, ol Gim made his entrance looking 'bout as excited as I've ever seen him.

"Gim, my man, only a few short hours, and me and thee will be in the Chariot with two fine women exploring the true meaning of young love and quite possibly being the envy of every able bodied man and woman in Newton County."

I actually tried from time to time to tone down my succinct rhetoric, but people had come to expect it, and I did have a reputation to uphold.

"You not just shittin' me, are you, Rango? You really think we got a chance to score tonight?"

Maw, of course, was totally wise to my bullshit and decided it was time for her to get in the game.

"Think you two young studs might just hit a home run tonight? Y'all got the big car; you the talk of the town for yo' big victory in the contest, and you got a little spending money after cheating poor ol' Maw out of half her winnings. Now, ol Maw been around the circuit a long time and sho' knows some things a woman likes. Ol' Maw can give you a few tips if you like."

Now Maw did have thirteen kids. If anybody knew about love, and better yet how to make it, it would be Maw.

"We'd be honored by any suggestions you can give us, Maw," I answered in my best butt kissing tone.

Maw looked thoughtful, "Well, boys, you know womens kinda like a little paddin' in the pecker, if you know what I mean. Ain't nothing get Maw hotter than to see jeans full of gonads. My last husband had a slop jar full of nuts and a weeny you coulda eat in one bite, if you catch my drift."

This talk began to embarrass even me. I had to look away. And when I did, I saw that Gim was paying rapt attention.

"Go on, Maw," he said, entranced.

"Boys, the point I'm making is dat you got to strut yo' stuff, show yo' manhood in the best light. And if you ain't got the real deal, das ways to overcome that."

I started to think that maybe Maw was having a change of heart, freely conferring her life experiences on two novices and for free. Usually, Maw's wisdom came with an alcoholic price, usually at least one bottle. Perhaps it was time for me and the Gim to be a little more trusting and forgiving. And, by God, if Maw could do it, so could we.

"Go on, Maw," I gently prodded. "Share your wisdom with us."

Or as Booger always says, "Wisdom is just shit you learn."

"Well, boys, if we's gonna enhance yo' manhood, first thing we needs is a roll of toilet paper."

"What's the toilet paper for, Maw?" we asked.

"Boys, we gonna put a few sheets around yo' manhood and make it grow."

"Maw, you telling me and Rango that by putting a few sheets of toilet paper 'round our talley whackers is gonna make 'em bigger. That's the biggest bullshit I ever heard. How the hell's that supposed to work?"

Oh, shit, one glance at the look on Maw's face, and I knew we'd been had...again. I thought Maw was gonna have a stroke before she delivered the punch line I knew was coming, "Worked on yo' ass, didn't it, Gimlet?"

And with that, Maw totally collapsed on the floor, tears, mucus and pee coming out of different orifices. I've never seen a woman get so much pleasure out of a totally tasteless joke. The only thing that made it bearable to me was that it seemed to be directed at Gimlet. It was pretty funny, just an innocent joke on a young innocent boy. So, of course, seeing Maw in her helpless state and seeing the pissed look on Gim's face, I, helpless in the matter, joined in the levity. This seemed to really piss off Gim more, which tended to make Maw and then myself really stroke out. By now, Gim had had enough and lashed out with his typical rejoinder, "Maw, you and Rango can both kiss my ass."

I felt almost sorry for Gim, cause me, the master of the one-liners, knew what was coming. Maw, taking deep gulps of breath, raised herself up on one elbow, "Gimlet, we could kiss all over you and never miss yo' ass."

With that, I collapsed on top of Maw, both of us laughing insanely. I really felt sorry for ol' Gim. After all, his protector and leader never should have so much fun at his expense. O', well, the boy was young, and, by God, I would make it up to him tonight. Note to self: Never, ever trust Maw. Love her, enjoy her cooking and mirth, her songs, but never trust her.

I knew I would find my boy down at Wheeler's Drugstore, drowning his sorrow in a double chocolate malt.

"Hey, ol bud, how bout another one? My treat. Lester, two more malts, two eggs each."

Gimlet was really down.

"Rango, you s'posed to be my best bud, and you always on my ass bad as Maw."

This called for some of my finest reasoning, not to mention oratorical skills.

"Gimlet, what you say is probably true, and I apologize if perhaps I went too far. But I think you know, I am always looking out for our best interests, and, if I hadn't gone along with Maw's joke, it might have spoiled her happy day and screwed up our night. You know she was singing "Drown in My Own Tears," good sign. I think I might get Maw to bake one of her apple pies, and we'll take our honeys to yo' house 'bout eleven-thirty tonight and have some pie and poon tang."

By now I had Gim's full attention. His emotions had done a complete three-sixty; damn, I was good.

"You really think there's a chance, Rango?" We might get 'em to spend the night. Maw'll be passed out, and we'll sneak 'em out in the morning."

"Now, you talking, Gim. I was thinking the same thing."

You know, one of these days, maybe soon, I'm gonna quit bullshitting Gim. But damn, it's so much fun.

Lester, boy wonder, put down our two shakes. And, surprise, surprise, two intact eggs were floating in each one.

"Uh, Lester, remember, I think we've had this conversation."

"Tell you what, if you'll bring me a spoon, I'll fish the eggs out and do it myself."

"Gotta keep our strength up, Gim. I hear eggs are a aphrodisiac, and I got a feeling we might need them tonight."

"Well, Rango, what's the game plan?" my innocent friend asked.

"First thing, Gim, I'm gonna go home and take me a long warm tub bath. Get me some'a Mama's bath salts and soak Durango, Jr., for 'bout an hour. Then I'm gonna douse my magnificent body with Old Spice, specially below the waist. Then I'm gonna put on my costume and come over to your house. The Chariot is clean and sparkling and awaiting us. If you're ready, we'll drive over, pick up our honeys, go to Betty's for a bite to eat, then make our grand entrance at the party 'bout seven. Then 'bout ten, we take our leave and see what carnal delights await us. Either hit the fire tower or go to your house for some, uh, pie."

"You still going as a baseball player, Rango?"

"Yeah, I guess so. You still going as a Roman?"

"Yeah, Maw is sewing up my sheet even as we speak."

"Gim, what you wearing under that sheet? Still wearing a jock?"

"Think so. Got to let my boys be free. Sides a jock under that sheet oughta make 'em stand out."

So Maw's sewing the sheet. The thought of never trusting Maw suddenly came to mind. Probably the excitement of the moment. If anything embarrassing should happen to Gim, cut my tongue out if I even think about laughing.

Besides, as Booger Scales always says, "A sucker born every minute, sometimes two."

"Well, Gim, you gonna let me see you in all your sartorial before I take my leave? Let me check yo out in that Roman outfit. Matter of fact, you and Betty Sue might just win the whole costume contest. I hear ol Betty's going as Joan of Arc. Got to show a lot of skin in that kinda outfit. You might really get to let yo' boys out and howl."

"Hot damn, Rango, Joan of Arc? That sounds hot. What kinda outfit is Joan of Arc?"

"Well, Gim, I hadn't actually seen her costume, but being burned at the stake and shit, I'd say just a sheet that barely covers her butt cheeks with a lot of holes where the fire burned through." I sneaked a glance at my fair-haired friend to see what affect all this talk was having. "I'd say you might be using those sheets for more than costumes later tonight. I can picture it now; you and Betty Sue exploring the pleasures of the flesh. Yo' first time, Gim?"

"Aw, Rango, you ought to know better than that. Told you 'bout the time my cousin fixed me up with that wild thing from Newton. A night to remember."

As Booger always says, "A lie is just some shit that ain't true."

"Oh, yeah, Gim. Damn near forgot all about that night of passion. What was it, three or four times?"

"Aw, Rango, you know a gentleman never kisses and tells. Actually, more like five."

Now, I know for an absolute fact the closest Gim had ever gotten to any part of the female anatomy was when Linda Lou Thomas, the town slut, had grabbed one of Gimlet's hands and put it on her tit. And that was only because Tommy Munn bought her a Coke. The mere written word cannot begin to describe what happened after that. Let's just say that Gimlet had to go home for a change of drawers.

"Well, Gim, you the man all right. Kinda wonder if you oughta buy you any kind of protection?"

"What'cha mean, Rango?" asked my young naive bud.

"Like a raincoat or something?" Yeah, ol Gim was a true cocksman, all right.

"Naw, Gimlet, I mean like some rubbers to put on yo' massive manhood."

"Hot damn, Rango, never thought about that. Don't want to have me no little Gimlets running around just yet. Where we gonna get some?"

"We, kemosabe, ain't getting any. Ol Rango, the stud muffin's got two, and I plan on using both of 'em," I lied through my teeth. "But Wheeler's drugstore has got plenty. You might want to get yours in the jumbo size though, Gimlet, with all that massive meat you toting around." You know the sad thing bout his whole sordid conversation was that it was all absolute bullshit, but my ace companion thought that it was the absolute gospel. When I went into my spellbinding oratory, I could make Gim believe that night was day, especially when the subject was the fairer sex.

"Uh, Rango, you mean you ain't gonna help me get any? How I'm gonna ask old man Larson for rubbers?"

"Easy as pie, Gimlet. Just go ask for a five pack, and Gim, never, ever use the word rubbers. Ask for intercourse enhancers. That's the scientific name. Go in and ask for rubbers, and people know you just a rookie. Go in and ask for intercourse enhancers or I.E.'s, and people'll think you been around the circuit a time or two. Sides, just sounds better than going in asking for rubbers. Kinda low class, if you know what I mean."

"Uh, Rango, you gonna walk with me over to Wheeler's? I'll buy you another malt. While I buy the rubb..., uh, intercourse enhancers."

"What's yo' best bud for, Gim? Sure I'll walk with you."

"So, Rango, I just walk right up and ask Mr. Larson for some IE's, and he'll know what I'm talking about?"

"For God's sake, Gim, the man's a druggist. How many times a day you reckon he's asked for shit like that? I mean, I figure most of the town's screwing. Gotta have their protection some where; sides when you had yo' session with the Newton girl, what's you do?"

"Uh, well, she was so hot for me, she had some in her purse."

"Well, Gimlet, you know a nice girl like Betty Sue ain't gonna have nothing like that. It's gonna be up to you to provide the protection."

"Let's do it then, my man. Might as well get this little task over with and be on our way to a night of passion."

"Two double chocolate malts, with two eggs each, Lester," my brave little buddy called out shaking. I almost took pity on ol Gim right then and there. The lad was sweating like a field hand and turning a darker and darker shade of pink as if he knew the possible total humiliation that awaited him. But, no, this would be an excellent lesson for my bud. And, in the game of life, there's always a thing to be learned. Besides, even if I wanted to stop this game, I'm not sure I can. I mean, I'm only human after all. And as the near great philosopher Booger Scales once said, "The true winner in the game of life is the man that neither ask nor receives but is always a rock in the face of adversity."

Lester brought over our two malts. "Where're the eggs, Lester? Already have 'em in the malt just like we like?" I asked hopefully.

"Gonna be a few minutes, Rango. My maw told me 'bout three minutes for a perfect soft boiled."

"That'll be great, Lester. Hell of a job."

Sometimes you just have to throw in the towel.

"Well, Gim, you gonna drink yo' malt first or you gonna go get you protection?"

"Might as well get it over with, Rango. Time's a wasting. Sides we only got bout an hour fore we have to get ready."

"Go for it, Gim." I already felt like getting up and hugging Gim, maybe kissing him on both cheeks or something. I did feel somewhat responsible for the scenario to be played out.

"Uh, Rango, where's Mr. Larson? Only person I see behind the counter is Miz Fox."

Now Fox was a pretty good description if you'd call somebody stacked like a brick shithouse foxy. Trust me, she was.

"Gim, my man, should make this even easier for you, you being a ladies man and all. Sides that, she'll know you a man of the world and all, ordering those rub..., uh, IE's that way. Wouldn't surprise me a bit if she came around knockin' on yo' door some day."

Whoa, Rango, Even that was a little much.

"Yeah, guess you right, Rango. Wouldn't hurt to line up some older stuff. Might be buying rub...er IE's every week after this."

Oh, the eternal optimism of youth.

"Well, here goes. Wish me luck, Rango."

"A stud like you don't need no more luck, Gim, my friend," I lied like a rug.

Sometimes the anticipation of an event is almost better than the real thing, but somehow I didn't think that would be the case today. It was almost like I was going into battle with my bud, apprehensive yes, but wishing the skirmish would begin. As Booger always says, "Anticipation is just wanting shit to happen."

Gimlet slowly but bravely made the long walk to Miz Fox and the pharmacy.

"Well, hello, Theodore. And how are you today?" greeted Miz Fox sweetly.

This provocative exchange caused Gimlet to turn a few shades pinker, and I guess Gim knew it was now or never. Shit or get off the pot; put up or shut up; when the going gets tough, the tough get going; Tippacanoe and Tyler, too.

"Uh, Miz Fox, I need some IE's, five pack, please, jumbo size." The boy had gonads, all right or was just incredibly gullible. You decide.

"IE's, Theodore? I'm not too familiar with that. Is that something like Visine? Got something in your eye, poor baby? And I'm not sure it comes in but one size. Let me call Mrs. Handy out here."

Miz Fox went behind the counter and yelled through the door, "Miz Handy, Theodore Anderson's out here, needin' some eye ease. We got anything like that?"

Miz Handy made her entrance. Mean as a yard dog. Could probably take Maw in a fair fight.

"Little candy ass probably got mascara in 'em."

Whoa, now, absolutely nobody could talk about my ace bud that way. Except, maybe Maw and Miz Handy.

"Get yo' butt over here, Theodore, and let me look at yo' eye. Got some drops there. Ought to fix you right up."

By now, Gimlet was sweating bullets, wanting to talk and explain himself, wanting to get his rubbers, but mainly wanting to get the hell out of Dodge, Decatur, and the great state of Mississippi.

It was time for the master to intervene.

"Uh, Miz Fox, Miz Handy, Gim...Theodore's eyes all right; he wanted something else," I blurted out. "He wants some protection."

I, as always, had said just enough, just enough that now the two ladies were bound and determined that Gimlet would not leave the premises without something.

"Protection, Theodore, why didn't you say so? You want some of those clear plastic goggles for your eyes? Speak up, boy."

Gimlet, bless his sweet soul, was now close to being a blubbering idiot. The boy had just never gotten the knack of being glib and convincing.

"I...I wanted some protection for below my eyes," stammered Gimlet.

"What the hell you want, Theodore? You talking 'bout a jockstrap. All you need is two band-aids."

Gim, now totally flustered, embarrassed, shamed, and humiliated, made one last valiant try. You really had to love the boy.

"No, ma'am, I need me some IE's; you know, some intercourse enhancers." Oh, shit, this was not good. Gimlet was sweating buckets now, not a dry thread on him, face as red as any barn, looking like he needed oxygen. Little I could do, though. I tried to talk him out of his hair-brained scheme. But some things are a matter of destiny and should not be trifled with. This was one of those occasions. My now good friend Lester and I were lying on the floor, laughing our asses off. It was funny.

"You need some what?" Miz Fox asked bravely, hoping she hadn't heard Gim say what he said.

"Some intercourse enhancers, peter protectors, cum catchers," babbled Gim, damned near incoherently. The boy had clearly lapsed into the kind of jargon that was best suited for the locker room. Damn, I was proud of that boy.

As Booger Scales always says, "If you gonna fuck up, might as well fuck up big. You fucked anyhow."

By now Miz Handy decided it was time to put an end to all this merriment. "Wait 'til I tell Miz Hortense her number one son came in to buy rubbers. What you gonna do, blow 'em up like balloons?" Miz Handy could not resist this little dig.

Gimlet drew himself up to his full height and with as much bravado and daring as he could muster, which was very damn little since he was red as a beet and looking like he just came out of the swimming pool, replied, "Miz Handy, they are not known to professionals as rubbers. The proper term is intercourse enhancers or IE's."

"I'm fixing to call Miz Hortense and Maw right now, and we'll see about yo' IE's. When they get through wearing yo' butt out, you'll wish you had some ass ease."

It was getting serious now. This could interfere with our big date. If Maw was home, we were in a shit pot full of trouble. The pressure was on me, but, by God, the kid was pressure proof.

"Uh, Miz Handy, Miz Fox, please forgive my young friend. He certainly meant no disrespect. He really thought Mr. Larson would be in today. You see, Gim is trying to get in a new secret academic fraternity and you know how boys are; getting condoms was one of the silly juvenile things he had to do today to get in. Gimlet's heart was really set on this fraternity, but he really went too far today. Boy's got top grades; only the best and brightest get in. Biggest honor of his young life." I was on a roll. "However, I can see where you two fine ladies would be offended by such talk. It just meant so much to him."

And now for the clincher. I lowered my voice and blinked rapidly, "You know, ladies, ol Theodore there had a pretty rough life, you know, with his Paw gone and all. Maw does the best she can with the boy with Miz Hortense having to work morning to night to put food on the table. I just wanted the boy to have a little happiness while he's young. Again, I apologize to you two nice ladies."

I chanced a glance at Miz Fox, bottom lip quivering. Good sign. Miz Handy, moist eyes.

"You two ladies have a good afternoon. I'll take Theodore home to Maw right now, so he can get the beating he deserves." Damn I was good.

"Hold on now, Sidney. Just a fraternity prank?"

"Yes, ma'am. One that probably went a little far if you ask me. I don't condone that sort of thing. But, it just meant so much to Theodore. I'd just like to see him happy for once in his life."

"Well, boys will be boys." Miz Handy now had a little liquid running down her face.

"And, Theodore, you need a pack of condoms to get in the fraternity, and that's all? What's the name of this secret academic fraternity?"

Now, I've told you that Gimlet's not the sharpest knife in the drawer. His eyes were darting back and forth between me and Miz Fox and Miz Handy, his tormentors.

"Do what?"

I intervened, "Ladies, Theodore is under an oath not to talk about this fraternity. I, however, have no reason not to. I know it's top secret and only admits fifteen to twenty of the best and brightest. And I may be mistaken, but I overheard one of the officers refer to it as C.U.N.T., the Center for Undergraduates in Nuclear Technology."

"Well, I had no idea Theodore was such a scholar," gushed Miz Fox.

"Oh, yes, Theodore is a man of many talents all right. Just a shame he won't get to use them all."

"Hold on, Theodore; hold on, Sidney," said Miz Handy. "Miz Fox, go get a pack of condoms behind the counter."

"Jumbo size, please, Miz Fox," said my totally dumb ass friend.

I intervened, "If you have jumbo, Miz Fox, that's what the fraternity asked for." I put my best evil eye on Gim.

"Of course." Miz Fox came out with the magic pack safely in hand and handed it to me.

"Thanks so much, Miz Fox, Miz Handy. Me and Theodore'll never, ever forget this. When Theodore grows up to be President or something, you two ladies can look back on this day and know that you were the reason that Theodore finally got his head screwed on right. And be secure in the knowledge that you have truly turned a young life around. Why, with all the challenges and difficulties modern youth face today, one kind act such as yours make all the...."

"Uh, Rango, it's time to go, if I'm gonna make that fraternity meeting," Gim wisely said. And with that we took our leave, not without some big hugs and possibly a few tears.

Safely outside, I unloaded my wrath on the unsuspecting Gimlet, "Gimlet, you dumb shithead. Peter protectors? Cum catchers? Are you out of your mind? What a totally fucked up scheme! And, if not for my silver tongue, you'd be touching yo' toes while Maw worked on that fat ass of yours. Plus we'd be grounded, and our big night would go to shit."

"Sorry, Rango, it just all fell apart in the drug store when I saw Miz Fox. Appreciate you bailing us out. Sides, Rango, we got the IE's. Just hope five's gonna be enough."

"Oh, I'm sure it will be. Hey, only an hour to pick up our two honeys. You excited, Gim? Might be yo' big chance to be with a woman in the Biblical sense."

"Whacha mean, Rango? I didn't know Joan of Arc was in the Bible."

"Uh, must have been thinking of somebody else, Gim. I'll meet you at yo' house in 'bout thirty minutes," I said, as we parted company.

The night we had anticipated for weeks was finally here. "Well, Gim, you lookin' mighty sharp in that toga. Who you supposed to be? Nero?" I must admit ol Gim did look pretty presentable; Maw had stitched his sheet up on both sides with gold thread, giving Gim a kind of regal look. She'd also fashioned a braided headpiece so he'd look like a Roman emperor. Rounding out the ensemble with his red shower clogs, Gim was ready.

"Thanks, Rango, with that baseball outfit, you're lookin' good, too."

"Uh, Gim, that wreath you got on yo' head. How come it's white instead of green? Thought those Romans wore ivy or some shit? What's it made out of anyhow?"

"Aw, you know, Maw wanted to put the whole outfit together. Did a good job, too."

If Maw put it all together, it had to be ok, didn't it? Hmmm…

"Ok, Gim, you drivin' or me? You drive, I get to suck face with Pamela Sue; I drive, you get the back with Betty Sue."

"Oh, Rango, you mostly responsible for us having the car and the condoms, uh IEs. Why don't you drive?"

"All right, Gim, get yo' magnificent self in the car, and we'll go pick up Betty Sue and Pamela Sue."

As we left, we noticed Maw was pretty much knee walking drunk, and I might add, in damn fine spirits. After much hugging and kissing and blubbering something about her two favorite honkys being all grown up and going off to their first real unchaperoned date, she began singing one of her all time favorites:

"Down on My Knees
When Trouble Arise,
I talk to Jesus
Beyond the skies
He promised me
He gonna hear my plea
If I will tell him
Lordy, Lordy
Down on my knees."

Uh, oh.

"Uh, Maw," I said, giving her an opportunity to strike. "Gim looks mighty fine in that nice outfit you made. Cuts quite the impressive figure."

"Oh, Rango, I's so proud of that boy, first real date and all. Good as that boy looks, bet he ain't gonna be in that costume long."

I'm sure it was just my imagination, but Maw looked like she had that look, the look right before she stuck it in Gim's ass. Probably just the lights.

We proceeded to the chariot and rather uneventfully picked up our two honeys. Only small glitch was when Gim went in to pick up his date. Seems ol' Betty Sue's father is somewhat of a jokester and he rather enjoyed himself with his questioning of my boy.

"Not going to try and take advantage of my daughter are you, boy?" asked the Grand Inquisitor.

This, of course, had the effect of turning Gim's face into the red hue seen on a monkey's ass.

"Uh, uh, no sir. Absolutely not," answered Gim, as big beads of sweat rolled down his face.

"You ain't got you none of them condoms, have you, boy? Wouldn't mind if I looked in yo' billfold?"

Ouch, how was my pathetic friend going to answer that? These rapid-fire questions, I must admit, would shake even an old salt like myself, but Gim was no match for the playful Mr. Walters.

"Uh, no, sir, I ain't got no IE's, and I ain't got no billfold with me. No, sir, I'd never have nothing like that."

"Ass ease, that some kind of cream you perverts carry around? Trying to turn my Betty Sue into a hussy, are you, boy?"

"No, sir, no, sir, Mr. Walters, but IE's what the pros call condoms. Mr. Larson hisself told me that," Gimlet lied.

"You buy rubbers from ol' man Larson, boy? I got a good mind to call yo' Maw right now."

Of course, Mr. Walters' gentle line of questions had the usual effect on Gim; his face turned beet red, his body a mass of soggy sweat. And by now, strangest thing, a rather vile odor seemed to be emanating from Gim's vicinity.

"You didn't shit in yo' pants, did you, boy?"

Well now, even Gim had his pride, as he tried valiantly to maintain some semblance of dignity, "I most certainly did not, Mr. Walters."

"Where that smell coming from then, boy?" I must admit there was a substantial odor coming directly from Gim.

"Uh, Gim," I asked, "seems like it's coming from yo' headpiece there." I leaned in a little closer. "That head band you got on smells like it's made out of garlic."

Braided garlic... Maw!

Gimlet, now thoroughly soaked with sweat, had garlic odor permeating from every pore and stitch of clothing. I must confess that I, much to my shame, was totally enjoying this. Whoa, on second thought, I had to be cooped up in the car with him. Oh, well, I'd faced hardships before. Besides, I didn't have to dance with Gim, did I? Poor Betty Sue. You know something; it's really a shame that fate always seems to take a dump right on Gimlet.

Mr. Walters, now tiring quickly of this inquisition game and wanting Gimlet out of his house ASAP so he could breath again, said, "Well, Theodore, y'all be running along. Don't want to make you late."

Poor ol' Gimlet. Unless a miracle occurred, the lad had absolutely no chance of even getting to first base. He had started the evening as a properly costumed young lad on his way to an evening of fun. Now, red faced and soaking wet, the boy smelled like a shit house on a July day. This was certainly not my fault. Maybe I could help, though.

"Gimlet, you and Betty Sue get in the back seat. We'll go by and pick up Pamela Sue. I'll come up with some solution," I logically stated.

"This shit's all yo' fault, Sidney. I bet you and Maw been planning this all week."

The boy knew how to hurt me and hurt me deep.

"Gimlet, Gimlet, my dear ol bud. I, for one, am thoroughly shocked by your attitude and demeanor. After all I've done for you. If I could change places with you right now, you know I would," I fibbed. "Got you the car, the date, got you out of the mess at Wheeler's. You want me to go on?"

"You right, Rango. I'm sorry, ol dude. What we gonna do?"

"That's more like it, Gimlet. You know I always got a plan."

I think Betty Sue, quiet as one of Miz Handy's farts, was totally enthralled by the evening's events. At least, she had a look of total disbelief on her face, or she could be riding the white horse. Hard to tell. Or as Booger was often fond of saying, "Sometimes a cucumber tastes better when it's a pickle."

"Let's go on to Pamela Sue's house. See if we can get Miz Banks to wash yo' toga real quick. Shouldn't take more than ten minutes, and then we on the way to the party. Maybe Mr. Banks'll let you use some of his fu fu water, see if we can't get that garlic smell off."

Well, Miz Banks, as always, was very accommodating and had Gimlet's garment washed and dried in twenty minutes. Mr. Banks let Gim use some of his Aqua Velva, and all was well with the world. We were finally on our way to the big party. Oh, Happy Day. But Gimlet, even with all the washing and scrubbing and scents, still stunk. Probably gonna take awhile to get all that garlic out of his system.

Finally, Gimlet and Betty Sue in the back seat. Me and Pamela Sue in the front. Pulling up to the school gymnasium. We made our big entrance along with the usual boyhood joshing and good-natured teasing we had come to expect.

"Something crawl up yo' ass and die, Gimlet?"

"Couldn't get a date, Betty Sue?"

The evening was all and all great fun. Good band. Good tunes. Good dancing. Good refreshments. And we eventually made our departure. Time to get in the love chariot and make our way to our love nest. Well, not exactly a love nest, more like the fire tower. See, this was the plan. When we got to the fire tower, Gim and Betty Sue would climb up to the top landing. Nice little platform, great view. Good place to make out. Me and Pamela Sue would stay in the front seat of the car. Comfortable, good radio, good place to make out. Even if I were a skeptic, I could see absolutely nothing wrong with this plan. And I tried.

When we arrived at the rendezvous. WLAC was playing the Drifters, "There Goes My Baby." For a moment, life was good.

Gimlet and Betty Sue made their departure. Romance was in the air. I leaned over and kissed Pamela Sue; she kissed back. I got hard as a nickel soup bone. Then, out of nowhere, a tap on the glass.

"Uh, Rango, I'm calling a huddle."

Calling a huddle? The ass wipe was calling a huddle smack dap in the middle of a romantic encounter. Gimlet could see by the look on my face I was pissed.

"I"ll owe you two chocolate malts and a full order of fries and gravy, Rango."

My boy meant business.

"All right, but make it quick, Gim."

So we huddled. "Uh, Rango, I need one of the I.E.s. You know, I ain't got no pocket in this sheet, so I can't carry my wallet with my I.E.s. I need to borrow one of yours."

"Let me get this perfectly straight, Gimlet. Betty Sue and you fixin' to bump uglies. You a damn fast worker. Ain't been gone a minute."

"Naw, this just in case, Rango. A gentleman got to be prepared. Sides, I think she's got the hots for me. She besotted."

"Yeah, but Gimlet, you ain't got a pocket in yo' sheet. Whatcha gonna do with the rubber?"

"I thought I'd go over behind that tree and go ahead and put it on. Save me a little time when Betty Sue's ready."

Chuckling aloud, I said, "Ok, Gim, here you go. Good luck."

"A stud hoss don't need no luck, dude."

Gimlet and Betty Sue finally made it up the fire tower. And me and Pamela Sue got back to doing what we was doing fore we was so rudely interrupted.

"Oh, Rango, oh, Rango." moaned Pamela Sue, as I proceeded to undo her bra. Damn, this was fine! What if this thing got totally serious? Did I have what it took to go the distance? A few moments later, I decided it was time to go a little lower. At first, I thought it was a light show in honor of me maybe losing my virginity. But then, I heard the siren. Two seconds later came the flashlight followed closely by the jocular voice of Sheriff Kincaid. Just like that, the big date was over.

"That you, Sidney? Who you got with you? Ain't Theodore, is it?" The sheriff was quite the jokester.

"No, sir, Sheriff. This here's Pamela Sue Burns. We've been to the costume party. Came out here to get us a little air. That's all."

"Where's yo' buddy, Theodore?"

No need to lie. "Uh, he's up the fire tower, Sheriff. Him and Betty Sue, his date."

"Ol' Theodore's got him a date. Thought his only date was ol' Rosy Palm." The sheriff slapped his thigh. "Theodore," boomed the sheriff. "Get yo' butt down here right now. And I mean right now, This is Sheriff Kincaid."

From way up in the distance came Gimlet's panicked voice. "We's coming, Sheriff. Just lookin' for fires; it being the dry season and all."

Well, the sheriff directed his big spotlight from the patrol car up the tower toward Gimlet's voice. This had the effect of temporarily blinding Gim causing him to miss a step and catch the sheet on one of the railings. Gim, blind as a house rat by now, tugged at the sheet causing it to split right down where Maw had stitched together her masterpiece.

Maw!

Anybody that's ever climbed a fire tower knows it's always windy up there. And, as Gimlet's luck would have it, extremely windy on this fateful night. I thought for a fleeting moment that just maybe Gimlet would grab the split sheet, just maybe he'd wrap the split sheet around his plump body, just maybe he and Betty Sue would climb down from the fire tower, just maybe we'd all have a big laugh and we'd all go home, and look back on this episode with fond memories. But as the great philosopher Booger Scales once said, "The higher a monkey climbs, the more you can see his ass."

Helped by the wind, the fateful sheet slowly unwound from Gim's body, and it looked like, just for a brief second, that Gim had the sheet under control. But then a fierce gust tore it from his hand, and the sheet sailed off to parts unknown; leaving Gim wearing nothing but a jockstrap and his sandals. The sight, lighted up by Sheriff Kincaid's spotlight, was not pretty, to say the least. I had always thought that maybe the sheriff had a cruel streak, and after he turned on his siren and his blue lights, my suspicions were confirmed. Why, this would only bring attention to Gimlet's plight and could possibly have the effect of drawing a crowd that would have their fun at Gimlet's expense. I always liked the sheriff.

As luck would have it, the first carload of gawkers were four couples from Booker T. Washington

High.

"Holy shit, look at dat white boy up the tower."

"What he wearing? Look like a jockstrap."

"Dat boy don't look like he need no strap, cut a inch off his dick, and he have a hole in his back."

The cruel comments went on and on. The Booker T. coeds, all cheerleaders, were now getting in the spirit of things and possibly getting in practice for the upcoming football season.

"Honky up the fire tower

Ain't no homewrecker

Anybody can see

Hardly got a pecker."

And even the sheriff yelled out, "Squatty, squatty, all butt and no body."

This thing was getting totally out of hand, but what could I do? After all, this was the sheriff.

And the black coeds again:

"Honky's dick hard to see

Wonder if he squats to pee."

By now, four or five other cars had pulled up, discharging various schoolmates, more Booker T. students, and even Reverend Hales, on his way home from a big tent revival.

"Who's that up the tower, Sidney? Looks like yo' buddy Theodore?" inquired the Reverend.

"Yes, sir, it is. I been trying to get him down and safely home ever since his costume got blown away by the wind. He seems to be frozen by the spotlight in his eyes."

Now the Reverend been knowing me and Gimlet a long time. "I know how hard you trying to get him down, Sidney?" The dig was not lost on me.

"Oh, I got to get home and get my sermon ready. Tell Theodore I won't tell his Mama about this, but I want you boys to clean the church the next four Sundays."

You boys? I was pretty much an innocent bystander in this little sordid episode. Damn Gimlet getting me in this shit.

"Yes, sir, Reverend. It'll be our privilege."

"See you boys Sunday. Good night, Sheriff."

And the coeds again:

"Whitey's dick so small,

Ain't hardly there a'tall"

Then,

"Peter, Peter, pumpkin eater,

Had a wife and couldn't eat'er.

But if he can't eat'er,

He sho' can't meat'er."

Mercifully, Sheriff Kincaid decided that just maybe Gimlet had learned his lesson and finally put an end to all these festivities.

"All right, everybody. Fun's over. Load your cars and get on out of here now."

"About time, Sheriff." I can only hope he didn't scar my friend Gimlet for life. Course, I'd have no choice but to tell Maw, and I'm pretty sure with our counseling, we'd get Gim through this little episode.

"Ok, Theodore, just stay where you are. This is the Sheriff. I'm coming up to get you."

Five minutes later, the sheriff and Gimlet were back on firm ground.

I decided to try the light approach. "Well, Gim, you always wanted to be in the spotlight. Sho' got yo' wish tonight. You ok, ol buddy?"

"Stuff it up yo' ass, Rango. Big help you were. I could hear you laughing down here at all those cracks. Thought you were my best friend."

"Gimlet, I don't know when I've ever been hurt more by a remark. You can just go ahead and cut my gonads off. Sure, there were a few off color remarks, but most of them were all in fun. Why come tomorrow, nobody gonna think twice about this shit. Heard a few of the women talking 'bout they didn't know you had such a good body. Kinda showed it off to advantage in that spotlight. Tammy Sue was really oohing and ahhing."

"What 'bout all them remarks 'bout the size of my dick. I'm the laughing stock of the town."

"Not so, Gimlet. From where I sat, seemed to me most of that was said in envy and jealousy. I can tell you honestly some of the guys said they ain't never seen such a dick."

"So Tammy Sue really said something 'bout my bod? Think she might want some of the ol Gimlet?"

"Well, Gim, ain't so much what she said…more like what she didn't say. When I looked at 'er, she just had her mouth wide open staring at that magnificent bod."

"Think she'll really go out with me, Rango?"

"Not a doubt in my military mind, Gim. Get the car, and we'll double next week."

"Rango, I take back all that stuff I said. You 'bout the best bud a man could have."

I was the best.

Sheriff Kincaid listened to this conversation with, I think, some small measure of admiration. He pulled me to the side, "Sidney, I ain't never heard such utterly total bullshit in my life. If you ain't a politician or lawyer when you grown, you sho' as hell missing yo' calling. Now get Theodore's ass home and get some clothes on that magnificent bod."

"Yes, sir, Sheriff. We leaving now."

"Oh, Rango, where our dates? They ain't in the car."

"Shit, our dates. Totally forgot about them with all the excitement. Maybe they got a ride home with somebody else. Betty Sue seemed kinda pissed with all those other girls ogling you."

"Hell with her. Plenty more where she came from. She'll just miss some o' the pleasures of the Gim machine."

"Well, whatever, Gim. We better get the car home if we ever hope to use it again."

We made our way to the main road back towards the big city of Decatur. About three miles from the fire tower, we spotted our two Sues, Betty and Pamela walking, into town.

"Hey, girls. Why'd you leave? Come on and get in the car, and we'll drive by the Toot-N-Tell It and get a Coke."

"We never want to see you two assholes again. I've never been so embarrassed in my life. We'll never live this down," Pamela Sue wailed. Betty Sue nodded in sympathy.

"Now, Betty Sue and Pamela Sue. What you got to be embarrassed about? It was me and Gimlet who screwed up," I said, shouldering some of the blame.

"All I know is that me and Gim had the two foxiest dates in town and that we was trying to show you a good time. I thought the night went really well up to the time at the fire tower. I know Gimlet and I never been with two ladies we admired and respected more. Sides, I heard some of the other couples talking 'bout how much they admired you two sticking with your dates even tho we hit a little bump in the road."

As Booger always says, "You can call a hoss turd a flower, but it still stinks."

Anyhow, it was time to go for the gold.

"And, ladies, we can't tell you how honored we were when you agreed to go our with us. This is all we been talking 'bout for weeks. We both been saving our money just so we could treat you two ladies like you deserve. And, this being Gim's first real date, we wanted it to be absolutely perfect. I take all the responsibility for the little mess-up, but I have always tried to look out for Gimlet, and I'm just so sorry I couldn't make this the kind of evening he'll never forget. I guess I'm just guilty of wanting my best friend to be happy and not afraid to date again. Can you find any way in your heart to forgive us?" My lower lip quivered ever so slightly, and I stared down at my feet. I sneaked a look at the two Sues, and I knew ol Rango had pulled it off again. Both the Sues had slightly moist eyes and looked like they wanted to cry. They looked at each other and nodded slightly.

"Why, sure, we'll forgive you guys. Guess it could happen to anybody," Betty Sue said.

Pamela Sue, not quite as forgiving, said, "I'm not getting in the back seat 'til Gimlet gets some clothes on."

"Ain't no need to put 'em on. You just gonna take 'em offa me in about fifteen minutes, so you can have some o' the ol Gimburger."

Oh, shit.

"Told you they were two assholes, Betty Sue. We wouldn't go out with you two again if you could pee sideways. Don't ever call us again. Don't even act like you know us."

Well, if I was a bettin' man, I'd say the evening was 'bout over. Nothing to do now except to get our rejected assess home. Damn, it'd be nice to have a normal day sometimes. I didn't even have the heart to get on Gimlet's ass about his somewhat inappropriate comments. Hadn't the boy been through enough? However, I really felt the need to make some remarks to Gimlet so he would know his rude behavior was not entirely overlooked.

"Gimlet, you totally worthless drop of shit. Everything was okay, and you fucked it up again. Any reason?"

"Aw, Rango, you know I'd never let two split tails get between our friendship. You mean too much to me."

Wow. The boy had clearly been around me too much.

"Well, ol' Bud, since you put it that way, I guess you're right. Pretty good day, huh, Gim?"

"Other than the fact I'm now the laughing stock of the town and no woman'll ever go out with me again, I guess not too bad."

"Oh, and we've got to clean the church the next four Sundays, but Reverend Hales ain't gonna tell yo' maw."

"Well, I guess it's a hell of a good day then."

And with that we both laughed; Gim punched me on the shoulder, and we made our way home.

Too Sweet meets the Recruiter

"Ya'll owe me and owe me big time!," was Maw's first statement when I walked through the door that morning. She was always in fifth gear in the A.M. before she got to sippin' the booze. Check back about four o'clock in the afternoon, and there's not a coherent, complete sentence to be heard. Gimlet was waiting on me in the kitchen.

"Calm down, Maw. What happened? Somethin' happen to Too Sweet?"

"Naw, Rango, Too Sweet jus' fine. It's about Too Sweet though. That big recruiter from Ohio State done called," Maw said, looking like she was gonna burst into tears or hit somebody.

"Why, hell, Maw, that's great news! If Too Sweet goes to Ohio State, he'll be a cinch for the pros. Why you got yo' drawers all in a wad? You oughta be poppin' the champagne. Ol' Too's a Buckeye. I hear them big schools like that usually got plenty of money to go around, if you catch my drift."

"Durango, you dum' little shit. 'Fore they give Too Sweet a scholah'ship, recruiter wants to meet us and take us to dinner. Make sure we Buckeye material, he say."

"Well, why wouldn't Too Sweet be Buckeye material? Best damn running back in the state right now. Boy could get a scholah'ship anywhere he damn well please."

Maw, still pacing the floor, "Well, you know, Too never been outta the county. Boy don' know how to act 'round real people."

"I'm real people, Maw. Me and Gimlet and our folks. Too Sweet always acts fine."

"Rango, you know Too Sweet don' say two words 'round any grown ups." Maw was still agitated.

"Well, Maw, what if me and Gimlet come to the dinner with you? We could tell soma our witty anecdotes, keep the ball rollin', so to speak. Too Sweet could nod and smile at the right moments and next thing you know, Too's a Buckeye."

"Ain't quite what I got in mind, Rango. Too Sweet a good boy, but he lible to mess the whole thing up. You know the boy ain't got no manners; likes to eat with his hands and shit, farts at the table, too. Naw, Too Sweet can't be at that dinner. Don't wanna fuck up the boy's big chance."

"Why don't you jus' call the man and tell him Too's sick and unable to meet with 'im?"

"Yes, that's what I'll do, Rango. I'll call the man up and tell 'im cram that scholah'ship up his ass.

That my boy's too sick to meet with his honky ass."

Sarcasm, imagine that coming from Maw.

"Well, Maw, what else ya gonna do? Get a double to go in his place? Why don' cha get Gimlet to go as yo' number one son to the big dinner?"

Gimlet peed his pants laughing at the thought.

"Well, well, well, Rango. Yo head cool for something more than holding up that football helmet after all," Maw said with a big smirk looking straight at me.

"Wait a minute. You tellin' me you gonna take Gimlet with you to that dinner? Gimlet, the white boy? The lard ass that out weighs Too Sweet a good seventy pounds? The one boy in Decatur that's double guaranteed to screw up any chance, beyond a reasonable doubt, that Too Sweet will ever, ever, see the state of Ohio? Is that the Gimlet we talkin' bout here?"

"Oh, no, Rango. Not at all, my little saltine. We not talkin' Gimlet at all. Even Maw knows that fool fuck up a one car funeral."

Whoa, wait a minute, time out. If not Gimlet…

"Ooh, no, you don't. Unless that recruiter's blind, I think he's gonna be able to tell I'm a little too light to be Too Sweet. 'Sides that, Maw, I don't owe you that big."

"Oh, no, Rango? With all the shit I let you boys get away wit 'round here? How many times have I turned a blind eye?"

"Are you counting the times you've passed out?"

"Hush, child, and let Ol' Maw have her say now, honey. Ol' Maw don't ask you for much. Maw jus a po' ol' black woman trying to make a way in the world for her and her chilren. I's had to be mother and father to them boys, and now one of um got a chance to get a real college education. You know ain't a one of Maw's people ever even had a chance to go to high school. Always working the cotton fields, plowing the crops, working for the man trying to get enough money together. Ol' Maw been working sunup to sundown since she was just six years old, and still deys never quite enough to eat. Yup. Jus an Ol' black woman trying to get by. This yo' one chance to do somethin' nice for Ol' Maw. Let her go to the grave knowin' one of her sons finally got him a college degree."

Maw was really milking it now. Her eyes were brimming, her lips were quivering, quiet sobbing sounds erupted every few seconds; I was waiting for the explosion sure to come. Of course, I knew that Maw had never picked cotton, and she'd damn sure never missed a meal. And as far as no education, I know that Maw's two brothers had graduated from Jackson State. In the end, I knew there was no winning with Maw.

"All right, Maw, let's listen to your little plan. Number one problem I see is how you gonna pass me off as Too Sweet, seeing how our complexions are uh, a little, how should we say, off?"

I sneaked a peak at my buddy Gimlet, who had something between a smirk and a shit-eating grin plastered across his moon face.

"Oh, Durango! Maw never forget you for this. You sho' nuff saved an Ol' black woman's life! Maw gonna bake you an apple pie anytime you wants one. But enough of this horse shit beating round the bush. Here's what we gonna do. We gonna get us a little eye shade like they put on you boys at the big game with the Curs."

I guess bad news travels fast, too.

Maw must have been able to read our minds because she suddenly burst into laughter.

"You two butt wipes think Ol' Maw got her head up her ass and didn't know who you were? Been saving this for the right time, and this is it! I was so pissed seeing you two assholes taking that victory ride. Well, Ol' Maw gonna take her ride now. See, Too Sweet gonna have him a little car accident. Nothin' serious. Gonna put us some tape all around his head, put a little eye shade where the tape ain't, and lawdy! we got us a genuwine brotha who gonna charm dey shit outta that Ohio asshole and get my boy a scholah'ship."

It was a plan that had 'fuck up' stamped in bold letters all over it. But since I was pretty sure you can't get arrested for impersonating a black man, and figuring that I could handle a little embarrassment, I vowed then and there that I would give it my absolute best shot. As Booger Scales always says, "A plan without action is shit anyway."

My only concern now was how to involve Gim in this little caper.

Of course, he was already in whether he knew it or not.

"You know, those recruiters love to go back to their colleges to say how well rounded their prospects are, you know, in terms of racial relations. I bet he really enjoy meeting one of Too Sweet's honky friends."

"Whoa," Gimlet erupted, "you two ain't getting me into this shit."

"But, Gimlet," I said, "don't you want to be there to see how it goes down? Look at it this way, you'll get a free meal out of it."

The mood in the room quickly shifted. Gimlet came to life, and Maw knew she had us.

"All right, here's the plan. Ohio asshole will be here next Saturday 'bout five o'clock. Coming by the house here to see the family and shit. Then, he's be taking us to the steak house to eat. You and Gimlet get here by three. We gotta get the bandages and the eye shade on. Wear a long sleeve shirt so we ain't got so much skin to cover," Maw said, now taking charge of the situation. I was starting to think this might actually be fun, and I allowed myself a moment to imagine Gim and I having ourselves in stitches, laughing over this one day.

When Saturday finally rolled around, I was a tad nervous. It was like being on stage, only this was the real deal. Act good, scholah'ship. Act bad, goodbye scholah'ship; hello, junior college. The stakes were high, all right, but this is the kind of stuff I lived for. If anyone could pull this thing off, I would modestly say it'd be me.

It was three o'clock sharp as I knocked on Maw's screen door.

From just inside she called out, "Rango, you sho' nuff a good friend to me and Too Sweet. Ol' Maw gonna take you to all the Ohio State games after we pull this off." As she opened the door, that familiar odor of booze hit me square in the face.

"You been drinking. You know that recruiter gonna be here any minute. You need to be sharp if this gonna work, damn it."

"Oh, just had me a nip or two, Rango. Just calmin' Ol' Maw's nerves."

About that time Gimlet came waltzing in.

"Here's yo' ace boon coon; I'm yo' pride and joy. I'm a sorry shithead, but I'm still yo' boy."

Well put, Gim. "All right, let's get ready."

Then Maw said, "We got bout forty-five minutes 'fore he shows. Better start getting yo makeup on. Gimlet, get me the tape and the face black. Got to get this boy lookin' like a brotha. We'll have Ol' Rango faking and fixing flats every Sunday afternoon. He be eatin' pigs feets and chitlins in no time."

The transformation was a success. When Maw got through with her handiwork and handed me the mirror, I wouldn't have recognized myself in a dark room until I smiled, of course. And since the Steak House tended to be dark, I figured, we just might pull this off.

"Damn, Maw, I could pass for one of yo' sons."

"One thing, Rango. You got to learn real fas' how to talk black. You sounding too much like some tight ass politician. Got to quit talkin' like you got a cob up yo' butt. Quit sayin' shit like four and street; got to say fo' and skreet. Basically, you gotta talk lazy."

"Maw, you know Too Sweet kinda shy. Why don't I just say 'yessuh' and 'no suh.' Let you and Gimlet carry on the conversation, and I'll just nod and smile every once in a while."

"Sweet Jesus, Me and Gimlet ass here carrying on an adult conversation? You as dumb as I just made you look?"

"Just a minute now, Maw," chimed in Gim. Proudly he stated, "I'll have you know, I was picked as an alternate on the debate team." He failed to mention the part about the fact that they needed six on the team, and only five showed up.

"Well, boys, I gots to have one mo' shot of tonic. Dat recruiter gonna be here any minute. Now, Maw love you two like you was her sons. We pull dis off, you get a apple pie and get to use the car again."

Then she said, eyes gleaming, "Maw heard Trudy May Brown asking if Gimlet got him a steady. Think she was out to the fire tower and saw Gim's fine bod. Also heard Trudy May could suck a baseball through a garden hose."

Ha!

I didn't buy it for a second, and I knew for sure Gimlet would see right through the horseshit.

"Trudy May, you say, Maw? Huh. I didn't think she even liked me. She usually turns her nose up when we pass in the hall."

"Oooh, she hot for you all right, Gim. She just afraid she'll lose control, she start talking to you."

Damn, my boy was weak.

"Ok. Last minute instructions, boys. First, yessuh and no suh to Mr. Ohio State. No eating with yo' hands, no talking less he talk, don't order no steak jest cause he buying, and no floatin' air biscuits at the table."

Together, Gim and I said, "Damn, Maw, we ain't in kindergarten."

Just then, the Ohio State recruiter knocked on the door. Maw took one final swig of Thunderbird and the show began.

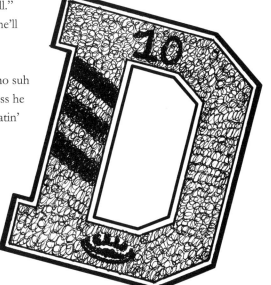

"Ah, you must be Miz Cunt, and this must be your son, Too Sweet. So glad to finally meet you. I'm Mr. Barnes. We can't wait to see Too Sweet in a Buckeye uniform."

I couldn't believe my ears. He had just called Maw Miz Cunt. As the words ran through my head, I let out a little chuckle as the name of the character I was playing dawned on me. Too Sweet Cunt. I knew in an instant that me and Gimlet would never make it through the evening if he called her Miz Cunt again.

Maw seemed to handle it in stride. "Uh, Mr. Barnes, dat name Miz Curt, C U R T. Too Sweet done filled out dat questionnaire you done sent him, and his spelling and hand writing ain't de best."

"Oh, so sorry. I sincerely apologize, Miz Curt. The lady in the recruiting office typed in Too Sweet Cunt and that's what I read."

Mr. Barnes, realizing his gaffe, turned three shades of red, and a thin film of perspiration appeared on his nearly bald forehead. I looked at Gim, and I could tell he was just about to lose it.

Mr. Barnes decided to change the subject.

"Uh, Miz Curt," he carefully enunciated every word, "is this one of Too Sweet's friends?"

"Yessir, Mr. Barnes. This honky, er, white gentleman here is Too Sweet's best friend, Theodore."

"Looks like he could play a little ball himself. Play football, do you Theodore?"

"Yessir, made all conference and honorable mention all-conference this year."

Gim had lost it. The boy barely lettered this year. He knows that most of his football career consisted of picking splinters out of his ass. But he also knew I couldn't contradict him in front of Mr. Barnes. As I glanced at him, he gave me a slight smirk.

"That so? We may be recruiting you next year. And Too Sweet, think you'd like to be a Buckeye?"

I stuck to the script.

"Yessuh."

"Like to visit our campus next week?"

"Yessuh."

"Think you can cut it in the Big 10?"

"Yessuh."

"Think you can handle the academic load?"

"Yessuh."

"Get along with your teammates, do you?"

"Yessuh."

As long as Barnes didn't mention the word cunt, I could keep this up forever. Once he had had enough of the small talk, Mr. Barnes said, "Uh, Miz Curt, you and Too Sweet and Theodore ready to eat?"

"Yessir, Mr. Barnes, thought we'd go over to the Steak House. Food pretty good there, and we can talk."

We all piled into Mr. Barnes' new Caddy and drove off.

"Miz Curt, you like a little drink before dinner? Got a fifth of Jim Beam there in the glove compartment. Help yourself if you like. Got some Coke in that paper sack."

"Well, Mr. Barnes, I normally don' touch the stuff, but seein' how this a speshul occasion, I guess one little drink won' hurt." Maw glared into the back seat, almost daring us to say a word.

Maw opened the glove compartment and took out the golden nectar, along with two paper cups and two Cokes. If I were a betting man, I'd guess that Maw had never had anything more expensive than Thunderbird or maybe some ol' rotgut whiskey. Now, she was in the big leagues.

"Like some, Mr. Barnes?" asked Maw graciously.

"Don't mind if I do, Miz Curt. Mix mine about half and half."

Maw poured herself and Mr Barnes a hefty drink that both consumed in one long swallow. It seemed to me that Mr. Barnes was just trying to get through the evening after it's inauspicious start, and Maw, well she was just being, Maw.

"How about another there, Mr. Barnes?"

"Well, don't mind if I do, Miz Curts."

Things were going just swimmingly. After one drink, they were both on their way to becoming shit-faced. This might turn out to be one of the finest evenings in mine and Gim's young lives. One more stiff drink, and Mr. Barnes and Maw would be slurring their words. "How 'bout one more, Miz Curt?"

"Don't mind if I do, Mr. Barnes. Oh, and just call me Heather."

Heather? Heather?

I was about ninty-nine percent certain Maw's name wasn't Heather. It was probably something she heard on one of her soap operas.

"Pleased to make your acquaintance, Heather. You can call me Stone."

Stone? Heather? Who's bullshitting who here?

I started to think there was some kind of sick attraction between these two.

"How 'bout one more quick drink before we get to the restaurant, Heather? There's another bottle in the glove compartment."

"Why, Barnes, thought yo'd never ask. Ol' Maw, er, Heather don' usually drink like this but it hard to say no to such a gentleman like yo'self," said Maw, giggling seductively.

Barnes had totally forgotten about his prize recruit and his honky buddy sitting in the back seat.

"Man on the road much as I am don't get a chance to run into many foxy ladies like yourself, Heather."

Had I been drinking, I think this would have made more sense to me. Barnes, the pudgy baldy lily-white honky, and Maw, black as the ace of spades, were trying to hook up. After just three drinks, they were asshole buddies.

"Oh, Barnsie, you say the nicest things. I's gonna have to fix you a home cooked meal one of these days."

"I'd like that, Heather. Don't get many home cooked meals in my profession. All work and no play. Speaking of play, that's my last bottle. What say we stop at the liquor store and get us another bottle to go with dinner?"

Gimlet spoke up.

"Uh, Mr. Barnes, this here's a dry county. Nearest bootlegger's 'bout ten miles away."

"Well, Heather, still kinda early. That ok with you boys?"

"Yessuh," I replied.

"Damn straight," replied Gimlet.

"Barnsie, I'd go anywhere with you," giggled Maw.

"Why don't I stop up here and get the boys a Coke or something. You and I can share our cocktail on the way," said Barnes, putting his hand on Maw's knee.

This was really getting interesting. This being small town Mississippi, we'd never seen a black and white in an obvious romantic situation, and the fact that it was our very own Auntie Maw made it even more surreal.

By now Barnes and Maw were for sure shit-faced, and I wasn't real keen on Barnes driving to the bootlegger, so I nudged Gimlet.

"Pull over at this Quick Stop, Mr. Barnes, and I'll get us some Cokes," said Gim.

"Right, Theodore, here's ten bucks. Buy whatever you want. Anything for you, Heather?" asked Barnes, grinning seductively.

"Wouldn't mind a couple of them pig's feet, Barnsie, and maybe a little stone later on," replied Maw with what, I guessed, was her best seductive pout.

"Be right back with pig's feet, Cokes, and snacks," he said, snatching the ten spot from Barnes' hand. Gim, living up to his reputation, returned in record time with two paper sacks full of refreshments.

"Here's yo' pig's feet, Maw, er, Miz Curt. Coke and Nabs for me and Too Sweet. Anything for you, Mr. Barnes?" Gim asked politely.

"Just another drink and maybe a little dark meat later on," he replied, now looking at Maw with pure lust. Hell, I was preparing to stop at a motel the way things were going. I decided right then and there that Too Sweet's scholarship was in the bank.

"Oh, Barnsie, you charmer, you. Bet you say that to all yo' women."

Breaking up the lovebirds, I said, "Uh, Mr. Barnes, suh. Suh, I got to work out early, got to stay in shape. Reckon we could go on and get yo' adult beverage pretty soon?"

"Why, certainly, Too Sweet. Forgot about you boys' bedtime. We'll go now, then get us something to eat, and your Maw and I can talk about the scholarship and all that. All right?"

"Yessuh," I replied.

The ten-mile drive to the bootlegger was basically uneventful. And after restocking the car bar, we finally made our way to the Steak House. And the flagrant sexual innuendoes continued.

"I think I's gonna order me a Barnsie Burger pretty soon," cooed Maw.

"How you want your Barnsie Burger, Heather?" Barnes asked.

"No dressing, I likes it raw," Maw replied.

As I was on the verge of puking, Gim seemed to be thoroughly enjoying himself. He just sat there through all this, making faces and trying to hold his tongue. After all, he had all the food and drink he could handle and a free meal coming up. He even took the chance to encourage Barnes and Maw in this shameful charade.

"Er, Maw, er, Miz Curt, you and Mr. Barnes make a nice looking couple. Look like you was made for each other."

Yeah, like Hitler and the Jews, I thought to myself. But, I guess everybody has a right to a little nooky now and then. Barnes' cup of tea just happened to be quite different from mine. As Booger Scales, the legendary philosopher, once opined, "Everyone has his or her idea of love. It may be the love of ideas, the love of music, of poetry, of quiet times beside a roaring fire, a quiet walk on a windswept beach, or just a good piece o' ass." I'm not real sure Booger said all that, not all at once, at least. It was probably more like, 'Is it lust or love, the troubadour sang, is love in your heart, or you just want poontang?'

Yes, I'm sure Booger said that.

"Thank you, Theodore. Don't know when I've enjoyed myself more. Got to thank you and Too Sweet and Heather for this wonderful evening. I'm gonna buy all of you the biggest steak and trimmings in the restaurant when we get there."

Mr. Barnes was by now what some would call three sheets to the wind. With that awful Yankee accent, who could really tell? About this time, Mr. Barnes had dropped his speed to about thirty miles an hour. My guess was it was on account that he was drunk, but then, it could have been that his attention was else where in the seat beside him. With only about three miles to go to a big steak dinner, we already had a million stories to tell.

The bright lights of a car fast approaching suddenly caught my eye as I glanced into the rear view mirror. Seeing how we were moving at a crawl, I figured they would just pass us. But instead, the car pulled along side, the occupants gawking at the idiot driving so slowly in a sixty-mile zone. I quickly recognized the people staring back at me.

Blubber Butt Brown. Booger Scales. And Erskine Brown in Tommy Munn's old Chevrolet. Tommy slowed down to keep pace with the unfamiliar Cadillac. The whole group did a double take when they saw a strange white man and a black woman in the front seat. Slowly, their gaze moved to the back seat where Gim and I were doing our best to be inconspicuous. Even in the dark, though, Gim stood out like a sore thumb. They began to take a little deeper interest as they recognized my buddy.

"Hey, there, Gimlet Ass!"

"Who the hell's that black boy back there with him, though?"

"Ain't never seen him before. Ain't that Maw up in the front seat?" "Must be Miz Hortense's boyfriend driving.

"Car got Ohio plates, though. Some Yankee bastard. Damn Yankees shot my great grand paw in the Battle of Vicksburg."

I sensed that Ol' Blubber Butt was getting irate at the thought of a Yankee parading through his town. I knew for a fact that none of his kinfolk had ever served in any organized army. Truth is, Blubber Butt came from a long line of drunks, con men, draft dodgers, and others probably not eligible for any social register. In fact, if Blubber had a family tree, it probably went straight up, and to him, that was reason enough to abhor any Yankee scum.

"Hey, Gimlet ass. What'cha doing riding with that damn Yankee bastard?"

Normally, Blubber was an all right guy, always smiling and joking around, but I'd bet he'd had a nip or two, it being Saturday night and all.

"Did that fat boy just call me a Yankee bastard?" asked Mr. Barnes angrily.

"No suh," I replied, just wanting to get to the Steak House and home.

"Certainly sounded like it. What'd he say then?" Barnes requested.

Before I could reply, I glanced over at Tommy's car, just in time to see that Blubber Butt had dropped his drawers and was in the process of sticking his wide ass through the passenger window. I had never seen a more awesome moon. Whoever stuck the Blubber Butt moniker on him was right on the money. Blubber Butt's ass had completely filled the entire window. Even Gim was almost speechless. Almost.

"Hot dam, look at that ass! Bigger than a U. S. government mule."

I don't know if the sport of mooning had made its way all the way up to Ohio, and I'm not quite sure Barnes could believe what he was looking at, but should he ever have the good fortune to be mooned again, he would never see such a sight. It was breathtaking.

"Is that fat boy sticking his ass out the window?"

"Naw, Mr. Barnes, he's probably just more comfortable riding that way," Gim answered.

"No, suh," I replied.

"Too Sweet, you mean you don't see that big ass staring us right in the face? You see it, don't you, Heather?"

"No, suh," I replied.

"Dat dat Brown boy? Look like his ass aw-ight," replied Heather.

"Most impressive," Gimlet confirmed.

Mr. Barnes, after seeing this amazing display of rear, had unconsciously floored the Caddy's accelerator, causing us to quickly reach eighty miles an hour. Tommy Munn, wanting us to enjoy the spectacle of Blubber's ass as long as possible, had kept pace. All we needed to make the evening complete was for Sheriff Kincaid to come on the scene. Low and behold, there in the crossroads was the defender of justice. For a moment I believed I was psychic. Tommy quickly jammed on brakes, causing Blubber's ass to wedge even tighter in the window opening. After the sheriff switched on his blue lights, Mr. Barnes also slowed to a respectable speed. Both cars pulled over near the sheriff's. And Sheriff Kincaid made his way to Tommy's car first.

"Well, well, Tommy, in a bit of a hurry tonight?"

"Naw, sir, Sheriff, Blubber Butt's got the squirts pretty bad. Trying to get him to a restroom. Real quick."

The sheriff, I'm sure, had seen some horrible things in his ten years of law enforcement, bad car wrecks, drownings, wife beatings and all the rest, but I would guarantee you he ain't never seen anything like he was about to see.

"Where is Blubber, anyhow?" the Sheriff asked as he switched on his flashlight.

"That's him over on the passenger side, sheriff," answered Tommy.

The sheriff swung his flashlight around the car and took in the sight of Blubber's massive ass, now tightly stuck in the window.

"Holy shit!" exclaimed the sheriff. The sheriff was a church going man, and until that night I had never heard him use any form of blasphemy. And he wasn't done.

"What the fuck's going on here? Why is Blubber's ass up in this window? Gezus Christ, get yo' butt back inside and put yo' pants on before I put yo' ass under the jail."

I guess some things just make you lose it.

"Uh, Sheriff, I think he's wedged in there. Like I said, he had him a little case of diarrhea," Tommy lied admirably.

"So he was crapping out the window on a public road? You gotta to be shittin' me."

At that, we all started to laugh. Except of course, Kincaid.

"I ought to run all yo' asses in. Month on the county farm and some of that ass'll disappear. You boys gonna unwedge his ass right now."

Tommy, Booger, and Erskine went into a quick executive session.

"I wouldn't touch his ass with a ten foot pole," said Erskine.

"I'm with Erskine. Sheriff can send me to Parchman 'fore I'll get close to that ass," exclaimed Booger.

"Guys, come on. We don't want to get in no trouble with the sheriff. He'll tell our folks, and hell, we'll be grounded for a month. I got me a couple of quarts of recycled motor oil in the trunk. All we got to do is pour some on Blubber Butt's ass, and he'll slide right out," reasoned Tommy.

"Bullshit, he's wedged in there tighter than Old Mis Dawkin's twat. Somebody gonna have to do some serious pushing, and it damn sho' ain't gonna be me," said Booger.

Tommy then said, "All we gotta do is find a couple of big tree limbs and pour a little oil on his butt. Me and Booger put the end of the limbs on each butt cheek and push. Blubber'll slide right out. Easy as pie."

"Yeah, but if he farts, I'm out. He can keep his ass in there till it falls off," declared Booger.

Blubber, hearing all these somewhat unflattering comments as if he weren't even there, remained quiet. Since he was helpless, it was probably a good tactic.

"Come on, guys. I promise I won't fart. Come on and get me out of here. My butt's falling asleep."

"All right, BB, but if you even look like you gonna pass ass gas, we out of here," threatened Tommy.

Meanwhile in the Caddy, Mr. Barnes and Maw, knowing they were completely bombed, decided to try to sober up with Kincaid just steps away. Gim and I were totally enjoying the spectacle in Tommy's window, but we knew it was just a matter of time 'til the sheriff got to us.

"Tommy, I ain't got all night. Get that boy's ass out now, or I'm gonna get on my radio with my deputy and have him bring all yo' parents out here."

That got Tommy's attention.

"Guys, find us two poles, and I'll get the motor oil."

A few minutes of searching and two large tree limbs later, Tommy was pouring motor oil on Blubber's massive backside.

"A little around the hips," chuckled Booger, as he and Erskine got in position with the poles, placing one firmly on each cheek.

Picture it. A massive ass, now black with oil and two of our buds with poles in hand, taking on possibly the most odious task of all time. That night it didn't get any better than that.

"Ok, now, push, guys, push… keep on pushing… I'm gonna pour some more oil… I think he's coming out… butt's moving… c'mon… push harder," said Tommy.

Tommy then poured the remaining oil on his butt, and the guys gave one massive push. Blubber's ass was now slowly moving. It was working. Blubber, feeling his ass slowly making it's way out and knowing he would soon be free, decided that maybe it was payback time for some of the rather mean remarks made about his dumper. He sensed that a lot of motor oil had run down between his cheeks and collected in his crack. Suddenly, he got this look about him as though an idea had just hit him. Then his face tensed up…

Braaaack, braaaack, braaaack!

The geyser had blown. Black gold, or in this case, Blubber Oil, spewed everywhere. Clothes. Shoes. Skin. Nothing was safe and everything was covered. I heard later that Erskine had been yelling something at the time and got it right in the kisser.

"Damn, Blubber! Son of a bitch!," screamed Tommy.

As convincingly has he could, Blubber replied, "Uh, jeepers, guys. Um, sorry. You know, about messing up–"

"Damn, I'm gonna have to burn these clothes," cried Tommy.

"Ooops?," Blubber offered sheepishly.

He was grinning from ear to ear looking like he'd just won the lottery. The sheriff meanwhile was trying to compose himself. He'd been attempting to suppress his laughter this whole time.

"All right, guys, looks like y'all have learned your lesson. Now go home, and don't let me see you out again tonight."

With little grumbling, the four quickly departed. Next, it was our turn. Sheriff Kincaid swaggered over to our car, blinding us with his flashlight. He paused as he took it all in. Maw and Barnes in the front. Me in black face and Gim in the back.

"Well, well, what have we here? Looks 'tho an OREO been cracked in two. Is that you, Theodore? Maw? Who's that in the front seat? Who's that in the back with you, Theodore?" Then, another pause.

"This whole car smells like a damn brewery. Y'all been drinking? The boy in the back; he been in an accident? I want answers right now."

Under pressure, Gim's not the coolest cube in the freezer. Fittingly, he spoke first.

"Uh, Sheriff Kincaid. This here's Mr. Barnes, the famous recruiter from Ohio State, and that there's Maw, uh, Miz Curt, our maid, and this is Too Sweet, Maw's son, who's being recruited by Ohio State. I'm just along for the ride."

"Mr. Barnes, Miz Curt, you two ain't been drinking, have you?" queried the sheriff.

Maw retreated into a more colorful dialect.

"Now, She'ruff, you knows Maw take a little medicine for her condition. 'Ritis be's pretty bad tonight. Had ta double de dose. But you know Ol' Maw never touch the hard stuff."

The sheriff rolled his eyes at that comment.

"What about you, Mr. Barnes? You got some kinda medical condition, too?"

Now Barnes was totally wasted, could barely focus on Sheriff Kincaid as he replied. "Occi'fer, here's uh, twenty dollars for the police benevolent… fund, thingy. If you'll escort us to the restaurant, I'll dub'lit. And, yes, I did have one drink with the charming Miz Curt."

The Sheriff actually used the flashlight on all of us to decide just who it was Barnes was calling charming. Sheriff Kincaid was from the old school, and bribery and bullshit were way down on his list.

"Not trying to bribe me, are you, Mr. Barnes? Pretty serious offense in these parts."

Once again it fell on my mighty shoulders to sort this all out. Damn them all.

"Uh, Sheriff, suh. Can I speak to you, suh? Over there?"

Once Sheriff Kincaid and I were out of earshot, I explained everything. He went through a range of emotional responses. At first, he was pissed. Then amused. Then, just downright hysterical.

"You got your driver's permit, don't you boy? I don't want drunk ass driving anymore tonight. Take him and Maw home and let 'em sleep it off. Then you and Theodore get yo' asses to bed."

Sounded like a plan to me.

"Mr. Barnes, I'm gonna let you off with a warning, but I don't want you driving anymore tonight. Too Sweet here's gonna drive y'all home." He shot me a wink.

"If I see you out again tonight, I'll put you in jail."

This got Mr. Barnes' attention.

So, Barnes reluctantly slid across, and I got behind the wheel. Me driving a brand new Cadillac, who'd thought it? If only I could show some of the local honeys. But seeing how I was stuck playing Too Sweet, it was probably just as well. Then, Gim had one last request.

"Uh, Mr. Barnes, you know me and Too Sweet never did get to eat. The sheriff said we had to take you and Maw home, but he didn't say nothin' 'bout us. You know Too Sweet got to keep his strength up to play ball. Wonder if we could have that twenty you offered the Sheriff? Me and Too Sweet'll go on to the restaurant. We'll drop you and Maw…Miz Curt off at the house, and you can get better acquainted. Maybe have some more medicine."

That's my boy. One trick mind when it comes to food and pussy.

"And Mr. Barnes, Too Sweet here's a good driver. We'll drive on to the restaurant in style and get yo' car washed 'fore you go back up north. You and Miz Curt have more time that way."

"Smart plan, Theodore. Here's forty. You boys have yo' a good meal and fill the car with gas before you get back. Take your time. I want to show Heather my rock collection."

"Oh, Barnsie, you devil," Maw giggled.

So, as fast and cautiously as I could, I raced home to drop Mr. Barnes and Maw off at Miz Hortense's house. We had to almost drag Maw and Mr. Barnes into the house, since both of 'em were having trouble navigating. But their wayward feet didn't keep them from flirtin'.

"Why they call you Stone, uh, Stone?" You got a stone or two for Heather? I's gonna eat you like a

Hershey bar, nuts and all."

"I'll show you 'em both, while I'm yodeling in your canyon."

"Gimlet, let's go, I ain't gonna be able to eat my supper if we hang around here." We left the two horn dogs on the porch and jumped into Barnes new Caddy and made our way to the Steak House.

"Gimlet, help me get this tape and paint off. Since Barnes is gone, I can go back to be a honky."

"Bet Stone and Heather gettin' it on right now in your bed. Bet you'll have pecker juice all over yo' clean sheet and probably some of ol' Maw's essence of ass on yo' pillowcase."

"Bullshit, Rango. That ol' bastard couldn't get it up with two Popsicle sticks and a roll of adhesive tape."

"Well, even if they can't, they'll wallow all over yo' sheets with their hot naked bodies. Be a lot of grab ass going on."

The visions in my head started to make me a bit queasy.

"Soon as I get home, I'm gonna throw those sheets away. Barnes and Maw, sweet Jesus," said Gim.

"Drop it, Gim. Let's go in and have us a big steak, onion rings, french fries, and a couple slices that homemade coconut pie. Barnes' treat."

After we ordered, Gimlet gave me a friendly elbow. "Not a bad day, huh, ol' bud. Got to ride in a new Caddy, got Too Sweet his scholarship, got Maw laid and most importantly, got us a free meal. Oh, and for a change, we ain't in trouble with the Sheriff. You even got to play a spook for a second time. Matter of fact, I think like you better cooned. You a hell of a lot quieter."

"Well, when you white you white, Gimlet." We both got to laughing.

"One hell of a day. I'll never forget Blubber's oil-spewing ass stuck in that window. Don't know if we'll ever top this one."

"Oh, we'll find a way, Gim. We always do."

Phylasho

The sun had come up on another fine day, and like clockwork, I was on my way to Gimlet's house. But before I could even knock on the door, I heard the sound of Maw bawling and wailing. "Oh, sweet Jesus, help me now. Lawdy, Lawdy, woe is me."

Then, just as passionate, came the sweet sound of Maw singing.

"Nobody knows the trouble I've seen. Nobody knows, but Jesus."

Gim met me at the door.

"Gim, what's with Maw? Haven't seen her this upset in a long time."

"Her daughter, Phylasho, got beat up pretty bad last night. Sheriff found her by the side of the road out at Deemer Mountain. She's in a coma; still ain't sure she's gonna make it."

He then went on to explain to me that Gim's Auntie Maw had ten daughters and one son, Too Sweet. Maw had named her oldest daughter, Phylasho. And as the sound of her name might indicate, rumor had it, she was quite skilled in certain areas.

"Oh, shit, what happened? They got any idea who did it?"

"Naw, not yet. Since she ain't woke up yet, nobody knows what happened. Sheriff's out there now looking for clues."

I suddenly felt a wave of emotion well up inside me. A sense of urgency. After all, I considered Maw like a second mother to me and Gim. And deep down, I think she loved us, too. And then it hit me light a bolt of lightning.

"Gim, if we wait around for the sheriff to solve this case, we'll be two old bastards. We gotta do something. We gotta do it for Maw."

"Guess you right, Rango. What'cha think we need to do?"

"Well, first off, we need to ride out and take a look at the crime scene 'fore the sheriff completely fucks it up. Then we need to go see Phylasho when she comes out of her coma."

"Damn, Rango, got to be ten miles out to Deemer Mountain. How you propose we get there? Maw ain't gonna let us use the car."

"Gim, damn it, we'll walk if we have to. Or ride our bikes. The exercise'll do us good. I'll even buy you a Barq's Root Beer and a moon pie over at Rich's Grocery. We gonna get to the bottom of this for Maw; then we'll get to use the car anytime we want to. I bet Maw'll be so grateful she'll let Trudy Lou sleep over one night," I said, sealing Gim's fate. I knew he had a snowball's chance in Hell of getting Trudy Lou to sleep over. But I just loved screwing with Gim's mind.

"Rango, you really think so? You heard anything 'bout Trudy Lou even liking me?"

"Now don't get all side tracked with Trudy Lou. We're doing this for Ma and Phylasho, and after we solve this case, we'll be able to do what we want to. Let me go get my bike and I'll meet you back here in five minutes."

Exactly five minutes later, Gim and I were on our trusty PF Flyers headed to Deemer Mountain. We were on a mission to make the Hardy Boys look like pansies. Not too hard, we figured.

About half way out, not surprisingly, Gim started bitching. "Damn, Rango, it's hot. My ass hurts. My underwear is stuck up in my crack, and I'm tired. Let's stop up here in the shade and rest."

"Gimlet, we 'bout halfway there already. We'll stop at Mossey's Grocery. It's only another mile. We've got to stay focused. This is our chance to be town heroes. Bet the mayor'll even give us the key to the city or some shit. And after that, there'll be a lot more nooky than Trudy Lou pining for the Gimster. You'll probably have to wear a disguise when you go out cause the women'll be trying to tear your clothes off and take advantage of you."

It was like a light bulb went on.

"Think I just got my second wind, Rango. Let's ride all the way – no more breaks. We'll get a drink on the way back. We got to solve this case for Maw and Phylasho."

Encouragingly, I offered, "Atta boy, Gim."

Fifteen minutes of heavy pedaling, a quick bathroom break at Massey's, and we were there. The crime scene was easy to spot, being right on the side of the road that went straight to the top of Deemer Mountain. Looking back, it really wasn't much more than a hill, let alone a mountain, but some ol' timer had named it years ago, and the name just seemed to stick.

When we got right up onto the scene, we found that the Decatur Police Department had cut a bunch of burlap feed sacks into strips and strung them around the area and hand lettered a warning on the back of an old Barq's sign: KEEP YOUR ASS OUT. DECATUR POLICE DEPARTMENT. So much for that fancy yellow crime scene tape, I thought to myself.

"What da you think we oughta do, Rango?"

"Well, Gim, we need to go over every square inch of the roped off area. I think we need to get down on our hands and knees and crawl all around. Anything that looks the least little bit suspicious, we'll pick up with a handkerchief and–"

"Uh, Rango, you got a handkerchief? I didn't bring one."

"Nah, I didn't bring one either. Hey, I thought Maw always made sure you had a hanky 'fore you left home, Gim. What happened to it?"

"Uh, I had it just a few minutes ago. Must have lost it somewhere," said Gimlet, turning bright red.

"Gimlet, you been chokin' your chicken again?"

The question turned out to be a rhetorical one.

"Damn, Gim. Only time you were out of my sight is when we went into Massey's for you to use the bathroom."

Gim turned even more crimson, almost purple.

"Damn, Rango. That Miz Masey was looking hot this morning in those shorts. You know a man's got only so much willpower."

"Gimlet, my boy, Ms Masey got to be at least fifty years old and has an ass bout two axe handles wide. You gonna' go blind you keep beatin' yo meat five times a day. I guess we're really gonna have to get you laid after we solve this case. Only thing I can think of now is we just gotta have to take our underwear off and use them like a handkerchief. Your drawers clean, Gim?"

"Fresh this morning."

"Somehow I doubt that."

Then I added, "We might as well take our shirts off too, Gim. This is gonna be a nasty job. No need to mess up our clothes."

For some reason that morning, perhaps it was the clean mountain air, but for some unknown reason the idea of two naked boys crawling around the ground with a pair of underwear in their hands didn't strike us as being odd in any way. But we were so focused on the task at hand that nothing was going to distract us.

"What if somebody comes down the road, Rango? We crawling round naked; got to be a law against it."

Undressing, I said, "You worry too much, Gim. Everybody that lives out this way has already gone to work. And should someone come along, all we got to do is lay flat on the ground. Ain't nobody gonna see us. 'Sides, everybody in town done seen yo naked body already."

"Hardy har har."

"Ok, Gim, you start over on the left side; I'll start on the right. We'll meet in the middle and, remember, anything that looks suspicious, pick it up."

"OK, Rango, I just wish we didn't have to get naked."

"Well, fine, Gim, keep your clothes on. See what Miz Hortense does when you show up with dirt all over your clothes."

With that exchange, we began our delicate task, crawling ever so slowly over every inch of ground inside the crime scene. After about ten minutes, Gim and I were drenched in sweat and dirt, making us almost unrecognizable.

"Finding anything, Gim?"

"Nothing so far. Damn, this is hard work. You 'bout ready to take a break?"

"Hell, no, Gim. We just got started. I told you we gonna solve this case one way or the other. Now keep crawling. We'll stop in a few minutes."

Ten minutes later, Gim found something.

"Rango, Rango, I got something. Looks like a Lucky Strike pack. It was crammed down in this hole like somebody was trying to hide it."

"Damn good work, Gim. That just might be our first clue. Make sure you pick it up with your skivvies and put it in the sack."

"Uh, Rango, why ain't we just pickin' this stuff up with our hands? We ain't got any way to fingerprint this shit anyhow. What difference does it make?'

"Quite simple, Gim. It's possible we'll contaminate the evidence if we go around picking it up with our bare hands."

"Oh," said Gim.

"We need to find us one more clue so we can narrow down our suspects. I can name ten people that smoke Luckies."

"Yeah, Rango, but these got filters. That's gonna eliminate a bunch. Most people smoke Luckies with no filters."

"Well, why didn't you say so, Gim? Yeah, that'll really narrow our suspects down. Excellent work."

I was beginning to get optimistic. If we could get one more break or two, we just might be able to solve this puzzle. Of course, that was assuming our cigarette pack was, in fact, discarded by the guilty party. And we could get the perp to confess, assuming we could get him or her to do it in front of witnesses. Unfortunately, I was well aware of what can happen when you a.s.s.u.m.e. something.

"Gim, we need another break. Let's really concentrate here. When we get through, we'll run over to Stovall's pond and wash all this dirt off, and I'll buy you a root beer on the way back to town."

"Uh, oh, I hear a car coming, Gim. Lay down flat 'til they get by."

We got as low to the ground as we could and out of the corner of my eye, I saw Rufus's three-hole chariot slowly making the turn and stopping right beside the crime scene. My other favorite drunk, Early Rue, was riding shotgun. Well, at least if they spotted us, it's for damn sure nobody would ever believe them.

"Got to take a piss, Rufus. What all dese croker sacks doing here? Look like some kinda arena fo goat ropin or somthin."

Early Rue stumbled over to the crime scene and looked over the ground trying to digest all that he was seeing in his pickled brain. I swear he was staring right at Gimlet's naked ass, but I'm sure he had no frame of reference for what he was seeing.

"Rufus, it looks like a dead hog laying dere in de pen, but seems de thing gots hair."

Rufus came staggering over and through half closed eyes tried to come up with some simple solution.

"Ain't no hog, Early Rue. Ain't never seen a hog dat had a ass dat fat. Looks like a cross' tween a hog and a Jack Ass. Tink de called a hogass."

"Bullshit, Rufus. Ain't no such thin'. Dat's one ugly as a bal' headed pussy all right. Why don't you poke dat thang wid' a stick, make sure it's dead?"

"I ain't gettin' no closer to dat thing than right here. Damn', look over dere Early Rue, look like another one dere on de ground; Must be some kinda Indian burial ground. Dat one look a little better than dey fat one. Shiiit, I ain't gonna never eat me no' pork after seeing dis. Dat thang ought'a be in de circus. Biggest ass I ever saw."

"Rufus, why don'cha throw one of dem dirt clods at that fat one; see if it moves."

"I ain't throwin' shit at dat ugly motherfucker. What if dat thang's alive and jumps up and eats us both? Dat thang didn't git to be dat fat eatin no collard greens."

Suddenly, the beast awoke.

"Who you ol' piss drunk assholes calling fat?" yelled Gimlet, getting up off the ground.

"Oh, sweet Jesus!" yelled Rufus, fainting dead away.

"Holy shit, dat hogass alive," hollered Early Rue moving faster than he probably ever had in his life. However, his equilibrium was a little wobbly, and he fell headfirst into his car door. A lesser, or rather less drunk man, would have been knocked unconscious, but Early Rue just shook his head and began screaming at the top of his voice.

"Oh, Mr. Hogass, don't eat me. Early an old man. Dis meat tough. Don' eat me, Mr. Hogass."

Now Gimlet was really pissed. "Stop calling me Hogass. It's me, Gimlet and Durango. We're out here searching for clues for the Sheriff. Now get yo' asses out of here."

Early Rue finally stopped screaming and tried to focus on Gim.

"How it be dat you be talkin'? How you know my name, Hogass?"

"You drunk mother–"

"Wait a minute. Gimlet, dat you? Who dat udder out there? And why in de hell you naked?"

"I already told you, ya drunk son of a bitch, that's Durango. We on a secret mission for Sheriff Kincaid."

"Really, what kinda secret mission involves getting neked? Come on out, Rango. You boys out here having a circle jerk or somethin'?"

About that time, Rufus sat up and took a long look at me and Gim.

"Y'all playing hide de pork? Can't ya'll find a better place to play grab ass?"

"We naked cause it's part of our undercover operation for the Sheriff. We out here investigating Maw's daughter's beating."

"Well, why didn't you two goober gobblers say so?" said Rufus.

"Me and Early be glad to stay 'round and help you boys look for clues," he continued.

"You boys want us to go undercover, get naked, too?" said Rufus.

"Keep yo clothes on, Rufus. This is serious. You two could help us look for clues outside the crime scene. Just don't get in our way," I said.

"Ok, let's quit standing around with our thumbs up our asses. Let's see if we can get another break."

Thirty minutes later we had nothing new.

"I got to pee," said Rufus.

"Damn, Rufus, just make sure you go far out in the woods. We gonna go over this area again tomorrow and make sure we didn't miss anything. We don't need you contaminating the place."

Rufus walked over to the edge of the woods to pee.

"Rango, come quick, might be a clue."

I went running over to Rufus.

"Whatcha' got?"

"Look like some big animal done shit right here in de woods. Look at dat pile."

He pointed to the biggest pile of dog shit I had ever seen.

Gimlet piped up, "Told you these two sots be useless as tits on a boar hog."

Pondering, I said "Wait a minute now, Gim. Who we know that's got a real big dog and smokes filtered Lucky Strikes?"

We looked at each other, and the name came out simultaneously, "Deputy Brown".

"Dat da skinny ass white deputy dat walks like he got a cob up his butt? Dat bastard run me in fo' drinking tree or fo' times. Sheriff usually just lets me sleep it off. Brown put me out on the work farm. I'd like to fix that tight ass honky," declared Early Rue.

"Well, this jus'might be yo' chance, Early. One thing's for sure; he's definitely a suspect. Y' all got any ideas on what to do next?" I asked.

"Oh, Ol' Early might have an idea or two."

"Let's hear it. Anything's worth a try," I said halfheartedly.

"Dat Deputy out to de colored quarters bout ever night. Always got dat big dog wid' em. One night tho, he was walking house to house lookin for booze, and his dog started runnin' for a cat. Left Brown right in de middle of de quarters by hisself. Well, I tellin you, de honky scared shitless in de dark wid out dat dog. Started runnin' like a scared ass ape back to his car. Ran right into Miz Lucas boy, Troy. You know de one ain't right in de head? That jive ass honky took one look at dat tree hunderd poun grinnin' idiot and started screamin' like a woman. Thought he was gonna have a heart attack 'fore he got back to de car. Guarantee he had skid marks in his drawers."

I already had the start of a plan in my head. We knew that Deputy Brown was scared of the dark and, especially, without his dog. As the plan began to form in my head, I realized that I would need a way to get everyone involved to help it all come together.

"Good info, Early," I said, trying to stroke his ego. "We might need you and Rufus to help us with our little plan."

"You can count on us, Rango. Wud love to put dat asshole under de jail. Wha'chums want us to do?"

After discussing everyone's roles, me and Gim prepared to leave our two black sleuths.

"Me and Gim gonna ride our bikes over to Miller's creek and wash some of this mud off. Then we'll head into town. I'll holler when we need you. Just be ready."

"We stay ready, Rango. Be glad to give you boys a ride tho. Put you' bikes in de trunk."

"No thanks, Early. We've seen you drive. Just be careful, and don't give Deputy Brown any reason to pull you over."

"Oh, we's be careful all right, Rango. Don't you worry 'bout a ting. See ya', Hogass," they said as they jumped into the car and sped off out of control.

When the dust settled, I glanced over at Gim. He had both middle fingers up as if to wave the drunks good-bye.

"Never mind them, Gim, we got a lot work to do. Let's go get cleaned up and get back into town."

The Decatur General Hospital was a place you didn't want to be a patient in and a place you didn't want to visit. As we walked through the main doors, we could hear Maw's soulful voice singing to Phylasho.

"Will de circle be unbroken bye and bye,

Lord, bye and bye, dere' s a betta home awaitin in de sky,

Lord, in de sky. Undertaker, undertaker,

undertaker take it slow. Cause dat woman that you haulin',

Lawd, I hate to see her go."

I hated to see Maw in this condition. She was singing her sad death song, and it was up to me and Gim to cheer her up.

"Maw, Maw, me and Gim're here now. Everything's gonna be all right. We gonna find out who did this to Phylasho, and we gonna see that they're punished."

Maw, on seeing us, stopped her mournful singing and gathered us both in her ample bosom. "Oh, boys, ol 'Maw love you both just like you my own chil'ren. You both a big comfort to me in this time of sorrow."

"How's Phylasho, Maw? Is there any change in her condition?" Gim asked with moist eyes.

"Bless you for asking, boy. Doctor say no change, but she holdin her own. Say it may take a week 'fore she come outta her coma. Maw don't know how she gonna pay for that. Ain't got no insurance, no savings, no nothin'. Ain't got a pot to piss in. Just don't know what I'm gonna do. Guess I'll have to go to the po' house. You boys gonna come visit me there?" Maw was as down as we'd ever seen her and, as if on cue, went into another sad refrain.

"Ever time I go to town,

de fellahs start kicking' my dog around.

Make no difference if it is a hound,

You better stop kicking' my dog around."

"Don't worry, Maw. Rango and I'll take care of you. Don't want to hear no nonsense 'bout no po' house. If we have to dig ditches, me and Rango gonna raise all the money you need," blurted Gimlet through watery eyes.

"Oh, Gimlet, you and Rango come here and give Maw a big hug." She said almost crushing some ribs in the process. Tears were now freely flowing down Maw's shiny black face. I glanced over at Gimlet, whose lips were trembling and whose eyes were brimming over. I did my best to stifle my own tears and keep from outright weeping. Then the control just washed away in a sea of tears. I was blubbering like a baby. The more we hugged, the more we all cried. After a few moments, we all regained our composure.

"Boys, Maw doubly blessed to have two fine boys like you as friends. I'll love you till the day I die."

"Maw, I got just the idea for a fund raiser," said Gim. I'll get Booger and Blubber, and we'll do a benefit concert over at yo' church, the Mount Mariah, " he added.

"Gimlet, you sure, ol' buddy?" I asked.

"Yea, Rango, I'm gonna do this for Maw. If Booger & Blubber won't do it, I'll do it by myself."

"I'm proud of you, ol' buddy. I'll help any way I can," I said, with the tears starting again.

"Gimlet, Maw ain't gonna ever raise her voice to you again. You gonna be my number two son," said Maw, now bawling openly.

I finally mustered up enough strength to put an end to this cry-in.

"Uh, Gim, what date you got in mind? We gotta have time to promote the concert, and you gotta have a little time to practice."

"Today's Tuesday. What about next Sunday? I'll get with Booger and Blubber and see if they'll do it. If not, I'll go solo. I'm gonna do this, Rango, whatever it takes. Maw's done a lot for me, and now it's payback time."

I don't think I've ever been prouder of my friend than I was right then. Except, perhaps, the time he ate all the beans in the Coach's science project and took his ass whipping like a man. But this was different. I know how Gim dreaded singing in public, and here he was preparing for a big concert to raise money for Maw and Phylasho.

"What'cha need me to do, Gim?" I asked, acknowledging the fact that this was all Gim's show.

"Rango, see if you can get Tommy and Erkine to help you make a bunch of posters promoting the concert. We gonna have it next Sunday at two o'clock. Y'all put 'em in every store in town and on as many telephone poles as you can. Make sure you make it right with Reverend Billy that we can use the church," said Gimlet, really taking charge.

"Leave Reverend Billy to me, Rango. He won't dare say no to me. I used to wipe that boy's ass," said Maw, giving us a lot more information than we wanted.

"Uh, Gim, we gonna promote this with just you or with the three of ya. You think Booger and Blubber'll do it?" I inquired.

"Just put me and special guests. If they don't do it, I'll have you come up and harmonize with me on Amazing Grace or somethin'. You can be my special guest, and also, Rango, write down at the bottom of the posters: 'See if he splits his pants again.' Put a little humor in it."

I quickly recalled the incident that my friend was referring to. A time in Jackson when he had been on stage and fell victim to a childish prank. But with him taking charge as he was, I saw no reason to relive the embarrassment at his expense.

"You got it, Gim. We'll get right on it." I called Tommy and Erskine and asked them to begin designing some posters that read:

"BENEFIT CONCERT"
WHERE: MT. MORIAH HOLY SANCTIFIED MISSIONARY BAPTIST CHURCH
WHEN: SUNDAY, JUNE 18
TIME: 2 PM

~ FEATURING THEODORE THOMAS ANDERSON, JR., & SPECIAL GUESTS. THIS
WILL BE A SPECIAL BENEFIT CONCERT FOR "MAW" HEATHER CURT AND HER
DAUGHTER PHYLASHO TO HELP PAY HOSPITAL COSTS. ~

A SPECIAL COMEBACK TOUR FOR THEODORE "GIMLET" ANDERSON.

WILL HE SHOW HIS BUTT AGAIN?

Gim overheard me calling and said, "Ain't that a little bit long, Rango? It's good, but how you
gonna have time to make up a couple hundred posters? And, Reverend Billy ain't gonna like that butt
remark, now that I think of it."

"Well, what if we put derriere in place of butt? Reverend Billy won't have a clue, and he'll be
ashamed to ask."

"Ok, leave it in. Sounds kinda classy."

"Oh, and Gim, I'm gonna get L.T. over at Dorsey's Printing Co. to run us about two hundred. He
owes me a favor. I used to date his daughter."

"He's still speaking to you?" asked Gim.

"Yeah, I guess he believes she's still pure," I said with a wry smile.

"But since we broke up, she started going with that punk in Union. But me and L.T. are still cool.
Speaking of Union, we gonna put posters up in Newton and
Union, too."

"Good idea, Rango. Get the whole county coming.

You think we oughta charge admission or just rely on donations?"

"I think donations are the only way to go. I'll bet some of the businesses probably give a couple a hundred bucks. Everyone knows Maw. She raised 'bout half the town."

After Tommy and Erkine finished the posters, we met up at Dorsey's to get them printed. It took a while, but considering the cost, we managed to wait patiently out front and in the end, they didn't look half bad. As soon as the last one was done, we divided up the lot of em and set out to post them everywhere. As the final poster went up, our two favorite drunks turned the corner.

"Hey, Rango, jest saw de poster. Who dat Theodore Anderson? Dat ol' Gimlet Ass? Didn't have no idea dat boy musical. Didn't know he could play nuthin' but a skin flute," said Early Rue, laughing uproariously.

I didn't have time to get into a prolonged conversation with Early and Rufus, so I did my best to make a hasty exit.

"You boys just be at the concert Sunday. You might be surprised. See ya."

"Oh, we be there, Rango. We could use us a good laughin'" I heard them say as I turned and walked in the opposite direction.

For the next few days, we visited Maw and Phylasho in the hospital. We spent our time away from there getting everything ready for the big concert and formulating a plan that just might trap Deputy Brown into admitting his involvement with Phylasho. Gimlet, Booger, and Blubber were practicing several hours every day and to my untrained ear sounded better than ever. Booger and Blubber were as serious as I'd ever seen them. The only down side I could see was that since the two B's were now totally committed, I wouldn't get to sing with Gimlet. I thought that would probably be best, anyhow.

Finally, Sunday arrived. I walked over to Gim's house, and before I even got to his mailbox at the street, I heard the sweet sound of Maw's voice.

"Oh, happy day. Oh, happy day.

When Jesus washed my sins away."

"Good news, Rango. Phylasho is still in a coma, but there has been some signs of improvement. Doctor Login said she should make a full recovery," announced Gim upon my arrival.

A second later, Maw came into the front room.

"Maw, this is the big day. How's my favorite tenor doing?" I said, referring to Gimlet.

"Dat boy didn't hardly sleep a'tall last night. Walked de flo' til bout tree dis mornin; ol' Maw never forget what dc boy doing for her and Phylasho. Bet de boys ass pucker factor 'bout a ten now. Mystery to me where he gonna get de courage to sing after showing his ass dere in Jackson."

"Gim's gonna show everybody, Maw. Where is he, anyhow? Eating another breakfast?" I said, realizing my friend had disappeared.

"Naw, Rango. He be calling Roy all night, bent over the porcelain. Been pukin' his guts out. Hugging the commode. Nervous as a 'ho at confession."

I walked down the hall and pushed open the bathroom door. "Gim, you ok? Maw said you'd been up all night pukin and pacing. You gonna' be all right for the concert?"

"Aw, Rango, I'm scared shitless. Whatever made me think I could sing in front of a crowd again?" Gim said, on the verge of totally losing it.

I took a moment to reflect on the severity of the situation before I began.

"Now, Gimlet, you and I have stood toe to toe on hundreds of occasions, and we've never lost a battle. When you get right down to the nut cuttin', Gim, who besides your mother means more to you than me and Maw? No matter what you do, me and Maw'll be behind you. So I'm asking you, Gim, if Maw and me are behind you, what the hell difference does it make to you if some people say you're fat and lazy and can't sing and laugh at you behind your back? What if a lot of people saw you naked at the water tower? What if a lot of people said you had a dick like a Vienna sausage? I ask you, friend to friend, Gim. What if you go on the stage naked today? What if you forget your lines? Me and Maw are always gonna' be behind you. In the great scheme of things, opinions are like butt holes. Everybody's got one. But me and Maw got

the only opinions that should count to you, Gimme. What if people say—"

"Who said I had a dick like a Vienna sausage?" blurted out Gim, suddenly completely over his nausea and ready to take on a three hundred pound linebacker.

"Relax, I'm just making a point on what's really important and what's not. And letting you know that me and Maw'll never desert you. You'll always be my best buddy, no matter what," I said softly, putting my arm around Gim's neck.

"You ready to do this for Maw?"

"Damn straight, Rango. Screw everybody else. Me and you and Maw. That's all we need."

"Well, that and a few split tails from time to time, right, buddy?" I threw in for good measure.

We finally made it out of the bathroom and headed into the kitchen.

"You ok, Gim, honey?" asked Maw.

"Never better, Maw. I look, feel, and smell like a million bucks. Screw everybody else but you and Rango. Everybody else can kiss my round brown."

"Hey, Gim, I don't want to make you nervous, but while we were putting up the posters, Mr. McKay told me there might be a scout here from Ted Mack Amateur Hour. Might see you on TV soon."

"Screw 'em, Rango. I'm singing for you and Maw."

"Just sing yo' best, Gim honey. Me and Rango proud of you," said Maw, borrowing a page from my book.

"What time you wanna' go over to the church, Gim?" I inquired.

"Told Booger and Blubber I'd meet em there' bout twelve-thirty. We gonna do one last practice. Wanna' come?"

"Wouldn't miss it for the world. You wanta' go that early, Maw?"

"No, you boys go on. Mr. Barnes in town. He gonna' come over and give me a ride."

"You mean the Ohio State Recruiter, Maw? What's he doing back in town? Scouting somebody else?"

"Think he scouting me," said Maw, grinning wickedly.

And on that note, Gim and I made our exit.

Since we had an early start, we took the long way to the Church, anything to get away from Maw talking sex acts with the Yankee from Ohio.

"Uh, Rango, you think Becky Sue'll be at the concert? Thinkin' bout asking her to the movie next week; thought we could double. You could get Betty Sue, and we'll go to the drive in over at Newton. After this concert, Maw gonna' let us have the car anytime. Mama's out of town."

"Maw said that, Gim? You sure? Anytime we want it? Damn, our sex life just improved. You better start eating your Wheaties, bud. Your left hand is about to get quite lonely. Or was it your right?"

"Screw you, Rango."

We laughed for a bit, and I could tell that all this guy talk was keeping Gim loose. I highly doubted he had any kind of shot with Becky Sue, but I thought talking chicks would help get him through the concert.

"Yeah, Gim, I'm sure Becky Sue'll be there. You know Maw was their family's maid for a couple'a years. Her whole family'll be there. Wouldn't surprise me at all if Becky Sue didn't ask you out after the concert. She's gonna be so impressed. You might even get to have your way with her in one of the cloak rooms. You'll probably fall right in, cause she's gonna be so wet after hearing you sing. But, Gim, for now you got to concentrate on the concert. There'll be plenty of time for the mossy jaws later. After today, I got a feeling you gonna' be fightin' off women with a stick."

The Church appeared around a bend, and we stopped talking immediately as we both were hit with a very unexpected and unnerving sight. It looked like the whole town of Decatur and most of Newton County were making their way to the Mt. Moriah Church. As we drew a little nearer to the church, we could see that Reverend Billy had put up loud speakers and grandstand seating outside the church. Cars were backed up all the way to the main drag, and folks were rolling down their windows to show their support for the Gimster.

"Gonna' show yo' crack again, Gim?"

"Hey, pencil dick, why don't you wear a tarpaulin this time?"

"I hear you sound so good on account of you ain't got no balls."

"Well, Gim, nice to know that the town's behind you," I remarked.

"Screw' em all, Rango. Got a feeling this is gonna be my finest concert ever. They'll be kissing my ass tomorrow. Today is for me and Maw and Phylasho."

"That the kinda talk I like, Gim. If I had to have one man lead me through the shark infested waters off the Coast of Borneo, you'd be it."

"Thanks, ol' buddy. I'll always be there for you, too. And today I'm gonna make you proud."

"You always do, Gim."

Finally inside the church, we found Booger and Blubber waiting backstage.

"Hey, Gim. Kick some ass today," said Blubber.

"Guys, let's get ready. Only 'bout an hour fore we start."

In honor of the occasion, the boys had purchased all new outfits, light blue trousers and blue and white stripe dress shirts, with a blue bow tie to complete the ensemble. Since all the participants tended to be in the pleasingly plump category, it somehow put me in mind of awnings.

"We gonna' do the same concert we did in Jackson?" queried Booger.

"Well, I mean minus the butt crack, of course," he added.

At that, maybe out of nervousness or a genuine appreciation for the humor, everyone laughed, even Gim.

The group ran through a few scales, harmonized on a few old standards, and went to take a final pee.

Show time.

Reverend Billy, the self-appointed master of ceremonies, finally stepped into the back room.

"You boys oughta see the size of that crowd. Looks like the whole county's here. Folks having to stand out in the church cemetery. De church and grandstands full. Ain't seen a crowd dis big since Wider Brown got married fo' de tenth time. Musta had five hundred relations here. Dis here concert oughta pay all Maw's bills and have enuf' left to get ol' Reverend Billy a new baptizing dunkin' pool. Hot damn."

"Say, you boys got a name you go by? Gonna' be introducing you here soon."

"No, no name, but it's a good idea. Ya'll need something people can identify you by."

"What you suggest, Rango? You the one always spouting all this bull shit. You oughta be able to come up with something seeing how you got the silver tongue."

"The Three Ton Trio?"

"Tons of Fun?"

"Ok, just kidding, I have a perfect name for this group, a name that fully reflects your many talents, a name that may soon be recognized in most states, if not foreign countries–"

"Cut the bullshit, Rango. The concert'll be over 'fore you quit talking," said Booger.

"Ok, you asked for it. Little drum roll please. The Three Cunning Linguists – That says it all."

"I like it," said Gim. "Kinda classy. What's it mean?"

"It means, my three fine friends, that not only are you smart and cunning like a fox, but that you are also linguists, purveyors and students of the spoken word, clever in the use of language and song."

"Damn, I like it, too. Gives us a touch of class. Way to go, Rango. Whatcha think, Booger?" asked Blubber.

"Fine with me," said Booger.

Together they declared their new title.

"The Three Cunning Linguists!"

"What be dat name, the Three Cunnin' Lingles?" asked Reverend Bill.

"No time to explain right now, Reverend Bill. Show's bout to go on."

The reverend headed toward the crowd, and I took one last look at the talented trio. They looked smashing, almost debonair. Then Reverend Billly, with all the sanctimonious pomp and grandeur he could summon, finally took the stage.

"Good afternoon, brudders and sisters."

"Good afternoon." echoed back from the audience.

"We's come together today fo' dis benefit concert to raise money fo' our own Auntie Maw and her lovely daughter Pbylasho. I want you to reach way down in yo' pockets today and give till it hurt. All dis money gonna pay Phylasho's hospital bills. As everyone know, Phylasho been lying in a coma for several days, but de Holy Ghost gonna heal dat child. De loving spirit gonna lay his hands on dat precious fo'head, and dat child gonna wake rite up outta dat deep sleep, and she gonna' point out de lowlife dat done attack her. Vengeance be's mine, say the Lawd. The Lawd gonna smite dat sum'bitch, just as sure as I standin' here. De Lawd givith, and de Lawd take away. De' fires of hell sho nuff gonna burn hot fo' dat sinnah. In my father house dere be many mansions and I be's wid you even to the ends of the earth, and in Bethlehem dere be Mary and Isaac who be turned away from de Inn. Just like de culprit gonna be turned away from the golden gates of heaven. When St. Peter meet him at the Pearly Gates he gonna say, 'Dude, take yo' sorry ass away from my door. For verily, I say unto you, if you done screwed wid one o my flock, it be like messin wid me.'"

I looked out into the audience to see if I could spot Deputy Brown, our number one suspect. I finally saw him standing guard at the back door, and maybe it was my imagination, but Brown looked even more pale than usual. Maybe the Reverend's little talk was getting to him. In fact, it was getting to the entire audience. They were absolutely eating up Billy's speech. Every sentence, every exclamation was greeted with shouts of "Amen! Sweet Jesus! Tell it like it is, Brother!," and the occasional, "Hell, yeah!"

The reverend continued.

"Fo' God so love de world, he gave his finest robe dat Jacob didn't want no mo to clothe the Baby Jesus, who later be found in de bulrushes wid Moses. Jus' like he gonna find de dude done lay his hands on Phylasho, and he gonna smite him down."

As much as I loved hearing the little sermon, I knew my boy Gim was getting more and more nervous. Before long, I could see the sweat was dripping profusely from Gim's chubby cheeks. If Rev. Billy didn't introduce them soon, I was afraid Gim might melt. So, to move things along, I did the only thing I could think of.

"So Solomon done parted de Red Sea, and put Lot's wife on de left side and de money changer, er–"

"HEY! Let's give it up for Reverend Billy! Wonderful sermon, Bill. Now let's say we raise a little money for Maw," I said, striding onto the stage applauding like a madman. The crowd joined in with gusto and stood en masse.

"Bravo, Bravo, Reverend Bill," from the audience.

Now I could tell that Reverend Billy was momentarily pissed, but I kept on going, and I went over and shook his hand until the applause died down.

"One of the best sermons these ears have ever heard, Reverend Bill," I said to a renewed round of applause. "And I know you can't wait to introduce this magnificent trio waiting backstage to entertain our fine audience," I said, trying gently to nudge Reverend Bill toward the real reason we were all here.

"Oh, yes, de Coon Lickers."

"The Cunning Linguists", I whispered in his ear.

"Right. Ok."

Then, turning to the audience he made the announcement.

"And now, ladies and gentlemen, wid out any further ado, comin' all de way from cross-town fo' yo' listening pleasure, finally reunited and back from dere hiatus, put your hands together and give it up for de one, de only, de fabulous Cunt Lickers!"

The crowd went wild. Apparently, they too couldn't understand a word the Reverend had said. And on cue, Gimlet, Blubber, and Booger stepped onto the stage amid deafening applause. The boys must have worked up a little skit earlier, because they strutted around the stage several times. Then, in perfect synchonization, they turned their backs to the audience, bent over, and shook their butts.

Then the chants from the audience began.

"Coon Lickers, Cont Liters, Cunning Littles, Coon Liters…"

After the applause and fan-fair finally died down, Booger hit a harmonizing note, and Gimlet's angelic voice launched into the most beautiful rendition I'd ever heard.

"I come to the garden alone while the dew is still on the rose, and the voice I hear, as I tarry there…."

The others joined in.

"And he walks with me, and he talks with me, and he tells me I am his own."

All the women and most of the men had their snot rags out and were openly weeping. As Gimlet hit the last drawn out note ending the song, there was dead silence for a good fifteen seconds. Then the applause started and swelled and grew and culminated in a standing ovation.

I looked over at my boy Gimlet, hoping to make eye contact. Gim, rightfully so, was eating this up. He had overcome his fear, done himself proud, and most importantly, was on his way to helping Maw and Phylasho.

After that, things came easy. They hit all their notes, stayed in harmony, and sang several more old standards until Reverend Bill announced a twenty-minute intermission. The crowd went outside to smoke and stretch their legs. I sought out Gim and his heavyweight partners and congratulated them all.

"Hell of a job, guys," I said, as I put my arm around Gim's shoulders. "Knew you could do it, old buddy. I'm proud of you."

"Fore you two start pullin' each others pork, what the hell Reverend Billy call us, the Cunt Lickers? Durango, you gotta straighten that out. My girlfriend ain't gonna like that one bit," said Blubber.

"Ah, Blubber, nobody could understand a word Bill said. Half the crowd thought ya'll named the Coon Lickers anyhow. Nothing to worry about," I said.

Reverend Bill came rushing out, "Good news, boys, dis here concert done raised over ten thousand dollars so far. Oughta be plenty to pay dem horspital bills. Might even be a little left over to build ma dunkin' booth. Ya'll 'bout ready to go back on, boys? Ol' Billy gonna'a try and milk a little mo' money outta dis thang."

"Yeah, we ready, Bill," the trio answered in unison. "Bring it on."

The audience was settling back in their seats eagerly awaiting the finale to this great concert. To thunderous applause, Reverend Billy strutted onto the stage, "Brudders and Sisters, I happy to announce we done raised over ten thousand dollars." Wild applause. "I also happy to announce de sheriff got him a prime suspect in de Phylasho case. Gonna get dat bastard and hang him up by his nutsack."

Truth was, the Sheriff didn't have a clue or a suspect. I asked the Reverend to say that in hopes of flushing out the guilty party. As he said it, looked right at Deputy Brown, who looked guilty as sin.

"Yeah, be jus' a matter of time 'fore de Sheriff put de asshole in dat little cell wid one of dem fudge packers. Boy's butt gonna be hangin' like a coat sleeve. Kinda' like de coat sleeve on ol' Jacob's coat when Moses done come down from de mountain wid de thirty pieces of silver and slew the Philistines. And de forty days and...."

"Let's give it up for Reverend Billy again for that wonderful news," I yelled, interrupting. "But didn't you mention backstage about asking the good folks to dig a little deeper? See if we can't raise fifteen?"

"Right, yes, my dear friends, brudders and sisters, I want you to reach down deep in yo' wallets, yo' purses, yo' pockets, and give all you can. Remember, now dis here fo' sister Phylasho and Maw. If Brudder Jonah, when he done come outta dat whale's belly, and de rich Pharisee ain't give him de frankincense, de boy have to go back in de wilderness fo' forty days and nights jus' like de asshole gona get reamed in dat jail cell..."

"Ok!," I yelled again. I glared at the reverend and rolled my hand over and over to get him to wrap it up.

"Oh, de encore, yes, ok folks, welcome back our very own, Cunt Lunchers!"

Their encore stage routine mimicked their opening, and again Booger hit a harmonious note, and Gimlet led in with "Peace in the Valley."

"There will be peace in the valley someday,

there will be peace in the valley for me,

no more trouble, no sadness, no sorrow I pray

there will be peace in the valley for me."

Again came the thunderous applause as the trio finished. I knew they had planned on singing Elvis' "American Trilogy," and when I heard the first note, I knew it was going to be as good as the King.

"In Dixie Land where I was born, early on one frosty morn', look away, look away,

Look away, Dixie Land

Hush, Little Baby, don't you cry,

You know all men are born to die

Glory, Glory, Hallelujah, Glory, Glory,

Hallelujah, Glory, Glory, Hallelujah,

His truth is marching on."

As they hit the last stanza, I couldn't even hear the trio above the crowd. They were on their feet. They cheered for a good five minutes until the group made their way off and on stage for several curtain calls.

My boy had done it.

Backstage, I found Gim.

"Way to go, dude. Great concert."

"You been crying, Rango?"

Poking the corner of my eye, I said defiantly, "Psshh, me? No way, man. Nope, not me." He could tell I was lying through my teeth, but thankfully kept it to himself.

"Man, I could eat the ass out of a rag doll," he said.

Reverend Bill came over and hugged Gim, Blubber, and Booger.

"Come on boys, Reverend Billy gonna treat all you boys. Concert done raise over seventeen thousand' dolla's. Ya'll can eat all you want down at Slim's BBQ. Got some o' de best BBQ you done put through yo lips. Got some chitins and pig feets, too. You boys want some? Tripe and pig ears, too. Treat's on me."

Now Slim's BBQ was one of those places that catered to blacks and whites, a totally unpretentious wooden shack with a half dozen picnic tables outside.

"All we want, Reverend Bill?" asked Gimlet, now salivating.

"All you want, boys. Ya'll done de concert for free. Least we can do is feed you. Some uh you boys lookin' on de skinny side."

So we all piled into Reverend Billy's brand new gold Cadillac Deville and made our way down to Slim's. Billy parked right by the front door, which was quite a trick considering that the parking lot was full. Seemed the whole town had the same idea.

"Aw, Reverend Billy, we'll never get anything to eat here. W'hole damn county's here," Booger said.

"See dat reserved sign, boys," said Billy, pointing to the sign in front of his car.

"See what it say?"

"Yeah, 'Reserved for Owner.'"

"Well, I de owner. We gonna go sit down in my private room and eat till we can't."

We didn't need another invitation. We all quickly piled out of the car and followed the reverend back to the private room. Once in, he said, "Boys, let me says a few words in a prayer of thanks."

"Lawd, we thank you for dis food we's gonna devour.

Thank yo fo' dese fine young men and de successful concert.

Help us find de' a-hole who done hurt Phylasho. Amen."

"Amen," we all declared.

We must of sat there in that private room with gold wallpaper, gold paneling, gold rugs, gold ceiling fans, gold furniture, and gold lamps for over two hours eating pork ribs, pulled pork, pork chops, pork roast, steak, beans, slaw, corn, potato salad, chitlins, pig ears, pig feet, and tripe along with peach cobbler, banana pudding, chocolate pie, and the sweetest coconut cake I ever had. By the end of it all, there were pig bones on the table, on the floor, and even a few in Blubber's pockets. We all had some amount of dessert on our faces.

"Oh, Sweet Jesus," said Booger.

"Amen," said Blubber.

Reverend Billy drove us back in his gold Cadillac and let us out. "Thank you boys again. You ever need anything, anything a'tall, you just call on Reverend Bill, and he get it done."

"Uh, Reverend Billy, we just might need yo' help on one little matter. We gonna' set a trap and see if we can catch Phylasho's attacker. We gonna' work on the plan and get back to you in a day or two," I said.

"Anytime, boys. Let Reverend Billy know. If you need more people, jes' say de word. We'll screw, blue and tattoo dat a-hole. Be a pleasure."

"And, Booger and Blubber, we gonna need your help, too. You boys in?" I asked.

"Damn straight, Rango. Count us in," said Booger, as he ripped a loud, long fart.

"Damn Boy, oughta make you register you' butt as a lethal weapon," said Billy, as he sped away in his Caddy.

When the air cleared, I said, "Fellas, enough clowning around. We need to figure out a way to trap Deputy Brown into a confession. Got to come up with a foolproof plan."

"So you really think Deputy Brown's guilty, Rango?" asked Booger.

"Do your farts stink?"

"Yeah, but what if he ain't?" asked Blubber

"What if we trap Brown, and he ain't the one? We all gonna be up shit creek. Every time we get in our cars, Brown's gonna be there with his ticket book and his little nightstick. Course, anyone of us could whip his butt, but assault on a lawman's pretty serious stuff. Naw, you got to be right on this, Rango. We can't take no chances. I don't wanna be walking from now on."

"You bring up a good point, Blubber, my old friend," I replied. "And I can assure you, I have thought of any and all possible consequences, and if I even thought that I could be wrong, I'd back off so fast, it'd make your head spin. You guys haven't heard me say this too often, but I look on all of you like you were my brothers, my family. When we're behind seven to six, fourth quarter, first down on the ten yard line, fifty seconds to go, what play do I call? I call a dive play right behind my three brothers on the line. I know that my family, my brothers, will open up that hole, and we'll win the game. If I can't count on my very own family, who can I look to? Same way, you know you can count on me. No way, I'd let you risk anything if I was not absolutely, one hundred percent sure that

Brown's our man. And, I'll make ya'll this further guarantee. If you guys will help me, and if we don't have Brown behind bars in thirty days, I'll quit the football team."

"Quit the football team. Hell, Rango, you our starting Quarterback."

"Never the less, men, I feel strongly about this. If I can't count on my family, my brothers, to help me out, what kind of leader am I? If I don't have your confidence and trust, what kind of team do we have. Not much, I'm afraid. So, hell yeah. I feel very strongly about this, guys. Brown's the culprit all right, and I'll not rest till that asshole is behind bars. So I ask, are you with me?"

"I'm in," said Gim.

"Yeah, me, too, Rango," said Blubber.

"What about you Booger?" I asked.

We all looked in his direction. He paused thoughtfully for a brief moment.

"Do my farts stink?"

So it was off to the Toot-n-Tell It to hatch our plan.

"Three Mountain Dews, please, Latrina. On me," I said.

Latrina and her older sister Placenta were institutions at "The Toot," as we called it. They started when the place opened some twenty years ago and had managed to save enough to buy the place.

"Three Dews coming up, Rango. How you boys' hammers hanging? You boys gettin' any?"

Latrina always tended to be a little on the brash side, maybe even a little ribald, but people tended to like her, and she had really made The Toot the place in Decatur. People countywide came for her chicken fried steak sandwich and fried onion rings.

"Gim, you still whackin' off five times a day? Prob'ly why that thing looks like a pencil."

With his confidence still riding high, he sarcastically fired back, "Well, let's see, Latrina, only four times so far today; I saved number five for you."

"You boys want sumpon to eat? Looks like y'all fadin' away."

"Not now, Latrina. We here to talk business. Gonna try and lay a trap for Phylasho's attacker. We gonna catch that bastard," I said.

"Who you think it is?" queried Latrina.

"Deputy Brown," we all answered.

"I just might be able to help you with that, boys. That bastard's always making passes at me and Placenta, always trying to cop a feel."

No pun intended, neither. Comes here 'bout once a week like he's making an inspection or somethin'. He done ask both of us out a dozen times. You know, he got a thing for black women. Wouldn't go out with that honky if he had a ten-inch dick. Well…"

She paused for a moment, contemplating all ten inches. Then resumed.

"But, let me tell you somethin' I ain't told another living soul. You know the night Phylasho got attacked? Well, I'm pretty sure I saw the her sitting out in Brown's patrol car. And Brown came in and got two shrimp baskets to go. I happen to know that shrimp sandwich Phylasho's favorite. So, if you boys got a plan to nail that shit head to a wall, count me and Placenta in."

"Very interesting, Latrina. How come you didn't tell the sheriff what you saw?" I asked.

"You think I'm crazy, Rango? Black folk try and stay away from the law if they can. 'Sides, I figure the sheriff and Brown in the same boat; one of them farts, the other one smells it."

"Naw, you wrong, Latrina. I don't think the sheriff likes Brown at all. He'd love to get rid of him if he could. And we're gonna give him a reason. So, you're in, Latrina?" I asked.

"Long as that bastard don't touch me, I'm in," she said.

I slowly processed all the new information.

"Let's see now, Brown likes the sisters; he's deathly afraid of dogs, particularly without his gun; he's afraid of the dark…I think I got a plan, guys. Listen up," I said confidently.

When I got through spelling out the plan, Latrina, our main player, excused herself to make a phone call. The phone was right by where we were sitting, and we could easily hear her as she placed her call. A moment later, someone picked up.

"Hey, Oscar, this Latrina. Been thinkin' 'bout yo' offer to go out. If you free Saturday night, thought me and you might go out jukin'."

While we couldn't hear the other side of the conversation, it wasn't hard to read between the lines. "Yeah, I done changed my mind 'bout you. Been thinkin' 'bout that big gun you got. You gonna let me touch it Saturday night? Bet I can make it shoot. Ok, that sounds good to me. See you later, big boy."

She hung up the phone, and turned back toward us.

"Deputy dip shit is in."

"Good work, Latrina. We're gonna nail that bastard. With yo' body and my mind, Oscar Brown's good as in jail. Let's go over the plan one final time and make sure we got it right."

Saturday morning we all met at The Toot to commence Operation Deputy Dog, or ODD, as we were calling it.

"Where's Brown picking you up, Latrina?" I asked.

"He'll be by here at seven. Knowing that horny bastard, though, he'll probably be early. He'll have a pint of Crow with him, and we'll have a nip or two 'fore we leave. That should kill some time."

Gim spoke up, "Hey, Latrina, you could show him a little of that Southern moss. That might buy you some time."

"Gim, I'm gonna rip that little nub you call a dick clean off, if you make a crack like that again," Latrina said angrily.

"You plan on using your teeth for that?"

Although I was enjoying this, I knew we had to focus on the task at hand.

"Shut the hell up, you two. We got work to do," I said.

Then I asked Latrina, "You know if Brown gonna be in uniform or not? Think he'll be wearing his gun?"

"Naw, he'll be in civvies. Don't wanna be too conspicuous. He'll probably have his gun though."

"Nevertheless, we need to get his gun, first thing. Don't need anyone getting shot," I said.

"Yeah, I'll figure out a way to get it away from him, " she replied.

"Ok, Blubber, you got that army cot in the house?"

"Yup."

"Booger, all the windows nailed up?"

"Done, Rango."

"Gim, got us a big mudhole?"

"Yep. Been raining all week, Rango. Didn't have to do much digging."

"Latrina, you gonna wear that low cut dress and that sexy perfume?"

"Rango, when Brown sees me, he gonna have trouble keepin' in his pants."

"Ok, and I got new batteries for the tape recorder. Good job, everybody. RC's and rings all around on me. ODD is officially a go."

"Hey, Placenta. R.C. Cola's and onion rings all around."

Over rings and RC's, we filled Placenta in on the plan. I figured it couldn't hurt to have back-ups. At approximately six o'clock, Booger, Blubber, Gim, Placenta, and I left to take up our positions in the quarters, where the colored folk lived. Latrina went home to freshen up and get ready to meet Deputy Brown at The Toot.

We pulled into the quarters about six-thirty with plenty of time to fine tune our little plot. The quarters had not a single street light, and the dark was setting in rapidly.

"Ok, guys, which one of these shacks did we set up as our little love nest? All these places look alike to me," I said.

Gim spoke up, "There's the big mud hole there, Rango. Got to be that one on the left."

Blubber said, "Yeah, the door's open, guys. That's it."

"Well, men, let's take up our positions."

Now all we had to do was wait.

I checked my watch and for a moment thought it was broken. It read seven-forty. Where the hell was Latrina?

Just then, I heard the mighty roar of Brown's patrol car. We could see the headlights very slowly coming our way.

"Gim, put yo' flashlight on and leave it on the cot pointing out the window. Let's give Latrina a little help."

Gimlet quickly did so, and we all made ourselves scarce. The patrol car, now very near, was slowing by the love nest. The lit flashlight had done its job. The car stopped, and Brown got out shit faced and almost fell on his ass. Apparently, Latrina had done her job, too.

Latrina's voice came from the car window. "See, Oscar, told you I had a love nest back here. Think you gonna be able to handle some of Latrina. Dat booze makin' me hot as a firecracker."

"Yeah, baby, ol' Oscar got the fuse for that firecracker right here in my pants. That's one Latrina I'm planning to fill up."

"From de looks of yo' gun, I think you might be able to flush dat Latrna pretty soon. Dat thing look like it 'bout ready to shoot."

"My gun's smoking, baby. Let's go in dat love nest and see if we can light that fire."

"Ok, Oskie, but 'member now, no touchin' till we get in bed. I so hot now, my joy juice be's bubblin'."

Getting out of the car, Latrina continued, "I's gonna go on ahead, Oskie. I be waitin' for you in dere. Take all yo' clothes off and meet me in bed. I been wantin' some ol' Deputy Brown fo' a long time."

"You just get in there, baby. Oscar and his joy stick be right in."

As planned, Latrina went in ahead of Deputy Brown and made straight for the bedroom.

Oscar was so hot for that trim that he practically tore his clothes clean off. Naked, Oscar stepped into the first room of the two-room shack, then tried the bedroom door. It was locked.

"Open up, now Latrina. Ol' Oscar gonna have you climbing the wall and howling at the moon."

Latrina unlocked the door.

"Oskie, I got to tinkle 'fore you pound my pee hole. Gonna take 'de flashlight and go right outside. Go ahead and get in bed. I be right back."

Stepping into the bedroom and closing the door behind him, he said, "Don't be long, Latrina. My gunpowder's gettin' dry."

With that, Latrina took the flashlight and went out the side door. As soon as she stepped outside, we sprang into action. Booger and Blubber had come right behind Brown and now had all his clothes in a paper sack. Simultaneously, Gim and I quietly crept in the side door and locked the bedroom door from the outside. For good measure, we each had three two by fours pre-drilled with nails ready to make Brown's prison secure. We nailed them as fast as we could over the door and windows. With the noise, Brown suspected something wasn't exactly kosher. He started beating on the walls and bedroom door and yelling.

"Latrina, you fuckin' whore! Better let me out now 'fore I put yo' ass in jail for good. Fuckin' with a lawman's a felony. Put you in Parchman for that."

With everything going on and my nerves shot to hell, I barely managed to push play and record on the tape recorder just before he said the magic words.

"You don't let me outta here, I'll give you some of what I gave Phylasho."

I got you, you womanizing piece of shit, I thought to myself.

According to plan, when Booger and Blubber finished boarding Brown in, they went to his patrol car and pushed it in the big mud hole. I found out later that it took a tractor to get it out.

To add a little insult to injury, Placenta had enlisted the help of one of her cousins, Diploma Massey, to bring her three mean-ass looking hunting dogs to the quarters. The beasts, each standing about waist high, weighed over 150 pounds each and made grown men cross the street when they saw them. But, they were all bark. We knew that about the only harm they could do was to drown someone in their slobber or leg hump you to death. Of course, Brown didn't know that. So as soon as we heard the dogs nearing the shack, we all started yelling at the top of our voices, "Mad dogs loose. Mad dogs. Run for your life. Oh shit. They're coming!"

As they came up to the shack, Diploma Massey led them right around to the side door and went inside. She immediately had them raising hell and trying to tear down the door that led to Brown.

"Oh, sweet Jesus, don't let them monsters in here." Brown was blubbering like a baby. "I'll do anything, Lord. Just don't let those mad dogs in here."

This was sounding better and better. But we were just softening Brown up. Might as well keep the pressure on.

Diploma Massey led the dogs back outside and around to the side of the shack to its only window, which was now boarded up. We yanked off a few of the boards so that Brown could get a visual of the barking in his head. We all switched our flashlights on Diploma Massey and her team.

"Oh, sweet Jesus. Don't let them get me. What you want? I'll do anything."

As instructed, she yelled out, "Who done fucked over Fasho?"

As if on cue, the hounds of hell all got to their hind legs and put their paws, which were the size of baseball mitts, on the ledge.

Brown's whole body, lily white in the darkness, was quivering violently. So was his voice, which now sounded more like a squeak.

"I don't know no Fasho."

Assuming Brown would stall as long as he could, I quickly went around to the back of the shack where Latrina and the rest of the gang were keeping out of sight and explained to Latrina what I needed her to do. Then I went to the side and motioned Diploma Massey and the hounds over. As soon as they cleared from Brown's vision, I sent Latrina screaming around to the window.

"Oh, Oscar, Oscar! Save me from da monsters. Dey gonna come right back, and she gonna let dem hounds get me and tear yo' balls out! She kept screamin' sumpin' 'bout me getting Phylasho hurt. You know anythin' 'bout dat, Oscar? You gotta help us. And your balls."

From around the corner of the shack, I could see that Oscar was shaking big time. With the barking now off in the distance, I was able to make out the sound of liquid dripping onto the shack's wooden floor.

"Said if you done tol' de truth, she just turn you over to de sheriff; udderwise, dem dogs gonna be snackin' on some white meat."

"Tell her to keep them dogs away, Latrina. I'll tell her everything. I was just trying to get some of Phylasho's nooky, and things got out of hand. I hit her a couple of times when she wouldn't spread those legs. I didn't mean to hit her so hard, but, hell, I'd bought her a shrimp basket and a bottle of Jim Beam. A man's got a right to expect something."

I pulled my recorder from my shirt pocket and smiled when I saw that it was still taping.

"Ok, I knock dis window out wid dis stick, and you run to de patrol car, and I meet you back in town later. You can tell de Sheriff everything you just told me. But before I go, I need a little spending cash to buy me dat new dress over at Gilfoy's."

"Ok, fine, anything, anything at all, Latrina. Got $100 in my pants pocket, but I ain't got no clothes. Find me my pants and $100's yours."

"I go look fo' yo' clothes, but you ain't got time 'fore dem dogs get back. Dey gonna bite yo' dick off when dey get back."

"Ok, just knock that damn window out, and I'll run to the car. Got me a spare key under the floor mat."

Latrina knocked out the window and helped Brown down to the ground.

"Latrina, you just made yourself $100. Let me get my ass to that car, and I'm getting out of this madhouse. Oh, and I made all that stuff up about Phylasho. I didn't have nothing to do with that. Heard it was her old boyfriend, that Perkins fellow."

What did he just say?!

You wanta ride with me, Latrina? Hate to leave you out here with these crazy folks."

"No thanks, Oskie. Dey ain't really after me. Dey thought you did it. You go ahead, and I'll meet you in de Toot in a hour."

Brown quickly made the distance to his car and got the key out from under the floor mat, not noticing he had just stepped into a mudhole. Brown cranked it up, threw the car into drive and slammed on the gas. He went nowhere. With every rotation of the whistling tires, the car went deeper and deeper into the mud. He tried several more minutes and finally gave up. Just about that same time, Diploma Massey and the hounds rounded the corner, looking more ferocious than ever. Brown immediately checked all the doors, making sure they were locked.

The dogs barreled toward the car, full steam. One vaulted onto the hood, denting it. Then the massive animal proceeded to get up on the windshield, howling right at Brown. Another made it to the roof and dangled his paws over the edge covering the top of the driver's window. The third, for some odd reason, made a beeline for Brown's door and rammed his head straight into it.

Diploma Massey came running, approached the mud hole, and calmly said, "Got anything on your mind you'd like to share with me, Deputy?"

"Yes, it was me; it was me. I'm the one who hurt Phylasho. It was an accident. Just take me to jail, and don't let them dogs get me. I confess. Please, don't let them dogs in here."

I had him. On tape and with witnesses.

Earlier, Placenta had lined up about thirty of her relatives from the quarter, who were probably just minutes from arriving. I thought before things got really ugly, I should probably make my appearance.

"Deputy Brown, is that you? What you doing out here at night naked in your patrol car? You on some kinda stakeout or somethin'?" I asked innocently.

"Rango, oh, thank God, go get help! And tell Diploma Massey to get these dogs away from me!"

About that time Diploma Massey pretended to whisper in my ear.

"Deputy Brown, she says you were the one that put Phylasho in the hospital. She wants a full confession, or she's gonna let those dogs rip out your nut sack."

The mob of relatives had come within a quarter mile of where we were. We could hear them singing.

"Swing Low, sweet chariot…"

"Uh, Deputy Brown, I hear people coming."

Again, Diploma Massey pretended to whisper in my ear.

"Uh, Deputy Brown? She said that's the locals making their way over here… something about avenging Phylasho, I think."

Brown was again shaking like a holy roller at revival.

"Rango, I'll start talking. Jes' keep them dogs away from me."

A moment later, the motley crew had arrived. Each had sticks and pitch forks in their hands as instructed. They circled the mudhole.

Brown was now spilling his guts to anyone who'd listen.

"Yes, it was me that hurt Phylasho. I didn't mean to do it. I got carried away and hit her too hard. I'm sorry."

Gimlet finally came out of hiding.

"Gimlet, has the Sheriff been called?" I asked.

"Yup, here he comes now," Gim answered.

The mob parted like the black sea; the Sheriff parked his cruiser right behind Deputy Brown and made his way to the mud hole.

"Oh, sweet Jesus, Sheriff. You got to save me from these crazy sons a bitches. Them damn dogs trying to tear my nuts out. And all these crazy ass folks just keep grinning at me. Get me out of here."

"What'cha doing out here naked in the middle of the quarter, Brown? Rumor has it, you were the one that hurt Phylasho. Tell me about it, and I'll put you in a nice safe place."

Brown, knowing the game was up, confessed, "Yeah, it was me, Sheriff. I got carried away and hit her too hard. I didn't mean to. It was an accident."

"Well, Brown, I'm putting you under arrest for assault, indecent exposure, unlawful use of city property, being out of uniform, and a PD 6969. I wouldn't plan on spending the next few Christmases at home, Brown." And with that, the sheriff put the handcuffs on Brown and put him in the back seat of his patrol car.

Intrigued I asked, "Uh, Sheriff, what's a PD6969?"

The Sheriff, now about to split a gut laughing, replied, "Having an undersized dick, Rango." Then he faced the rest of the group.

"Good work, boys. Good work Placenta, Latrina, Diploma Massey. I'm gonna talk to the Mayor about the good job you did. See if we can't get you a little award from the city."

Everybody burst into applause.

We did it.

The Sheriff, true to his word, did talk to the mayor, and sho' nuff, the following week they did have a parade in our honor with a few high school bands from Newton County, a few speeches, and a ceremony where Gim, Blubber, Booger, Placenta, Latrina, Diploma Massey, and I were each given a key to the city.

When the pomp and circumstance wore down, Gimlet and I slowly made our way home.

"Well, ol' dude, I'd have to say we done good. Put Brown in jail; Phylasho's on the mend, and all her medical bills are paid. Most importantly, Maw owes us big time."

Gim replied, "The most amazing thing is that we didn't fuck up. I didn't get naked and didn't get humiliated."

I put my arm around him as we continued walking. "Yeah, but you know what, Gim? There's always tomorrow."

The Big Meridian Date

"First de tide rushes in
plant a kiss on de shore and roll to sea,
and de sea is very still once more.
Now I rush to you side
like the ongoing tide...."

Maw was in a good mood today. With Brown behind bars, Phylasho safe at home, and all the medical bills paid, she certainly had reason to sing.

"Well, Maw, you sho' are in a good mood today," I said, walking into the kitchen as though I lived there.

"Oh, Rango, my little hero," she said, coming over and wrapping me up in a bear hug.

"Ooh, and here come my udder hero," she said as Gimlet came walking in from the bedroom.

"You two sit down, and Maw gonna fix you a breakfast like you deserve. I gonna fix you eggs and bacon and sausage and ham and grits and pancakes and some o' Maw's fried apple pies. Ain't nothing too good for my lil' heroes."

Gimlet and I grinned at each other, already used to the idea of being considered heroes.

"An' den you boys come back for lunch, and Maw's gonna fix you summa her fried chicken and pork chops an' cream taters and an' gravy and peas an' homemade ice cream. Nuttin' too good for my boys. An' if you get hungry after dat, Maw'll fix you growing boys a lil' snack. Got to keep you strength up after all you work catchin' dat deputy."

"Thanks, Maw. You th' best," I said sincerely.

"Sho' are, Maw, thanks," Gim echoed.

About an hour later we were stuffed to the hilt, and we needed to get moving before we fell asleep right there at the table.

"Gim, let's get out of Maw's way so she can clean up. That was mighty good, Maw," I said, going over and giving her a big hug. Gim followed suit and we walked outside to the big oak tree and the two lawn chairs.

"Rango, you know we peein' in high cotton right now."

"Oh, yeah, Maw can put out some grub all right."

"Yeah, well, the food sure, but I'm thinking about the car. It's ours for the asking now. We ain't

116

got to bribe Maw or win no contest with her. Didn't you hear her? We are, and I quote, 'her little heroes.' That three hole Buick's just sittin' there waitin' for us."

"Gim, why don't you just spit it out. I know you got somethin' on your mind."

"Well, Rango, not only are we Maw's lil' heroes, we heroes to the whole damn town. I mean the parade, key to the city, our picture in the Newton County Record. It all adds up to 'hero.' I've even had white women come up and speak to me now. They used to cross the street when they saw me coming. I mean I think we could have our way with half the split tails in town now."

"Sure, Gim, but where is this going? Wanna get us a date with Mary Lou and Betty Lou and go to the steak house and the movie? Or is Betty Lou not speaking to you yet?"

Gim shot me a look of disgust.

"No, Rango, for your information, I don't wanna double with Mary Lou and Betty Lou. We got a hell of a lot bigger fish to fry. Town heroes don't go out with skanks." It's funny what a little confidence and praise from others can do to a man. Two weeks ago, Gimlet would've given his left gonad for another date with Betty Lou.

"That's your trouble, Rango. You always shootin' too low. I mean you play with shit, you gonna smell like shit. I'm talking prime meat here, my friend. Somethin' deserving of my one-eyed trouser worm."

"Ok, Gim, ol' bud, I'm listenin'. I'm not sure what I'm hearing, but I'm sure as hell listenin'."

"Rango, who would you say were the two finest white women in Decatur? Who would you like to be in the back seat of a car with now? Whose bra would you like to be slowly unhooking and placing her supple bosom and very erect, rosy nipple into your warm mouth and sucking it like it was a Tootsie Roll? Whose panties would you like to be sliding your gentle hand down until it reached her furnace?"

"Been reading Maw's 'Lady Chatterly's Lover' books, again?"

"Just answer the question," he snapped back.

"Well, since you asked, my two picks would have to be Melanie Sue Hooks and Sue Sue Scruggs. But we got 'bout as much chance of gettin' dates with them as Maw does of becoming a marine biologist."

"Exactly my two picks, Rango, Melanie Sue and Sue Sue. Personally, I think Sue Sue's got the hots for me. Came right up to me last week and congratulated me after the parade. Kept staring at my crotch the whole time. Think she definitely wants some of the Gim's goober."

Attempting not to chuckle, I said, "Tell you what, you line up the two honeys. I'll drive so you and Sue Sue can get it on in the back seat. Just tell me where and when."

"All right, Rango. Here's the plan. Miz Hortense is gonna be out of town next week, so I'm thinkin' Saturday night. And get this. Won't be no steak house and movie in Newton. Hell no, my friend. We goin' to the Triangle in Meridian and get us a couple a chick steaks; then we goin' to the Temple Theater. If we goin' out with prime meat, we're goin' first class."

"Sounds like a plan to me, Gim. Think Maw'll let us take the car to Meridian? You know, that's about forty miles. Didn't know she'd let us take the car out of Newton County."

"Leave Maw to me, Rango. We could prob'ly take the car to Memphis right now, she's so grateful. 'Sides, this ought to really impress our dates, going to Meridian and all."

"Well, it's your plan, Gim, and a damn good one. Only thing left is to line up our dates. I've saved up 'bout ten dollars; should be plenty."

"Leave it all to me, Rango. Snatching Deputy Brown was your master plan. Mine is getting our hands on the brown snatch."

Just then, Maw yelled out the kitchen door, "My heroes ready for lunch?"

"Comin', Maw, I'm hungry," said Gim.

"Imagine that."

After getting our bellies packed for a second time in less than three hours, Gim cut right to the chase. "Uh, Maw? Me and Rango wanna use the car next Saturday night. Reckon it'd be ok?"

Maw replied, "Anytime, Gim, my sweetie. You two boys go and have a good time. Stone s'posed to be here on a recruitin' trip, so me an' him prob'ly go out. Try and be home by one, though."

Seeing no reason to push it, Gim and I thanked her kindly and made our way out to the street.

"Gim, just in the unlikely event that Melanie Sue and Sue Sue won't go with us, have you got a contingency plan? We still might get Mary and Betty Lou."

"Rango, my ol' bud, I done told you to leave all this to me. Actually, I got a little surprise for you. I already got 'em screwed, blued, and tattooed. They just are' tryin' to keep their panties on 'til Saturday night."

I was speechless, but not for long.

"You mean you really got Melanie Sue and Sue Sue to go out with our sorry asses? How'd you do that, Gim? I am really impressed."

"Well, Rango, bein' the quarterback, our number one pitcher, startin' forward on the basketball team and able to date anybody you want, you always take these things for granted. But, see, this parade and all is a big ass deal to me. And it did impress Sue Sue, and she does wanna go out with me."

"That's all true, Gim, but you left out the part 'bout me bein' humble and kind and trustworthy and loyal and brave. And you know I tried to date Lee Sue Miles last year, and she told me to eat shit. Besides, Gim, who wouldn't want to go out with you? You're a hell of a lot of fun to be around."

"You really think so, Rango? I really do want to impress Sue Sue. I could get serious about her."

"Aw, yeah, Gim, I'm totally impressed. Got us the two best-looking split tails in Newton County, and we takin' them to the big 'M' Saturday night. And it's all your doin', my man. I tip my chapeau to you. And I'm drivin'. You might get to touch some of that moss if things go right."

Gim's eyes began to glaze over.

Saturday night was taking forever to arrive. Maybe it was because I was really looking forward to my date with Melanie Sue. I'd always liked her, but just never did get around to asking her out. I wasn't sure I could wait until the weekend. As fate would have it, we ran into our two Sues over at Wheeler's Drugstore on Friday.

"Hey, girls, me and Gim are really looking forward to our date on Saturday night," I said.

"Oh, us, too," replied Sue Sue, blushing as she looked at Gim.

"Yeah, me, too." said Melanie Sue as she smiled at me. Her big pearly whites, big dimple, and full lips were only surpassed by her perfectly round, ample tits. I was in love.

"And I want you two boys to tell us every single detail on how you caught Deputy Brown. Heard you did it single handedly. Must have been scary."

"Well, actually, Gim here had most of the plan worked out in his head. I'd say he was our main most man."

Gim looked at me with tears in his eyes.

"I always got your back, bro." I said, without so much as a wink in his direction.

"My buddy Rango exaggerates. It was a fifty/fifty deal all the way. It took both of us."

He had said it with just the right amount of modesty.

"But we'll tell you everythin' you want to know Saturday night. Right now let's get some cherry Cokes, and let's talk about our plans."

And so we did. We threw in just enough of the details 'bout Brown to be titillating, but mainly we talked about our date Saturday night.

"Wow, Meridian and the Temple Theater with you two guys. I've never been there except with my parents. I can hardly wait, Gim," said Sue Sue, blushing furiously.

Gim and Sue Sue. Not impossible, I guess. There have been stranger pairings, like Rock Hudson, a known fudge packer, and Doris Day.

"Well, ladies, we'll pick you up 'bout six o'clock. First movie starts at seven fifteen. James Bond in Dr. No. Then we go to the Triangle for some Chick Steaks. Should be a fun evening," I said, as Gim and I prepared to take our leave.

"Thank you for asking us," they said simultaneously, and then each one gave us a brief hug.

"We'll see you two guys tomorrow 'bout six. Bye."

As we walked out of hearing distance, Gim slapped me on the shoulder, "Rango, I'm in love."

"Slow down now, Gim. You barely know the girl. I don't want you to put her up on a pedestal and then find out she's got feet of clay."

"What the hell does that mean, anyhow, Rango? Feet of clay," asked Gim.

"That means I don't want you thinkin' she's a tight end and then find out she's a wide receiver."

"You mean sleep around, Rango? That's bullshit. Tommy Munn dated her a dozen times, and he claims he never even got to French kiss her, and you know Tommy and his bragging. Now, Rango, you my best bud and always will be, but I don't wanna hear any more talk like that, or I'm gonna knock your jockstrap off."

Damn, the boy was serious. And standin' up for Sue Sue; well, it had to be love.

"Sorry, Gim, I just don't wanna see you get hurt. When you hurt, I hurt. But I'll keep my mouth shut."

"Rango, I know you mean well and are only looking out for me, but I'm really serious about this girl. If things go right, I might ask her to wear my letter jacket."

This was more serious than I thought. Gim's letter jacket was prob'ly his most prized possession.

"Gim, I hope it works out. And, if I can help, I will."

"Thanks, Rango, I can always count on you, and right now, I'm countin' on you to help me wash and wax the Buick."

"You got it, Gim."

Friday evening was spent sitting out on Gim's porch talkin' guy stuff. Cars, chicks, movie stars — those sorts of things. The next day I was up before the sun. I think we both were. We had been looking forward to this date more so than any we ever had. I mentally declared that Melanie Sue just might be the first girl I asked to go steady.

After another one of Maw's delicious feasts and a short nap, it was time to get ready. I laid out my khaki slacks and my dark blue polo along with my genuine penny loafers. I took a good long shower, followed by a liberal dousing of Canoe. I paid particular attention to ol' Druango, Jr., splashing the man perfume all around the shaft and base. Although I was never a Boy Scout, I was always prepared. When I got back to Gim's house around five-thirty, Gim was waiting in the living room lookin' freshly shined and shaved.

"Lookin' good, Gim. Like that cologne you got on."

"Think it's too much, Rango?"

"Prob'ly didn't need that second bottle. Naw, I'm just messin' with you, dude. What is that? Aqua Velva?"

"No, I went down to Wheeler's and got me a big bottle of Brute. You know the one Joe Namath uses?"

"Joe Namath sucks, Gim. He couldn't carry Johnny Unita's jockstrap. Heard he services all the guys in the shower after the game. I just as soon have Sandra Dee pee on me."

For some reason, any putdown of Joe Namath riled Gim. I could say the most outrageous things about him, and Gim took them as gospel. But my idea was that if I pissed Gim off, he'd be nice and loose on the date.

"Johnny U's got to be pushing forty. Heard they had to give him a vitamin shot 'fore each game just to get his heart started. His ass sucks canal water," Gim angrily defended his hero.

Mission accomplished.

"Well, Gim, ol' dude, ready for our big date? Could be a night in paradise."

"A little nervous, Rango. But I beat off twice in the shower, so I think I'm ready."

"Gee, thanks for sharing that little tidbit. Ok, let's make sure we got everything we need," I said.

"Mints and gum."

"Check."

"Rubbers."

"Check."

"Money."

"Ten dollars, check."

"Gas."

"I'll prob'ly have some after all them beans I ate at lunch."

"In the car, Gim."

"Half a tank, Rango. We'll buy more in Meridian. Heard it's twenty cents a gallon cheaper."

"Ok, Gim, what else?"

"What about a blanket in case we park and one of us goes outside?"

"Good, Gim, get us a blanket and let's roll."

When we had everything we needed, we went through the house to find Maw and tell her good-bye. We found her in the living toom, three sheets to the wind.

"Look at my two precious angels goin' out on dere first big date, all dressed up and smellin' like French whores. Bet you boys get yo some GASH tonight. Y'all just be careful and have a good time," Maw said, wiping away a tear. We each hugged Maw and quickly got in the Buick before she really got in a maudlin mood.

"You boys be careful. Maw gonna fix you a big breakfast in de mornin'."

We picked up Melanie Sue first. I parked and went to the front door and knocked. Her father came to the door, and we exchanged a few pleasantries. Melanie Sue came out, and we headed to Sue Sue's house, where Gim excitedly made his way to the front door and back to the car. We were on our way. The thirty-five or so miles passed quickly and pleasantly. Everybody was in a festive mood, and the chemistry was good. We talked about school, the band, football, who was dating who and other topics high school youth likes to discuss. Gim and I learned that the two Sues had a lot of extra circular activities also. They both were in the choir, were both cheerleaders, and took ballet lessons after school.

Gim spoke up. "That reminds me of a joke I heard the other day about a ballerina."

I had heard the same joke, and the two Sues definitely did not want to hear this joke. But since Gim told me this was his show, I reluctantly and humbly remained silent.

"Oh, tell it, Gim. "I'll tell it in class next week," gushed Sue Sue.

"Yeah, go ahead, Gim," encouraged Melanie Sue. "I like a good joke."

I think Gim was half way expecting me to come to his rescue after he realized all the implications. But, eventually, a baby bird has to leave the nest.

Gim nervously chuckled and began, "This really scruffy woman went into a bar and looked around. Seemed she hadn't shaved her legs or armpits in months. She raised one of her hairy arms and shouted, 'Is there a gentleman in this bar that will buy a lady a drink?' All the patrons except one very drunk old man in the back of the bar avoided looking at her. The old man shouted, 'Barkeep, buy that ballerina a drink.' So the bartender set her up. Fifteen minutes later, the lady stood up, raised her arm in the air and shouted, 'Is there a gentleman in this bar that will buy a lady a drink?' The old drunk immediately jumped up again, 'Barkeep, give that ballerina a drink.' Fifteen minutes later, the same routine. Immediately, the old drunk bought her another drink. Finally, the bartender couldn't stand it any longer. He walked over to the old drunk, 'Mister, I'm not trying to tell you what to do with your money, but just what makes you think that lady is a ballerina?' The old drunk replied, 'Mister, anybody that can raise her leg over her head like that has got to be a ballerina.'"

Dead silence. Then, the two Sues said simultaneously, "I don't get it, Gim."

A light sheen of sweat appeared on Gim's fore head. "Well, you see, the thing is that the lady hadn't shaved in a long time, and she had a lot of hair on her legs and under her arms."

"Yeah, we got that part, Gim. But what does that have to do with being a ballerina?"

Gim stammered, "Well, that's the whole point. You see her hairy armpit reminded the old man of a hair pie."

Sue Sue asked, "What's a hair pie, Gim? Is that something like a rabbit stew?"

"Well, actually, Rango told me the joke, and I really didn't get it either. What is the point of the joke, Rango?" asked Gim, grinning maliciously at me.

"Don't you remember, Gim? You actually told me the joke, and I think Gim was referring to hair like's on your head and not a rabbit."

"Well, Gim, that just makes no sense. I never heard of a hair pie. Do people actually eat 'em?" Gim's whole face was now sweaty and red. He looked at me for a life preserver. I could see the desperation in his eyes. As long as the boy knew who the king was, I figured I would help him out.

"Uh, ladies, I think the point of the joke was that all ballerinas are so neat and scrupulously clean, that the irony would be that anyone would think an ol' scruffy woman like that could be a ballerina. Only somebody that had way too much to drink would make that mistake."

"Oh, that is funny, Gim. I can't wait to tell my ballet teacher. Thinking some ol' woman with hair under her arms could be a ballerina. That's just too funny." Sue Sue moved a little closer to Gim.

Melanie Sue joined in the laughter, "That's cute, Gim."

Another few miles and we were in downtown Meridian. I started humming an ol' Jimmy Reed song, "The bright lights, big city went to my baby's head."

We passed Wideman's, the Triangle, Potsie's, and finally pulled up in front of the Temple Theater with twenty minutes to spare before the main feature. "The name's Bond. James Bond," Gim mimicked, sounding a whole lot like Sean Connery.

"Oh, Gim, you're so funny," said Sue Sue, leaning closer to my boy. At this rate, the lad might actually get to second base, possibly even third. A home run? Well, stranger things have happened. I mean the Dodgers did win the World Series last year.

The Temple Theater was an impressive sight. Compared to the old Decatur Theater, which was open only on Thursday, Friday and Saturday nights, it was a palace. There was a huge marquis lit up like a Christmas tree and a lobby as fine as the King Edward Hotel's in Jackson. This certainly had to impress our dates.

"Oh, Gim, this is such a nice theater. Nice as the one in New Orleans," gushed Sue Sue.

"Nothing but the best for you, Money Penny," Gim mimicked in his best James Bond voice.

"Vodka martini, shaken not stirred. And a little caviar on buttered toast."

Sue Sue was smitten. Gim was saying all the right things and making all the right moves. I had been so worried about Gim's performance that I was totally forgetting to be my own cool self. I might be lucky to get a good night kiss if this continued. But, I had plenty of time.

"Popcorn and cherry Cokes, ladies?" I asked.

"And some of those chocolate covered raisins," said Melanie Sue.

"Coming right up," I said, as Gim and I made our way over to the concession stand. When we were out of ear shot, I said to Gim, "Good show, ol' dude. You got Sue Sue eatin' outta your hand. You might get to play a little stink finger tonight. Maybe even get some stanky on your hang down."

Gim's eyes got huge.

"You're not just saying that, are you, Rango? I feel like I need to go lope my mule again 'fore the movie starts. If Sue Sue touches me, I'm gonna mess my pants."

"Well, Gim, it wouldn't be the first time. 'Sides you might need all that ammo for later the way things are going with you and Sue Sue."

We got the refreshments, went back to the ladies, and a real usher showed us to our seats. If anything, the inside of the movie was nicer than the lobby.

After 007 had dispensed with half a dozen villains, seduced several women and saved the world from mass destruction much to the satisfaction of M, the movie ended. We made our way out of the theater and to the shiny buffed Buick.

"How 'bout some chick steaks over at the Triangle, ladies?" I asked.

We drove the six or seven blocks over to the Triangle, and every place we passed was jumping and jiving. The Triangle was no exception. Just as we walked in, two couples were leaving, so we grabbed their booth.

"This is the best date I've ever been on," said Sue Sue, as we settled in.

"Me, too," echoed Melanie Sue. She continued, "And the nicest guys we've ever been with."

They both looked at us with what could be interpreted as young love. I really didn't have a game plan for this scenario. Gim looked at me with a confused expression.

"Thank you, ladies. I can assure you the feeling is mutual, and we've never been out with nicer ladies."

Gim chimed in, "And the prettiest."

They both blushed.

Everything was perfect.

After dinner we made our way to Highway 80. I glanced down at the gas gauge. "Uh, Gim, is this gas gauge accurate?"

"Yeah, far as I know, Rango. What's it showing?"

"It's flat on empty, Gim. Guess we better find a service station pretty soon."

We passed by several, but they were all closed up tighter than my bunghole was getting. We drove on another four or five miles and nothing.

"Gim, there's a joint right up the road. Why don't we pull in and ask somebody where a gas station is? We don't wanna run out of gas in the middle of nowhere. The girls can lock the car doors while we go in, and we'll be on our merry way in no time. Sound like a plan to you?" I asked.

"You bet, Rango. Hate to leave you lovely ladies out here, but we'll be right in and right out and bring back some Cokes."

"You ladies be ok? Be sure and lock the doors."

"We'll be ok, guys. We'll know our two strong brave men will be right back," Sue Sue said.

"Be right back, ladies."

The parking area we had pulled into belonged to the Embassy Club. Of all the joints in Meridian, it probably was one of the nicest. That simply meant there were less fights, less stabbings, and very few shootings. We had chosen well. We walked up to the door that was guarded by a big ass bouncer.

"How old you two punks?" he challenged. "Got to be twenty-one to get in here."

"We both twenty-one, mister. Both of us. We both go to Meridian Junior College," I lied.

"Show me some ID."

"Please, mister. We ain't drinking. Just want to go in and get some Cokes for our dates, and we'll be on our way. Oh, and is there a gas station around here? We're running on fumes."

The bouncer looked as if he might be sympathetic to our plight.

"You cake eaters shit out of luck. Nearest gas station's over at Hickory. That's 'bout eighteen miles." Gim and I looked at each other.

"Rango, I don't think we can make eighteen miles. We better see if we can get somebody to drive us over and bring back a five-gallon can," Gim said.

"Come on, mister, give us a break. We just need to get a ride. We ain't gonna be drinkin'. Let us go in."

The bouncer broke into a booming laugh. "Just shittin' you, boys. If you got a warm body, you can get in the Embassy Club. Just leave all the whores alone," he joked.

At last we were in the inner sanctum. It took a few minutes for our eyes to adjust to the surroundings. The only light in the joint was from the beer signs, but it looked like it was packed. The smell of cigarette smoke, body odor, beer, whiskey, and cheap perfume hit us from every angle. There was a huge dance floor loaded with couples who were doing little more than belly rubbing. The country band was laying down some sounds that only a true shit kicker could love.

I hate country music, but the ambiance was awesome. Several of the fillies spotted me and Gim from across the dance floor and made motions like they wanted us to dance with them.

"Hot damn, Rango. Look at those two over there ogling us. Look like they want us to dance. Boy, that one's got a butt like a U. S. Government mule. What say we dance one dance, Rango?"

"Gim, we got two of the hottest dates right outside that door. What we gonna do is buy some Cokes and get somebody to drive us to Hickory. How much money you got, anyhow? We gonna have to give somebody a few bucks to drive us."

"'Bout four bucks, Rango. What about you?"

"'Bout the same, Gim. Should be plenty."

We maneuvered our way around the dance floor, squeezing in between couples. I could only hope those pinches on the butt I was getting were from women.

"See a friendly face, Gim? Somebody that might give us a ride?"

"That card player over in the corner looks friendly, Rango. Keeps grinning at me. I think I'm gonna ask him."

We walked over to the card shark. "Hey, mister, how ya' doin'. Playing a little solitaire?"

"Hey guys. No, 3 card Monte's my game. Wanna play?"

"No, actually we tryin' to catch a ride to Hickory so we can get a little gasoline. We running on empty now. You got time to help us out? Be glad to pay you a few bucks for your time."

"Tell you what, boys. I'm gonna be leaving here in 'bout thirty minutes. Be glad to drive you over for five bucks. Prob'ly more than I'm gonna make here tonight."

Gim piped up, "What kinda game you playing anyway, Mister?"

"Real simple. I got these three cards that I shuffle around. All you got to do is pick out the ace, and you win. Here, lemme show ya."

With that, he turned the three cards up showing us the eight of diamonds, the two of clubs, and the ace of spades. He quickly turned them face down and began rapidly sliding them around the table. Finally, he stopped and looked at Gim.

"Which one's the ace?" the stranger asked.

Gim pointed to the middle card.

"Correct! See, if we'd been playing, you'd have won a buck."

Gim said, "Let's try that one more time, mister, just for fun."

Same routine, Gim pointed to the card on the right. Same results. The ace of spades.

"Let's huddle, Rango."

We walked out of hearing range. I calmly turned to Gim before he could speak. "You dumb crazy asshole. I know exactly what you gonna say. You wanna bet on that fixed card game, don't you? Can't you see he's suckering you in, Gim? He's puttin' a crimp in the ace every time, so you can't help but spot it. Hell, even Early Rue could pick the ace out. But, when you start playin' for real, he's gonna clean yo' plow. And, Gim, we only got eight dollars between us, and five of that's got to go to our ride, one dollar for Cokes, and two dollars for gas to get our asses home. And what about Sue Sue and Melanie Sue, Gim? Forget about them? I bet they're getting pissed right now, and we had a good chance to score tonight. Get you head outta your ass for once, Gim."

Gim looked offended. "I know I can beat that dude, Rango. 'Sides, I only wanna play him one time, and we'll go. If I lose a buck, that'll still leave one to buy gas with, and that'll be enough to get home on. But, then again. I might win enough for us to take the girls out again next week. Can you imagine how good our second date's gonna be? Just one play, Rango. That's all and then we'll go."

I wondered at what point Gim and I had switched roles, him doing the scheming and me doin' the following, but his plan did make a little sense. After all, a second date with the two Sues was worth takin' a chance on. The worst that could happen is that we'd only have a dollar for gas.

"Ok, Gim, but one buck. That's all. Then we'll go."

So, against any better judgment I'd ever had, we walked back over to the card game. An old wino, who looked like he'd had his face beaten with a pair of track shoes, was sitting across from our player. The old sot pointed to the table, and the card shark immediately exclaimed, " Oh, no, not again. That's three in a row you've won."

I pulled Gim aside. "You see that, Gim. That ol' wino's his shill. He didn't point to shit. Guy just turned over the winning card cause he's trying to sucker you in."

"Just what do you take me for, Rango. I saw exactly what he did, but the dude's never run up against the Gim Master."

The old drunk shuffled off to drink whatever dregs he could find.

"Hey, boys, come on over and let me buy you a beer 'fore I take you all the way to Hickory. Don't give no body a ride I can't drink with. What's you pleasure, men?"

Gim and I both looked over at the advertisement over the bar.

"Schlitz, please, mister." We said it at the same time.

"Three Schlitz, Gertrude," he yelled out. "And forget that mister shit. The name's Slick Booty." He pronounced it Slick Boo-Tay.

"Pleased to meet you, Slick. I'm Rango, and this is my buddy Gim. We live over at Decatur. Been to Meridian on a big date, and we runnin' low on gas."

"Ol' Slick get you over to Hickory and back in no time. First, though, let's enjoy our beers. Oh, Gertrude, bring us three pickled eggs to go with that beer. You look like growing boys. Don't want you to go hungry."

In the meantime, the old sot had drained the remainder of all the beer cans and whiskey bottle in sight and came back over to us.

"That one," he cried out, pointing somewhere at the table. Slick, ever obliging, turned over the ace of spades.

"Correct again, Valentino; that's four in a row. No more now, you too good for me."

"Ah, here's our beers and eggs, boys. Enjoy," he said, as he shuffled the three cards around. Since this was mine and Gimlet's very first beer and our very first pickled egg, neither of us knew what pleasures awaited us.

"Damn, that's good," said Gim, draining about half his can.

I followed suit. "Good stuff," I opined. "Thanks, Slick."

"Yeah, thanks, Slick," said Gim, as we both took a bite out of our very first pickled egg.

"Oh, Sweet Jesus, that's good!" Gim exclaimed.

Not to be outdone, I yelled, "Oh holy shit. Have we died and gone to heaven?"

"How 'bout 'nother, boys? On me, of course."

"Thanks, Slick, don't mind if we do."

"Three Schlitz and three chicken turds, Gertrude."

Gim and I laughed uproariously. Really not that funny, but we were like whores. The beers and eggs came and went in no time flat.

"One more round, boys? The night's still young."

By this time, the beer had run its course.

"Uh, Gim, what about the girls? Think we oughta go out and tell'em what we doing? Trying to catch a ride and all."

"Fuck'em, Rango. Anybody stupid enough to trust us oughta be eating oatmeal over at the mental institution, anyway.

Well, for some reason this struck us as exceedingly funny. So funny we giggled 'til tears came to our eyes.

"Yeah, you're right, Gim. They should realize that sometimes a man has to make tough choices. And they lost."

"Think a blow job's gonna be out of the question tonight, Rango?"

"From me or them?" That set off another ten minutes of hysterical giggling.

Slick seemed to be enjoying our little repartee. "Set'em up again, Gertrude," Slick yelled.

Gertrude did. And with all the hilarity and good vibes taking place at our table, we began to attract attention. The first wave of attentiveness came from the two road whores who had invited us to dance earlier. They sat down at our table with their drinks.

"Hey, Slick, who your friends?" they asked, rubbing their hands on mine and Gim's privates.

"Now be nice, ladies. This is Rango and that's Gimlet. Guys, this here's Passion Knight and Foxy Furr."

"What about another round, everybody?" Slick asked.

"Five Schlitz and five eggs, Gertrude."

They came; we partook. And one round led to the next round and the next. Soon, Gim and I were completely shit faced.

"You boys wanna dance?" asked Passion.

Looking at them amorously in the harsh light of a beer sign, I said, "Don't mind if we do."

"Love to dance, Foxy. Let's go," Gim said, as he stumbled over a chair and made his way to the crowded dance floor.

When we left Decatur, Gim was all neat and tucked. His blue dress shirt and khaki pants were all pressed and in order. Now, however, he was a hog ass mess. He was burping, tripping, and talking way above a reasonable volume.

"C'mon you two, catch up!"

All was right with the world. Gim and Foxy were groping each other on the dance floor and Passion, Slick and I were consuming red neck caviar and vast quantities of beer.

Then with one massive hiccup, it hit me. We had totally forgotten about our dates. We were fucked. I had to think of something fast. I ran over to Gim on the dance floor.

"Gim, we need to talk now. We got to get the girls home somehow. It's damn near midnight now. We got to make a move."

Gim looked at me blankly, "What girls, Rango?"

"Gim, you dumb shit, our dates we left sitting out in the car who we told we'd be back in fifteen minutes."

"Oh, those girls. Well, Rango, we been trying to get us a ride ever since we been in here. I mean, hell, we the ones doing all the work. Not that easy getting a ride on a Saturday night. I mean it's not like we want to stay here," Gim looked at me drunkenly, giggling like an idiot.

Heading back to Slick, he sensed my urgency and stood as I approached.

"Uh, Slick, you got time to take us over to Hickory and get some gas? We got two dates outside we got to get home before one."

"Tell you what, Rango. I've taken a shine to you boys, so I'm gonna help you out. How much money you boys got on you?"

"'Bout seven dollars between us, Slick," I said, holding back a dollar for insurance.

"You boys give ol' Slick seven dollars. I'll buy your dates a couple of Cokes, and we'll go out and siphon some gas outta my car. That way you can be on your way now. Save driving all the way to Hickory and back. And the beer and eggs are on me."

I was in no position or condition for that matter, to negotiate.

"Thanks, Slick. Lemme go round up my drunk friend, and we'll be on our way."

I walked over to Gim, who now had a double liplock on Foxy. The boy was not going to be pleased. Time to get tough now.

"Gimlet, get your sorry ass in gear. Slick's gonna siphon some gas out of his car. We gotta get our dates home, pronto."

"Fuck'em, Rango."

It was time to play my trump card. "You the one that's gonna get fucked, Gim. You remember the last thing Sue Sue's daddy told you when we left her house? He told you to have Sue Sue home by one, or he'd rip out your nutsack with his bare hands." Actually, we didn't even see Sue Sue's daddy, but I figured that in Gim's weakened state, he wouldn't remember anyhow.

"Oh, yeah, Rango. I do kinda remember him saying that. Thanks, ol' bud. Let's go."

"Give me all your money, Gim. We got to give it to Slick for gas."

We staggered over to Slick, "Here's you seven dollars, Slick. Let's go get some gas. We got to get home."

Foxy spoke up, "What's you hurry, boys. You two stud muffins can spend the night with me and Passion. We'll take you home early in the morning. After a good breakfast of poon and tang."

Gim's eyes had the thousand-yard stare, "Uh, Rango, maybe that's not such a bad idea with us having so much to drink and all. Maybe we can get ol' Slick here to drive the girls home, and we'll pay him next week after we get our allowances."

"Have all your brains gone to your dick? I'm sure the girls would love to ride home with a total stranger, even one as charming and debonair as Mr. Slick Bootay. And, even if you get some gash tonight, that'll be the last you'll ever get. I heard it's hard to screw without any balls. Sue Sue's daddy'll have yours mounted on the wall after tonight. So the best thing we can do is go apologize to the girls and take'em home as soon as we can. If we're completely honest with'em, maybe they'll speak to us again in a few months."

Gim cocked his head like a dog and sobered up, if only long enough to reply. "Did I hear you say completely honest, Rango?"

"Gim, ol' bud. I've always heard that honesty is the best policy, and that's gonna be my motto from now on. No more bullshit. Nothing but the truth. Let the chips fall where they may. You, my young friend, are talking to a changed man. There will be no more untruths uttered from the mouth of Rango Spears. If I say it now, it's just like it came form the mouth of Jesus Christ."

"Oh, I get it now, Rango. You gonna act like you're a changed man. You gonna use your old sincere, trust me, and I won't come in your mouth act. Yeah, that might work."

"Gim, don't you get it? I'm talking about nothing but the truth from now on. No more schemes, no more scams."

"That's just the beer talking. Ain't a way in hell you can even go an hour without some bullshit scheme."

I quietly replied, "You'll see, Gimlet."

Slick walked over, "Ready, guys? I'll drive my car over, and we'll siphon directly into your car. Oughta have you on your way shortly."

I replied, "Yeah, thanks, Slick. We in the fifty-five dark blue three hole Buick at the back of the parking lot. Slick, would you mind if we didn't go with you right now? Our dates are probably highly pissed at us, and we don't wanna see'em til we get ready to leave. If they ask, just tell'em we sent you over. Oh, and their names are Sue Sue and Melanie Sue."

"Sure, boys, anything you want. I'll be back shortly after I gas you up. Want another beer? My treat."

Gim answered, "One for the road would be nice, Slick. Thanks a million." I look at my pathetic friend and just shook my head.

"What?"

Ten minutes later, our new friend returned.

"Got you enough gas to get you back to Decatur, boys, but I ain't real sure I'd get in the car with those girls. They look beyond pissed. Kept talking about what their daddies and big brothers were gonna do to y'all. Never heard young girls talk that way before, and it all sounded painful. Sure you guys don't wanna spend the night? Let'em cool off a little first."

Gim turned his head to look at me.

"No, Gim, for once we're gonna tell the truth. We went into this joint, had way too much to drink, danced with some road whores, and just completely lost track of time. We're sorry it happened, and we beg your forgiveness. Nothing but the truth, Gim. That's my policy from now on. Now, let's go face the music, my friend."

Slick looked at us sympathetically. So did Passion and Foxy. "Good luck, boys. Come back and visit with ol' Slick anytime."

Foxy also gave us a fond goodbye, "Anytime you boys wanta dip you wick in a real woman, just give me a call."

Passion's added, "Yeah, I can do a lot more with that egg than just eat it."

Barely able to stand straight, we said our good-byes and headed for the door.

"The truth now, Gim. If they don't like it, tough shit."

Gim signed resignedly, "Your call, Rango. But I gotta tell ya, I've gotten kinda attached to my gonads."

"Not to worry, Gim. Haven't I always gotten us through the rough spots? Leave it to me, ol' bud."

I suddenly understood how a condemned prisoner feels taking that last long lonesome walk on death row. I thought to myself, that if there's nothing like a woman scorned, what the hell would these women be like?

As we approached the car, the two Sues were sitting out on the hood. They were smoking, and I don't mean cigarettes. We let them start in first, hoping they'd cool off, then listen to our side of things. The barrage of anger came at us so fast, I had no idea which one was screaming what.

"You two low bred, chicken shit assholes."

"You lying, no good sons a bitches."

"My daddy's gonna stomp your ass flat."

"My brother's gonna rip your lungs out."

"Cock suckers."

"Jack offs."

"You two assholes take us home right now. I'll bet our daddies are looking for us right now, and you two are in deep shit."

"Gimlet, get up front with your lying fucked up buddy. We don't want you two fudge packers sitting that close to us. And, Rango, get this car rolling right now. We want to get home and never lay eyes on you two sorry asses again. After we tell all our friends how sorry you two are, I got a feeling you two gonna be playing with yourselves for a long time, cause ain't no white woman gonna go out with you," Sue Sue said.

"Yeah, and what little social lives you mother fuckers had is now over," Melanie Sue echoed.

Funny, they seemed so sweet just a few hours ago.

I knew we'd fucked up royally. We had left them alone in the car, gotten drunk, cavorted with other women, and stayed gone over three hours. But I couldn't just stand idly by.

"Ladies, granted that we should have told you what we were mixed up in before we drug you into this whole sorry mess. And for that, we sincerely apologize. But I'm not gonna sit here and let you talk bad about my good friend, Gim. He really wanted no part of this, but, as a favor to me, agreed to help me crack this case. This is supposed to be top secret, but I feel like you two ladies are entitled to the whole truth. Cause in all honesty, I'm not sure we could have pulled this off without your help."

I paused and took a deep breath and looked around. The two girls looked interested; Gim looked his usual puzzled self.

"Ladies, I'm afraid what I'm about to say is top secret; everything that took place here tonight was part of a well laid plan, from us running out of gas at this particular club to our drinking beer with one of our contacts. It was all conceived months ago, and I'm just sorry we had to get you involved, but after you hear the whole story, I think you'll realize how important this mission is. If you choose to hate Gim and me after I explain, we'll understand. But, I would like to say that you are both very precious to us, and you will always have a special place in our hearts, no matter what you decide."

I paused and looked around again. I could see real doubt now in our dates' eyes; Gim just looked as puzzled as hell.

"So, ladies, before I continue, I must ask for your absolute and complete silence on this matter. If it ever comes up, we'll just have to deny it, and we could be in real and immediate danger if word gets out."

"Rango, you have our word that this conversation never took place. No way we'd do anything to put you guys in danger; you two are our heroes," Sue Sue said.

We had gone from 'low-life-shit-headed assholes' to heroes in just five minutes.

"And we kinda thought you guys might be on a secret mission. Two nice guys like you could never treat ladies any way but nice," Melanie Sue said.

"Ok, ladies, here goes. Not a single hint of this ever, ever leaves this car."

"You got our word as virgins, Rango," Sue Sue said.

"Virgins tonight, but who knows about tomorrow," Melanie Sue said, blushing furiously.

Then I launched into what could only be described as a masterpiece.

"Well, sometime ago the FBI recruited me for this secret mission here in Meridian. They needed a high school student to infiltrate some of the clubs around here. I can't go into any details about my contacts or anything, but I can tell you this mission has been going on for about six months, and thanks to you two ladies being our cover, I think I am allowed to say that arrests are imminent, and that this whole sorry mess is almost over. Ladies, I feel like I owe you both an explanation. If not for you two, we probably would have been another three or four months cracking this case. It's strictly top secret, but it's mine and Gim's case, so I feel like I can tell our two best girls. It seems that a big crime syndicate out of New Jersey was buying defective condoms from a factory out of Mexico and sending them to all the bars and nightclubs around Meridian. This was just the tip of the iceberg. If they'd gotten away with it here, they already had plans to send the defective condoms to every state in the country. Seems they could buy the condoms for pennies in Mexico and sell 'em for a dollar or so in the states. Every condom me and my inspectors checked had pinholes in the tip so they were totally no good for what they were intended. Well, as it so happens, this crime syndicate is linked to some area hospitals and others around the country, and they stand to make a lot of money on the rising number of OB/GYN visits to these hospitals. It's like they are creating doctors appointments which can only lead to some type of insurance payoff. I mean, can you imagine how much disease could be spread around and how many illegitimate babies would be born for one single night of passion?"

I was on a roll.

"Anyhow, the FBI's supposed to be picking up the kingpins even as we speak. I think I'm allowed to say that there will be no more defective rubbers in Lauderdale County. I just hope we don't have to testify against the mob, but if we do, we do. They can't kill us but one time, and I know Gim and I would give several lives to make life in this great country of ours better. And, ladies, I'm sorry we had so much to drink. We had to go along with the mob boys until we could find out where those shipments were coming from. But, when Gim and I are on a mission, we'll do anything, and I mean anything, to crack the case."

The two Sues had tears running down their cheeks. Simultaneously, they both kissed us softly on the cheek.

"You two are the greatest guys we know," Melanie Sue said.

"Just two average guys, my love, trying to do our part to keep America great," I said modestly, hanging my head.

"Our two FBI stud muffins," Sue Sue said.

"Stop the car, Rango. I wanna get up front with my man," Melanie Sue said.

"Me, too, Rango. Gim, you got one minute to get back here with me," Sue Sue said.

I pulled over, and the seat changes were made.

Then Sue Sue spoke up, "I think we just might have to check out Lover's Lane when we finally get back to Decatur. Being that close to danger makes me feel all tingly. Weren't you guys ever scared?"

I modestly replied, "Danger is just part of our job description. When you're doing this for your country, well it just makes our lives seem so insignificant. Gim and I have been lucky so far. A few times I thought we were about to buy the farm, but our training has carried us through so far. That's why we just live day-to-day and try to squeeze all the gusto we can out of life. Most of our agents don't make it in this business over five years, so we try and live each day to it's fullest. That's why we're so lucky we ran into you two precious jewels. If we don't see the light of another day, I think I speak for Gim as well as myself in saying that our perilous dangerous jobs have been made more bearable by your friendships."

"You two wonderful guys are a whole lot more than friends right now, and we're gonna prove it if you'll ever get this car back to Decatur."

Just then, through the rear view mirror, I spotted Sue Sue putting a double lip lock on Gimlet and placing one of his hands over her perky breasts.

Gim finally came up for air. He didn't look giddy as I had expected. In fact, he looked sick.

"Stop the car, Rango. I gotta pee like a racehorse plus all these eggs kinda rumblin' round in me. I feel like I might be sick."

"I'm pulling over at this roadside park, Gim. Plenty of bushes around here." I eased the car over to the side of the road, and Gim started to crawl over Sue Sue to get out of the two-door Buick. As he did, I heard a sound that I still have nightmares about, even to this day.

"Braaaaack, braaaaaack."

Gim, probably though no fault of his own had, done the unpardonable, the unforgivable. He had blasted a horrendous air biscuit made up of eggs, beer, and what ever was still dissolving from dinner, right in Sue Sue's face.

Before she could recover from this ghastly attack on her delicately powdered button nose, Gim began giggling and soon after, howling uncontrollably. The result was a series of machine gun-like farts that came in staccato bursts that buffeted poor Sue Sue's head and blew her hair like she was in a wind tunnel. Gim was out of control.

"Har, har, snort, snort, hee, hee. Braaaaack! Braaaaaack! Hee, hee, hoohoo, snort, snort. Braaaaack! Hee, Braaaaack!"

Although Melanie Sue and I had long since vacated the car, we too fell victim to the overwhelming essence of sewage erupting from Gim's ass.

Finally, the door to the gas chamber flung open, and my best good bud stumbled from the car. Sue Sue looked dazed and confused. Holding my breath, I pulled Sue Sue out. Her whole body smelled like eau de asshole. Sue Sue collapsed with her back against a big pine tree, trying desperately to inhale as much oxygen as her lungs would take. Gim continued to laugh and break wind.

I sternly addressed Gim, "I hope you're proud of yourself, Gim, after this shameful display here tonight. You have totally disgraced yourself and the FBI. What do you think Maw would say if she was here tonight?"

"Maw'd be proud, Rango. You know how she always farts on my head when I'm trying to eat."

"We gotta get these ladies home as soon as the car airs out. You about over your gas attack?"

"Braaaaaaaaaaccck," echoed through the roadside park.

"And another thing, Melanie Sue and I still have a little unfinished business at Lover's Lane. What about you and Sue Sue?"

Sue Sue looked up from her daze, "Don't let that gas man get close to me. I'll walk home first."

Gimlet looked contrite. "Aw, Sue Sue, I'm sorry. It's not like I embarrassed myself like that on purpose. I had too much to drink and got sorta sick to my stomach. I really, really tried to hold back 'til I got out of the car, but I couldn't. Come on. Let me help you up from there, and let's all get on home. I understand if you don't ever wanna see me again. All I know is that you mean the world to me, and I know I'd never do anything to make you unhappy. I know I was ready to give my life for you tonight if necessary. Things got pretty rough inside that club, but the mob was gonna get to you only over my dead body."

"Oh, Gim. I can't stay mad with you. Let's get home and both get a good night's sleep, and we'll talk tomorrow. Right now all I want to do is get out of these clothes and take a nice hot bath. We'll sort it all out tomorrow."

Wow, from the shithouse to the penthouse. I taught you well, my friend. I taught you well.

Another five minutes or so and the car passed the smell test, which meant that if you rolled all the windows down and didn't take deep breaths, you could ride without puking.

The ride home was fairly uneventful. Gim nodded off and farted several more times. However, that could be excused as "sleeping slippers." So, the ladies and I rode back to Decatur with our heads partially out of the windows. We finally reached Decatur. We pulled up to Sue Sue's house, and before I could even stop the car, she was out the door. Luckily, her brothers and old man weren't around.

"Melanie Sue, I'm not sure we want to go to Lover's Lane in this car tonight. Is there any other place we can go? I really need to be with you tonight, 'specially after the danger I've been through. I just need somebody to hold me and tell me I'm safe. I don't think I need to be by myself right now."

"Oh, Rango, I'm not about to let you be alone now, not after the danger and stress you've been through. My bedroom's way in the back of the house, where no body can hear us. Why don't we go there?"

Done.

I parked the car in Melanie Sue's driveway, opened all the doors to the car, and left Gim asleep, still farting his little heart out.

Two hours after I taught a lesson in carnal knowledge and learned a thing or two myself, I went out to the car, rousted Gim, and drove home. It was about three in the morning when we made it to down town Decatur. It was deserted. Except for one other car.

The blue lights of Sheriff' Kincaid's patrol car reflected right into my eye off the rearview mirror, and I pulled over in front of the drugstore.

"Let me do the talking, Gim. You just sit there and nod and try not to fart."

Sheriff Kincaid parked behind us, got out, and walked up to my window.

"Oh, hey Rango. Just checking to see who was out this late at night. You boys must have had a hot date. or y'all been out to old Man Stomper's farm. Hear he's got some stump broke cows up– Damn! What the hell is that smell, Rango? Somebody shit in your car?"

"Uh, Hmm, well, Sheriff Kincaid, the reason the car smells so bad is that Gim has got some serious stomach trouble. We been trying to get home for hours now, but we can only go so far, and I have to pull over so Gim can go to the bushes. Well, a couple of times, I couldn't stop fast enough, and I'm afraid Gim's got skid marks on his BVDs."

With that lovely visual firmly planted in the Sheriff's head, he let us be on our way.

Finally, we pulled into Gimlet's driveway. "Been an exciting night, Gim. I think I might be in love."

"Tell me the truth, Rango," said an almost sober Gimlet.

"Did I screw up royally tonight or what? Think Sue Sue'll ever go out with me again?"

"Naw, Gim, I think Sue Sue'll get over you farting in her face, not once, not twice, but several dozen times and then laughing like a mad man. I think she'll get over having to burn her clothes that were exposed to your noxious cheeses. I think she'll get over you getting knee walking drunk and trying to pick up a real whore… Of course, you did play the FBI bit just right, and the movie and the meal went very well. So, I'd say, Gim, it really depends on how offended she was by your farting. But since it's a natural body function, I can't imagine anybody staying pissed over something so trivial for long. What I think would be totally fair is to offer to let Sue Sue fart right in your face until she feels like she's paid you back. You could even offer to let her stick her bare cheeks right up against your head. Now that would be fair."

Then I got serious, "Just trying to add a little levity, Gim, ol' bud. I know how stressed you are about this and to answer you honestly, yes, I think Sue Sue will get over your obnoxious farting. I think she will want to go out with you again, and I predict that y'all will prob'ly be going steady within the next month. I also think that if you play your cards right, you'll get some of that trim. But, Gim, does it really matter? I mean, as bad as you fucked up tonight, I can promise you that you'll fuck up much, much worse in the future. In fact, one of the great pleasures of having you as a best bud is the sheer anticipation of knowing that somewhere, somehow, down the road, you will totally and utterly disgrace yourself in a way that very few ever do. You, my friend, are truly one of a kind, and I salute you."

"Thanks, Durango, I needed that. You're a true friend."

"You're welcome; now go take a shower, you fucking stink."

Maw Shoeman's first Football Game

"I could eat the ass out of a rag doll," said Gim, as I walked into his house.

"Yeah? So what's new?"

"Well for one, Maw's trying to lose a little weight, so she's serving a lot of healthy, tasteless shit."

"Aw, Maw's just looking out for your best interests, Gim. It wouldn't hurt you to lose a few pounds."

"But, right before our first football game? I need to be putting the pounds on. I feel kinda weak from all this dieting."

"How long you been dieting, Gim?" I asked.

"Well, what time is it, nine?"

"Yeah."

"'Bout an hour."

"Shit, Gim."

"But you know I got to keep my strength up. I might get to play a little tonight. Coach said if we got far enough ahead, he'd let everybody in the game."

"Well, Gim, we're playing Hickory tonight. We ought' a beat them like a drum. What'd we beat 'em last year, fifty-six, nothing?"

About that time, Maw came in from the kitchen.

"Hey, Rango. See how skinny Gim's getting? Got the boy on a diet. We're gonna both get skinny as snakes."

"Well, Maw, now that you mention it, the boy does look a little light in the loafers. You must have 'em on a diet of round steak. If he loses a little more, we'll put him on the cheerleading squad."

"Now, Rango, you don't be messing with Gim. I's countin' on you to help me make him stick with his diet."

"Oh, you know I will Maw. Just funning ol' Gim a little."

" I know I could count on you, Rango," Maw said, as she went back in the kitchen humming the old Monotones hit Book of Love."

"Rango," Gim said, "let's go down to Betty's Kitchen. I'm about to pass out from hunger. I could sure do with a double cheeseburger and a big order of fries and gravy. I just need something to tide me over 'til we eat our pre-game meal."

"Uh, Gim," I said, "the pre-game meal's in about two hours. You think you oughta be eating all that food before the game?"

"Well, Rango, it's not like I'm gonna' play much. I might get in if y'all get a big lead in the fourth quarter."

"I hadn't told you this before, but I've already told Coach Dick that you and I been working on a secret pass play that we gonna run in the first half."

"No bullshit, Rango? A secret pass play? But you know I normally play tackle, not end."

"Not to worry, Gim. That'll be the beauty of the whole thing. You'll come in a couple of plays at tackle, then you'll move to tight end, and I'll throw the ball to you. It's a piece of cake. Touchdown Decatur. Nobody'll be expecting it."

Although it sounded like I had this idea tucked away somewhere in the back of my mind, I had actually just thought of this whole scenario right then and there. I kinda' liked the idea of my bud Gim's being a hero for once. Only real problem now would be telling Coach Dick what was going on. But then again, since I was the quarterback and called all the plays, maybe I wouldn't have to.

"Oh, man, Rango, that'd be great. It's not like we don't play pass and catch all the time. You know I'll catch the ball if you throw it to me. Man, now, I'm really hungry. You know when I get nervous, I get hungry," said Gim.

"Yeah, and when you get mad, or happy, or sad, or sleepy, or pissed, or disgusted, or pretty much anytime you're not sleeping."

We headed to Betty's Kitchen, and Gim ordered his double cheeseburger and a big order of fries and gravy, plus a piece of chocolate cake. And while he ate, I said, "Gim, I've got an excellent plan to celebrate should our little secret pass play work. 'Cause if it does, you won't be just another third stringer that people look at with disgust. Nope, my man, you'll get immediate name recognition, and you'll be remembered as one of the legends of Decatur football, a young man able to have his pick of any woman in Newton County. Yup, if we succeed, this will be a momentous night for all."

I paused to let my bullshit settle comfortably in Gim's ears. And when I was sure I had his undivided attention, I said, "Gim, can you get the car tonight?"

"No problem, Rango. Miz Hortense is out of town on business, and Maw's got a hot date with that Yankee football recruiter, Stone. They usually shack up somewhere when he's in town. The car's mine for the taking. Why, what's up?"

"All right Gim, here's the deal. If this play works and you score a touchdown, why not celebrate with another touchdown later tonight? After all, you'll be a hero in the town of Decatur. Why not celebrate your new status by going to Maw Shoeman's and get your first piece of trim. Think about it. First touchdown, first trim. What could be a better way to celebrate?" I reasoned.

Maw Shoeman's was the notorious whorehouse located just outside the city limits of Meridian. For ten bucks a pop, any woman in the establishment could be had in the biblical sense. Rumor was that the Sheriff was paid off. So except for the occasional raid, the place operates with impunity.

"And Gim, iffin' you worried about finances, this will be my treat. You've got a birthday coming up next week, so this'll be an early gift from your best bud. But, Gim, and I'm not trying to put too much pressure on, the whole deal depends on you making the big play. Otherwise, you'll get the same ol' milkshake and burger I give you every year."

Actually, I was trying to put the pressure on. I mean, I wanted Gim to score both touchdowns, but ten bucks was ten bucks. It would be up to Gim – food or fornication. Either way, I'd come out like a champ.

Gim's eyes became glazed over, and I wasn't sure if he was thinking of all the delights that awaited him if he succeeded, or if it was time for another burger.

"Rango, I won't let you down. I got a feeling we gonna be in Meridian later tonight. You're a true bud for coming up with this. Gonna be the best birthday present ever."

"No problem, Gim. I guess we better mosey on over to the school cafeteria. It's bout time for our pre-game meal."

"Let's go, Rango, I'm starvin'."

Our traditional pre-game meal always consisted of steak, scrambled eggs, biscuits, and honey. When we were finished, we'd walk over to the field house to get dressed for the game. Coach usually gave us an inspirational speech at about six, at the end of which, we walked across the campus to the stadium between fans lining the way to give us a bit of last minute encouragement. You'd see people lined up, sometimes four and five deep. Yup, football was the only happening in town on a Friday night.

This afternoon, like most, Gim and I walked through the serving line and received our steak and eggs and pulled up a chair at a table with Booger and Blubber, who each had poured a whole large jar of honey over their food.

"How y'all eat that shit, Booger?" I asked. "Why don't you just drink a couple jars of honey and not ruin a good steak?"

"Eat me, Rango. We wouldn't expect some prissy ass quarterback to know 'bout energy food. You'll be back there prancing around handling off the football and trying to stay clean. Me and Blubber will be down in the bottom of the pile-up biting inner thighs, pinchin' gonads, and puttin' our fingers who knows where. You and yo' bone smokin' backfield butt buddies'll be back there playing drop the soap. Wouldn't surprise me if y'all are all bowlers. Bunch of candy asses."

I always liked the little give and take between the backs and the lineman, because I knew that when the game was on the line, I could count on each and every member of the team to give one-hundred and ten percent. Just then, Coach Dick came by the table.

"You boys ready to play? Hickory's got a tough team this year. Hear they got five or six players State and Ole Miss gonna be scouting. Y'all gonna have to be on the top of your game to stay on the field with these boys. Rango, I want you to stay real conservative tonight. I don't wanna see any of your off the wall sand lot b.s., unless we're lucky enough to get a good lead. I mean it, Rango. Nothing but straight running plays and flanker screens the first half. You got it?"

I acted indignant. "Coach, when have I ever let the team down? You know I always bust my butt for you. As long as I've been your starting quarterback, I've never run an off the wall play. Actually, I'm not sure if I've ever run a play that you didn't personally endorse."

Coach Dick choked back his words. He and I and the whole team knew I'd called plenty of horseshit plays, but most all of 'em worked. So no harm, no foul. Besides this was just another one of Coach Dick's standard speeches before each game. All that bullshit about what a good team Hickory had, well, that tended to be horse hockey. I'd played football for Coach Dick through pee wee, junior high, and well into high school, and usually the more he praised a team, the worse they were. I guess he just didn't want us to take anybody for granted. But for some reason that afternoon I just felt this was gonna' be the night for mine and Gim's secret play. We cleaned our plates and made our way over to the field house to dress.

"Nervous, Gim"? I asked.

"A little bit, Rango. I keep thinking about that play and just hope I don't screw it up."

"Don't even think that way, Gim. How many times have we passed the ball around, and you never dropped it? The only difference is that you'll have about four-thousand people in the stands watching, plus all your teammates counting on you, plus all the girls asking themselves if they really wanna go out with a loser that can't even catch a football thrown right in his gut. I mean, the worst thing that can happen is that you'll totally disgrace yourself again, and that people turn their back on you when you walk down the street, and the ones that don't, will simply look at you with outright revulsion and disgust. On the other hand, by some miracle, you could catch the ball and become an instant hero. Little kids might even be wearing your jersey number. White girls will be lining up to let you sample their wares, parents will let you into their homes through the front entrance, and maybe, just maybe, people won't wrinkle up their nose like they just smelled doo doo when they hear your name."

"You know, Rango, as usual, you're absolutely right. I mean I've been disgraced many times, and at least half the town's probably seen me naked. This won't be a hill for a stepper. If I drop the ball, big ass deal, right?"

"That's the spirit, Gim."

Once inside the field house the smell of old sweat hit us like a brick wall. We made our way to our lockers where the equipment manager had neatly laid out our uniforms and pads. Everything was clean, freshly washed, except Booger and Blubber's jock straps. It seems my two favorite heavy weights were very superstitious and, for reasons only they can explain, thought it very bad mojo should they have their jock straps washed before the end of the season. Because they were on either side of me, the odor emanated from both sides of my locker and engulfed me like a fog. It was an odor hard to describe. Let's just say it was way worse than what happens when Gim mixes eggs with beer. To keep their, well, streak alive, both tons-of-fun told Coach some bullshit story that their religion, Seventh Day Adventist, did not allow any of their undergarments washed except under a full moon and by a virgin. They would tell Coach that Booger's eleven year-old sister usually hand washes all offending garments, but Decatur being the kind of town it was, his sister no longer fit in that category. So for the time being, they were 'in between washers'.

Even as dense as Coach Dick was, he surely wasn't taken in by such obvious bullshit. He knew that Booger and Blubber were Southern Baptists and even as weird as Baptists are, most of them probably wash their underwear. Besides, as bad as the odor was, as long as we were winning, no complaints came from me. I've seen some of the opposing players come out of a pile-up. Their eyes would be watering, and they would suck fresh air like an asthmatic.

The Decatur Warriors' uniforms consisted of gold pants with two black stripes down the sides, a black jersey with gold numerals, and black helmets with two old gold stripes. I was almost dressed when Coach Dick entered the locker room to give his inspirational talk. Now the coach had no peer as an inspirational speaker. Black preachers, politicians, lawyers, even used car salesman took a back seat to Coach Dick. If he had been a black politician, he would have found his true calling. He began softly,

"Boys, here it is our first game of the season. We started back in July when it was hotter than Maw Shoeman's joy box. We practiced once a day and twice a day, 'til most of you were too tired to pull your puds."

"Tell it like it is, Coach."

"Some of you, after this game, will be heroes and might even play a little stink finger."

"Hallelujah!"

"And some of you," he said looking right at Gim, "will have to go home and say hello to ol' rosy palm."

"You de man, Coach."

"My point is that no matter whether you score after the game or not, the important thing is to score in the game of life."

"Amen, Coach."

"Some of you will go on to become successful businessmen, lawyers, doctors, upstanding citizens, while some of you," again he looked at Gim, "will be near-do-wells, bums, or town drunks."

"So the game of football is a lot like life, boys. Play well, you get the prime gash, cool jobs, and success. Play like ass and you'll be lower than whale shit, just another pimple on the ass of life, just hanging out at the pool hall or bowling alley. Succeed and you'll be drinking fine wines, eating prime rib, and driving the latest luxury cars. Fail and you'll be eating out of garbage cans, drinking Thunderbird. What's the word; Thunderbird. What's the price? Fifty twice."

"We gonna be drinking fine wine and eating prime gash, Coach. Ain't gonna be hanging out at no bowling alley."

Coach continued, "Now I've seen these Hickory boys

play. They gonna come in here like Hitler when he took Mexico. Comin' in here ready to rape and pillage. They gonna rape yo' sisters; they gonna break some of you down like shotguns in the shower after the game; they gonna make some of you suck their lollipops." Then he paused. "They gonna destroy yo' crops!"

"Oh, hell, no! Ain't no mother fucker from Hickory gonna destroy my crops, Coach! We gonna' stomp some Hickory Ass," yelled Booger, leaping up from his chair.

Blubber chimed in, "They'll get to my sister over my dead, stinking ass."

Even Tommy Nunn got in the act, "Worked too damn hard to let some pussies from Hickory come in here. And I hate lollipops."

Coach Dick did exactly what he set out to do. He had the team hanging on his every word. We were ready to rip off their heads and shit down their necks.

Coach Dick concluded, "So, boys, I want you to know the whole school, the whole town, you mama and daddies who worked so hard for those crops are counting on you. I just happened by the Hickory locker room on my way over, and they were all laughing and giggling 'bout what they were gonna do to ya'll after the game. Said sumpin 'bout dressing ya'll up in their sister's panties and making' ya'll squeal likes pigs." And he shouted from emphasis, "THEY GONNA DO IT RIGHT OUT IN YO' CROPS." At this point, the team just lost it. Every name in the book, and some that weren't, could be heard in the corridor outside the locker room.

"Damn Nazi pussies!"

"Let's go over to there right now and stomp their asses," yelled Booger, all red faced and striding for the door. Coach Dick got in his way.

"Sit back down, Booger. I'm about to see what kinda' man you are. I'm gonna' see if you lay down and spread yo' cheeks for these Hickory punks, or if y'all can sack up and stop these animals from rippin' through you like croton oil through a wider woman, destroying yo' crops and going down on yo' sisters."

"Let's go get them Hickory Dickory Cocks!"

"All right then! Let's go take our walk. Play the way we practiced, and we'll be fine. This Hickory group can be taken if you play your best and don't make any silly mistakes. Let's pray. Ya'll join hands."

Coach continued. "Lord, we don't ask that we win, but that we play to the best of our ability, and, if it's your will that our crops be destroyed and our sisters ravaged…."

"Ain't no damn crops gonna be destroyed," mumbled Booger.

Coach continued, "And if these Hickory boys do win and make Nancy boys out of my whole team, I just pray they will survive with some dignity intact, still able to hold their heads high, even though they have been violated in the worse possible way a white man can be violated, and over time and a healing period, be able to function as real men. Amen.'"

Booger slammed his fist into a locker, "We'll see whose crops get destroyed. Dirty cock suckers."

We filed out of the locker room and began walking over to the stadium. There were the usual parents, hero-worshiping kids, and other well wishers lining our path.

Booger's mom yelled out, "Have a good game, honey."

He replied, "I ain't gonna let no cock sucker from Hickory destroy our crops, maw."

Mrs. Scales, as sweet a woman as there ever was, pillar of the community, looked stunned. "What crops, Booger?"

"Maw, those crops been in our family a long time, and they gonna stay there."

Mrs. Scales looked at Mr. Scales questionably.

"What you think, paw? Steroids or dope?"

Next were everybody's favorite town drunks up ahead in the grove of trees.

"Hey, Rango. Where yo' fat buddy?" yelled out Rufus. "Sho' did want to see him in 'dose tight stretch pants. Boy has got him one fine ass."

Booger chimed in, "You know, Gimlet does have one fine ass. Hope them Hickory boys don't stretch it out too much after the game."

Gimlet fired back, "Knock it off, Booger, and you two old drunks get the hell out of here 'fore I tell the sheriff where you are."

"Aw, Gim, Rufus jus' messin' wid' you. Don't mean nothing by it," spoke up Early Rue.

"Sure, I do. White boy's got the finest ass I ever saw, and 'dem football pants make it stand out like two hogs fighting in a feed sack."

Finally making it to the stadium and finishing our drills, I called the fellas into a huddle. "Boys, I want you to calm down before kickoff. We don't need to start this game with a fifteen yard penalty or get any of you kicked out of the game."

Booger spoke up, "Rango, I ain't just gonna stand by while somebody fucks up our crops."

"You ain't got no damn crops, Booger. Coach just said all that shit to get you fired up. Forget about the damn crops, and let's play some football!"

"Well, crops or no crops, them Hickory shits stains ain't gettin' em."

"Whatever you say, pal."

A perfect end-over-end kickoff came right to me. It hit me in the numbers, and I took off. I followed the wall up the middle 'til about the 25, cut left, found a hole, and angled toward the sidelines. I knew if I could get the corner, I'd be gone. And I was. Eighty-six yards later, I was standing in the end zone. No flags. Seven, nothing. Us.

They fumbled the kickoff, and we recovered. One play later, I hit Tommy on the 10, and he took it in. Fourteen-zip. Decatur. Another two scores put us up twenty-eight to nothing at the half. We walked off the field, and I found Gim.

"Fourth quarter, Gim. We gonna work our little secret pass play."

"Coach OK with it, Rango?" asked Gimlet.

"Well, not exactly, Gim. But on the field I'm the boss. 'Sides, it's gonna' work like a charm. You, my young friend, will be the talk of the town tomorrow. Merchants will line up to give you free gifts, and they might even have a parade in your honor," I said, laying it on thick.

"Rango, I'm so nervous I feel like I might crap in my pants. What if I miss the ball? What if I catch it and fall down? My name'll be shit again. "

"What's the difference? Your name's shit now."

"You got a point."

"That's the spirit, Gim. But, somehow, I just have a real good feeling you gonna score that touchdown and lose yo' virginity tonight. I'll be proud of you what ever happens."

Gim misted over. He choked out.

"Thanks, Rango, ditto for me."

"On second thought, Gim, I'm gonna call the play early in the third quarter. We gonna' be so far ahead he's gonna' put in the second string start of the fourth quarter. Let's go ahead and get it over with."

"Ok, I'm ready, Rango."

"I believe you are, Gim."

In the locker room. Coach Dick was standing with his chalkboard.

"Heard them Hickory boys talking on the way off the field. Said y'all were a bunch of pussies they were gonna' beat in the second half." He continued on like usual for the entire intermission, but up by 28 points, it fell on deaf ears.

As we filed out of the locker room, Gim came running up.

"Rango, you ever used any stick-um to make the ball stick your hands? Thinking about spraying with it so I'll be sure and catch that pass. Manager had a tube of some new stuff called super glue he said was better than stick-um."

"I've never used any, Gim, but if it'll make you feel better, go for it. I know some of our receivers put it on their hands. Makes the ball sticky for sure."

We took the field. Two minutes later, we were up thirty-five to zero. I walked over to Gim, "Next series we on offense, come in the game. It's time. If we score again, Coach's gonna' take me out of the game."

You could just see the proverbial monkey jump on Gim's back. He started blinking and swallowing, and his voice raised about two octaves. "I'm ready, Rango," he squealed. "'Cept, I got to pee like a race horse."

"On all fours?," I joked.

"Rango!…"

"So pee, Gim. Get some of the guys on the bench to surround you, and you just pee on the sideline. I've done it many times."

Four downs later, we had the ball again. I wanted to drive the ball down to the five-yard line so Gim wouldn't have to run far to score the touchdown. Over ten yards and, no doubt, he'd trip over his own feet. I called the huddle.

"Guys, we gonna drive the ball down close to their goal line, and then I got a secret pass play designed for Gim."

"Gim?" asked Blubber. "That boy couldn't catch a pass with a butterfly net."

Everybody guffawed.

"Just do this for me. OK, guys?"

"Well, sure, Rango. Might be kinds' a fun to see how Gim's gonna screw this up," said Booger.

So we ran halfback right, five yards. Then the halfback left for ten yards. Finally, we were on the Hickory six-yard line.

"Time out, Mr. Ref.," I called.

I ran over to the sideline.

"Coach, Massey's hurt. I'm gonna take Gim back with me."

Coach, knowing we had the game won, couldn't care less.

So far, so good.

"Let's go, Gim. Time for you to be a hero."

Gim came running off the bench and promptly busted his ass. Funny thing, Gim had both hands on his crotch, almost like they were glued there. His teeth were chattering and not from the cold.

"Rango, put my helmet on. I put on too much stick-um and a whole tube of super glue, and I can't get my hands unstuck."

Just as I was about to really unload on Gim and tell him how ungrateful he was for blowing this opportunity I had given him to finally do something good for himself, I asked myself, what would be the use? I'm convinced that Gim probably wanted to change, but he really just was not capable.

"Here, Gim. Come on, let's go."

"But, Rango, how am I gonna' catch the ball with no hands?" Gim chattered.

"You just be there for the pass, Gim. Maybe your hands'll come unglued by then."

We ran on the field. Gim spawled out once more. Kinda' hard to run with your hands glued to your crotch. We made it into the huddle, and our teammates gave their usual support.

"Loping yo' mule again, Gim?"

"Damn, Gim, couldn't it wait 'til after the game."

"All right guys, listen up. Gim's gonna line up at tight end. Tommy, you move over to tackle. I'm gonna' fake a sweep around right end. Gim, you run right into the end zone, and I'll hit you right in the gut. Everybody got it?'

When we broke the huddle, Gim still had his hands glued to his crotch, trying mightily to get his hands free. Anyway, a plan was a plan, and I was sticking to it. The team got set. I started calling out the count.

"Down, hut one, hut two," I glanced over at Gim. He was trembling like a man with palsy. I was hoping the ref wouldn't throw a flag for motion. "Hut three, hut four". The ball was snapped. I rolled out right like I was running a bootleg. Where was Gim? He should be in the end zone. Then, I spotted his unmistakable large ass sprawled out on the ground.

"Get up, Gim," I yelled. "Get yo' fat ass up and turn around."

Gim scrambled to his feet and promptly tripped again.

"Get up!"

The whole team was now chanting.

"Get yo' lard ass up."

Gim, again scrambled to his feet. As for me, I was running for my life around in the backfield. Finally, Gim was turned toward me even though his hands were still glued to his crotch. Thinking I had nothing to lose, I stopped and threw the ball as hard as I could right at Gim's ample belly. The throw sunk right into his gut, knocking him back about six feet and then onto his ass. A whistle blew, and out of the corner of my eye, I could see a ref running with both hands raised above his head. We did it.

Gim was now a hero, and I ran over to congratulate him. The ball was still stuck in his belly.

"We did it, man! How you feel?" I asked.

Gim was too overcome with emotion to talk. Either that, or he had the wind knocked out of him.

"We gonna get you some skank tonight!"

Gim kinda' perked up at the very mention of skank, but he just laid there sucking air.

"Come on, Gim. Let's go over to the sideline. We still got a quarter to play."

I helped Gim to his feet and got the ball out of his gut. Gim's hands were still glued, so he tripped twice before we got to the sideline. Coach was there with open arms and clenched fists.

"Rango, what kinda' horseshit was that? Pull that again, and you'll be yanking bench splinters outta' yo' ass."

"Right, coach. My mistake," I said, deciding not to make any waves, knowing we had pulled off our secret pass play and were headed to Maw Shoeman's that night.

The game finally ended fifty-six to zip, and the team made its way off the field with all the pomp and circumstance you'd expect from a high school football crowd. Errant comments were thrown Gim's way regarding his cupped hands around his privates.

"Still trying to find it, Gim?"

"Never saw anybody try to fuck a football be'fore."

"Was that pigskin or foreskin?"

"What were you doing with that ball, son. Or don't ya have two?"

It was still a shame that his perceived goober grabbin' had overshadowed his miracle catch. But Gim took it all in stride; his attention now lay elsewhere.

We finally filed into the field house, took our showers, and got ready for our big trip to Meridian. Of course, the high school jock sniffers, hero worshipers, and kids were hanging outside our locker room when we emerged.

One of the people waiting was his old heartthrob, Pamela Sue.

"Good game, Gim. I just loved it when you made that touchdown catch," she cooed seductively.

I wasn't sure my ears were working for a moment. This was the same girl that promised to never have anything to do with Gim the night of the water tower incident. It just went to show that in the South, football, not time, heals all wounds.

Judging from her body language, I think Gim could probably have had his way with her right there in the locker room.

"You doing anything tonight, Gim? Touchdown catch like that needs to be rewarded."

I spoke up, "Uh, Pamela Sue, Gim and I promised Auntie Maw we'd drive her to Meridian to visit her sick sister in the hospital. But I know Gim'd love to see you tomorrow night. He talks about you all the time."

Pamela Sue lowered her voice and said, "Well, I certainly been thinking thoughts about him. That touchdown made me come to my feet."

Damn! She was verbally seducing my pudgy friend right in front of me.

Not wanting to get back late with the car, I quickly made our good-bye.

Still trying to take in what she just said, I stammered, "Uh, thanks , but we gotta go. Move, Gim."

Gim broke out of his trance, and we took off.

The three-hole Buick was right where we expected, and we started to get excited.

"Think I need to get some rubbers, Rango?"

"Nah, Maws got all that shit there. That's included in the price."

"Gonna be the best birthday present I ever had, Rango. Thanks again, ol' Bud."

"Nothing but the best for you, Gim. You bout' ready to roll?

We hopped into the freshly clean Buick and made our way through the mean streets of Decatur on our way to Maw's to enroll in her school of carnal knowledge. Ten miles outside of Decatur, we spotted the blue light of a sheriff's car.

"Slow down, Gim. Looks like a wreck."

We slowed as we got closer and saw that out directing traffic was none other than one of Decatur's finest. Officer Modine Gunch, the first female law enforcer in the State of Mississippi. Our favorite. Rumor had it that she was a carpet muncher of the card-carrying variety but would also spread 'em for anybody with a dick. A switch hitter. Rumor also had it that Modine would exchange a ticket fine in favor of a little man service.

"Damn, Rango, that's that Officer Gunch who's always hittin' on me. Making all kinds of sexual remarks and grabbin' my ass. I heard she makes guys screw her just so she won't arrest 'em."

"First time you told me that, Gim. You don't think she's trying to get in yo' pants, do you? I know if it was me, I'd have to put in to her. She's built like a damn wrestler, and I hear she's so mean she'll climb up a hog's ass for a ham sandwich. You wouldn't stand a chance with her. She'd have you screwed, blued, and tattooed 'fore you could yell 'calf rope'." But you go do ol' Modine in the back seat of her patrol car. Not sure if y'all both fit though, but, hell, it's worth a try."

"Not funny worth a shit, Rango; besides, rumor is she's got a taste for the Brillo."

"Rumors, rumors. Hey, just because Blubber says he saw her with her mouth south of Bertha Burnside's belly button doesn't necessarily mean anything. I mean, she could have been performing an emergency medical procedure or some kind of reverse CPR. And you know what the C stands for. Blubber said ol' Bertha looked like she was gasping and all trying to get her breath. Yes, I'm sure the whole thing was entirely innocent."

Slowly, we pulled up to the car wreck. Looked like a minor fender bender.

"Pull over to the side here, boys. I need to check your registration and driver's license. Let me get through with this accident report," said Officer Gunch.

One of the drivers involved looked familiar. It was one of Maw Shoeman's best girl's, Lulu Tann. A young blonde bimbo with huge jugs. With any luck, she'd be Gim's first sexual conquest.

Modine spoke, "Almost through here, Miss. Tann. One more question and you'll be on your way. What gear were you in when you rammed the other car?"

"Why, the same gear I'm in now, jeans and a blouse with some sandals," answered Lulu.

Luckily for Lulu, she had other talents that made up for her mental shortcomings.

Modine rolled her eyes and sighed, "That'll be all, Miss Tann. Drive safely now, you hear."

Judging from the polite and tolerant handling of Lulu, I got to thinking that Officer Gunch's reputation as a hard-ass was much overrated.

Gim was fidgeting in his seat. "Officer, we're kinda in a hurry here. Can you check my license now?" Gim asked politely.

Modine fixed him with a less than friendly stare. "When I want to hear from an asshole, I'll fart. Now, out of the car, both of you. Spread 'em over the hood of the car," ordered Gooch.

Gim started unbuckling his pants.

"What the hell are you doing, Gim?" I whispered as I bent over the car.

"Whatever she says," he replied.

There we were. The two football heroes of the day, spread out like soft margarine. Gim's pants were down around his knees, and he was holding his butt cheeks apart like a Parchman prisoner. To describe the scene as embarrassing wouldn't even come close. From behind us, we heard Officer Gunch stifle a chuckle. "Where you boys from?"

Gim nervously answered, "Decatur, Officer. We headed to Meridian to celebrate our football victory over Hickory. I scored a touchdown in the game."

"Do tell," she said sarcastically, before continuing, "Well, son, I'm gonna' have to put you in the patrol car with me while I call yo' license in. Yo' buddy here can sit in yo' car til we get through."

Gim looked at me, and I could tell he was thinking the worst..

"Yeah, looks like I'm gonna have to run an APB on you and, from the looks of things, a NEM report. Shouldn't take over twenty minutes."

Gim started babbling, "Officer, I got a sick Maw in Meridian Hospital. I think I'm coming down with Lupus. I got kicked in the groin in the football game, and I can't get a hard on. The Dodgers had another losing season."

Officer Gunch said, "Thought y'all were going to celebrate yo' victory. Come on now 'fore I have to run you in for resisting arrest."

Gim slowly made his way to the patrol car. Officer Gunch turned off the blue light and pulled a little deeper off the road. Now nobody could see them unless they happened to walk by. Nothing could save Gim now, but I seriously doubted anything of a sexual nature was actually going to occur. But that didn't stop me from wanting to see what's really going on in that patrol car.

Using my best deer stalking techniques, I soundlessly made my way over to the car. A full moon lit my way around the trunk. As I approached and knelt down in the blind spot off the back right corner, I saw a big, white object shimmering in the moonlight. It looked like a big bowl of very white jello quivering like the car was moving. But I couldn't quite make out what I was seeing at first. Then, as I slowly stood up, I got a crystal clear view of the interior... Sweet Jesus!

It was Gim's big ass, and it was moving like twenty-one jackhammers breaking up concrete. My boy was going to town. After about fifteen seconds, I heard what could only be described as what you'd expect from a wounded animal.

"Aaaargh. Aaspargh. Oh, baby. Oh yeah, Don't Sto– Arrwreegh, " Modine cried out with passion.

The retort that came from my friend wasn't much better. "Oh, ooh, uh, grugh, grugh, grugh, uh, oh."

I thought I was going to throw up, but instead I held it in as a thought passed through my spinning head.

My best bud had gone hoggin'.

Although I was happy that he lost his virginity, he might as well have been with a farm animal. Suddenly I heard a sound like an elephant in distress and saw the jello quiver again.

I quickly put my hands over my ears and moved briskly from the patrol car, not caring if they saw me. After what seemed like an eternity, I finally found the Buick and dove into the back seat. I shut my eyes and fell asleep trying to take myself to a far away place. Anywhere but where I was. I was startled awake when Gim rapped on the window. Cold sweat was pouring down my face.

"I think I'm in love, Rango," said Gim.

And as supportive as I could be I asked, "Have you lost your fucking mind?"

"I'm telling you, man. I've found the girl of my dreams."

"You're in love with fucking Officer Modine Gunch?"

"Yup, me and Modine're gonna go steady."

I paused for a moment as I took it all in.

"Have you lost your fucking mind?"

I then went on to give Gim every reason I could think of to convince him that what he was saying was utterly insane.

"She's too old for you. She's screwing everybody in town. She's a muff diver!"

"That'll change when she gets a steady diet of Gim's love luger. Besides, Rango, I like a woman with a little experience. I've outgrown these silly high school girls."

What have I done?

I had just one thing left in my arsenal to bring Gim back to reality. I took my time, letting out the words softly.

"Gim, Modine's a bowler."

What was a face full of joy and hope turned to complete disgust.

"That bullshit's not gonna work, Rango.

"No bullshit, Gim. Modine's a regular bowler."

"Rango, we been through a lot of shit together, but if you don't take that back right now, I'm gonna whip your ass."

"Gim, I wouldn't even joke with you about something this serious. Look, Erskine Brown and Tommy Munn double-date with two girls over at Newton, and they work in the sandwich shop right beside the Bowl-O-Rama. They just happened to mention that they see Modine and Bertha Butts every Friday night when they pick up their dates. They either going in or coming out of the bowling alley."

"Maybe Modine's going in to serve an arrest warrant or something."

I gently added, "Gim, they both got their own custom ball and shoes. I'm really sorry, buddy. I hate to be the one telling you this, but I can't let you throw your life away on someone in a bowling league. I swallowed hard and put the proverbial nail in the coffin.

"She's got a bowling shirt with her nickname on it, says 'Cuffs'. I'm so sorry."

"Wow. Now, I'm pissed. That bitch took advantage of me. And to think I would have thrown it all away – on a bowler. Thanks, man."

After a quick hug, which we swore to never tell anyone about, Gim and I continued on our big trip to Maw Shoeman's. Getting in the car, Gim said, "Uh, Rango, you wanna stop in the Embassy Club, see if Foxy and Passion are there? Might get some free trim 'fore we get to Maw's."

"I don't think so, Gim, I think you've done enough hoggin' this evening. We're gonna go to Maw's and get you some 'Grade A' puss. Your second piece is gonna be choice; I'm gonna see to that."

We finally pulled into the parking lot of Maw's. It was shabby and run down with three small mobile homes on the side where the girls lived and made their living. Their home office, as it were.

"Ready for your birthday present, Gim?" I asked.

Gim took a deep breath, "Ready, Rango. I'm a little nervous though. Why don't I buy us a beer first?"

"I'd love a beer, Gim, and don't be nervous. The worst that can happen is that you won't get it up, or if you do get hard, you cum like a jackrabbit, or you'll just get herpes. No biggie."

Gim said sarcastically, "Thanks, Rango, you're a real friend."

"Just jacking around with you, Gim. Ain't nothing bad gonna happen."

"You really think so, Rango? Think I'd have a shot at Pamela Sue?"

"Gim, my ol' bud, I predict you'll be throwing rocks at Pamela Sue 'fore this is over. I see you going out with some real beauty queens, maybe even the Meridian Stockyard Queen."

That last little confidence builder seemed to have done the trick.

"Let's go, Rango. Time to unroll the ol' love log."

When we walked into Maw's, a typical beer joint, a half dozen blinking beer lights greeted us. That, and five or six split tails sitting around in various stages of undress. Maw Shoeman greeted us from across the room. "Hey, boys, have a beer on me. I'm just interviewing a new girl."

We bellied up to the bar, got our free beer, and took a table near where Maw was interviewing the potential whore.

"Honey, on your application you checked 'No' under the question 'Active sex life,'" Maw said.

"Yes, Ma'am. I usually just lay real still," she replied.

Maw rolled her eyes, then continued, "It also says that you're from Chile."

"Yes, ma'am," she answered.

One of the other whores overheard and spoke up.

"Oh, I love chile."

"No, ya idiot, she's from Chile; it's a city in Canada," another chimed in.

Maw just went on with the interview, "Honey, it says here on your application that one of your goals is to promote world peace. How exactly would you go about that?"

The girl replied earnestly, "First thing I'd do is make a rule: all armies have to wear the same color uniforms; that way nobody'd know who they were spos'ed to be fighting, and everybody'd think they were on the same side."

Maw suppressed a chuckle and continued her questioning.

"It also says that some day you'd like to be a marine biologist."

"Oh, yes, ma'am, or an Air Force biologist or even a Navy biologist. I just kinda like the Marine uniform a little better."

Maw sighed and continued. "It says on your application you were born in July. You must be a Cancer."

"Oh, no ma'am. I never had cancer. Had a little VD once. Penicillin cured it right up. Had an aunt that had cancer, though. But I think it's in rebellion now."

Maw smiled to herself, "Welcome to Maw Shoeman's, baby. You can start tonight if you want. Maw looked at her application again. "Honey Potts? Is that your real name?"

"No, ma'am," she answered. "Real name's Ida Lou Clapp. Honey Potts' my professional name."

I broke in, "Maw, my dear friend Gim would be honored to be Miss Potts' first customer. It's my present to him on his sixteenth birthday."

Honey spoke up, "Oh, that's so sweet. Sixteen years old, huh? When were you fifteen?"

Gim looked puzzled. "Uh, a year ago?"

Honey continued, "So, you have a birthday every year then? See, I used to go with a boy only had a birthday every four years. He was born on leap year or something, or maybe it was the equinox. Anyway, when he was only five he already had a 10-inch cock." And apparently, I thought to myself, it had been used to bang her head against a headboard one too many times.

Maw spoke up, "That'll be ten dollars for your friend's birthday present. I'm knocking a dollar off the regular price for the special occasion."

"Gee, thanks, Maw," I said, handing over the ten spot.

"Happy Birthday, Gim," I said, patting him on the back..

His eyes got misty, "Thanks, Rango, this is the best birthday present I've ever had."

Honey chimed in, "And I'll make sure it's one you always remember."

"Ready, Honey?" Gim said eagerly, taking her by the hand.

Maw said, "Take Cabin number three, Honey. That mattress hadn't been peed on but a few times."

And so off they went, the future Rhodes Scholar and the hapless Gim, to engage in a night of lust not seen since the days of the Roman Empire. I stifled a sob and ordered another beer. Just as it arrived on the bar, so did a canopy of blue lights through the pine trees. Seconds later, the entire Lauderdale Sheriff's Department was in the parking lot, three squad cars and four deputies. They were led by the old warhorse, Sheriff Leland Dawkins. In the late 1950's in Mississippi about ninety-five percent of the county sheriff's departments were paid off in either goods or services. But while illegal liquor, games of chance, prostitution, nude dancing, and even midget tosses were wide open in Lauderdale County, Sheriff Dawkins was up for re-election. Which meant that they had arrived with the intention of making their annual bust for the benefit of the Southern Baptists. And so in they came.

"Hello, Leland," Maw said, addressing the sheriff. "What brings you out this time of night? Baptists on your ass again?"

The sheriff replied, "Hello, Lucille. Yeah, just making our usual rounds 'fore the election. Everything looks pretty good here. Looks like you got some new girls in, real lookers, too," he said, scanning the room.

"Yeah, Sheriff, a real crop of geniuses, but I don't pay 'em to think. Seems to be a good group, most of 'em out of New Orleans."

"Well, Lucille, we got to make our rounds so we'll be on our way. You take care of yourself now."

"You, too, Leland. Drop by one night, and I'll treat you to a free sample."

The sheriff laughed. "No thanks, Lucille. I might go into the hole on that deal. I never put my peter in my pocketbook."

With a wink and a smile, Maw said, "Into the hole? But Sheriff, ain't that the point?"

With that, the sheriff and his deputies were out the door. Before I knew it, I was right behind them.

"Uh, Sheriff Dawkins, sir. Can I speak to you a minute? I'm Sidney Spears from over in Decatur. I played Babe Ruth baseball with your boy Mike last summer. I go by the nickname of Durango."

"Well, pleased to meet you there, Durango. I've heard Mike speak highly of you. What's on your mind, Durango?" asked the sheriff.

"Well, I'd like to ask you a big favor. You see, I'm treating my best bud to one of Maw's girls for his sixteenth birthday, and I'd like to make this one that he'll never forget."

"Well, I'm very busy, but what is it you want me to do?"

"Well, sheriff, I was wondering if you and your men could go over to cabin number three and knock on the door and yell 'Police' like they do in the movies. Then act like you gonna arrest Gim and put him in the squad car. After a few minutes, I'll come over and ask you to release Gim into my custody."

The sheriff chuckled. "Hell, son, that don't sound like much of a birthday present to me. When he sees us, he'll need two Popsicle sticks and some duct tape to get his dick hard again. Might not get his birthday treat after all."

I replied, "Sheriff, don't worry about Gim. He'd screw a bush if he thought it had a snake in it."

The sheriff chuckled again, "You're the boss, Durango."

The sheriff turned around, "Come on boys, we gonna do a shakedown on cabin number three. Remember, this ain't real, just a little birthday joke."

One of his deputies spoke up, "You want us to cover the back of the cabin, Sheriff?"

"Hell, no. We're not trying to capture anybody. We just gonna have a little fun with Durango's buddy."

"Take your positions, boys," whispered the Sheriff as his men quietly lined up at the front door. The sheriff put on his game face. "Ready, boys? On my count. Three… two…"

"One!"

The door of the cabin nearly broke away as four police officers went crashing in. Flashlights were everywhere illuminating the musty love nest. Of course, I was right behind to make sure I would see the look on the Gim's face.

"Police!" they all shouted together. The darkness of the room made it difficult to adjust, and I had no idea of what I was seeing. I blinked a few times, but my brain was still receiving the same image. I began to make out the shape of a large person dressed in nothing but panties and a bra and sporting bright red lipstick. I began to make out large thighs, much larger than those of Miss Honey Potts. A second later I thought my brain had played a trick on me.

Gim!

Startled like a deer in headlights, he did what any normal person would have done in these circumstances. He ran like hell. Gim hit the back door of cabin three and knocked it totally off its hinges, then sprinted all the way to the swamp adjacent to Maw's. At the murky water's edge there was no hesitation; he continued on. For the first two steps he was literally walking on water, then gravity got the best of him, and Gim was up to his neck in swamp filth and alligator shit. I screamed at the top of my lungs.

"Gim, come back, it's only a prank!"

The sheriff and deputies were all down on the floor laughing insanely and trying to catch their collective breath. Miss Honey Potts, after her initial scare, was clearly pissed and had magically lost her southern accent.

"You mother fuckers! What you doing coming in here like some wop assholes?"

Knowing it was myself that caused all this, I quickly took off after Gim to confess to everything. I climbed into the three-hole Buick and slowly started driving back to the main highway. I switched the lights on high beam and began using the car horn to send out a steady beep.... beep, beep, that Gim and I had always used as a signal. I continued beating out the little beat on the car horn, stopping every hundred yards or so to listen for Gim's yell.

I heard the dogs barking first. It echoed through the swamp trees at a distance, but seemed to get closer and closer. Then I heard the scream. The barking and screaming were headed right toward me. I beat out another rhythm on the car horn.

"Rango, Rango, help me!"

I tapped the horn faster and faster.

"This way, Gim, I'm over here!" I yelled back.

Then I spotted him. It was The Creature from the Black Lagoon all over again. Every inch of my poor friend's body was covered with a black layer of mud, scum, moss, and other disgusting, unidentifiable shit. Then I heard the reverb of several shotguns being fired.

"Quick, Gim, get yo' ass in the car. Let's get the hell out of here!"

Gim shouted, "Get this fucking car moving, Rango! I ran across a 'shine still back there in the woods. Damn bootleggers after me, and they ain't playing games."

"Duck down, Gim," I said as I stomped down on the accelerator. The Buick peeled rubber just as the dogs and bootleggers burst out of the swamp.

"We're safe now, Gim. Roll down yo' window, though. You smell like ass."

I knew the time would come when I would eventually have to tell my best friend that I screwed him over more than Miss Honey Potts could ever have, so I figured sooner was better than later.

"Gim, there's something I need to tell you...."

Gim interrupted, " No, Rango, there's something I need to tell you. You saved my life tonight, and I'll never forget it."

I stammered, "No, Gim, you don't understand...."

Gim interrupted, "Here's what I understand. You're the best buddy anybody could have. I was dead meat back there. Damn perverts were gonna pull a Rock Hudson on me. And then you came along. I'll never forget this, Rango. Never."

"Aw, Gim, stop it. You'd done the same thing for me. Really, it was nothing. Only thing I regret is that I couldn't get to the cabin and warn you the deputies were there."

Gim replied, still breathing heavily, "Thanks again, Rango. I'll make it up to you if it takes the rest of my life."

"Aw, stop it, Gim. You're embarrassing me."

"Uh, Rango, you don't think any of this'll get back to Decatur, do you? That'd ruin my chances of getting a date with Pamela Sue."

I replied, "Gim, the only people that know about this are Maw and her whores and the sheriff and his deputies. Oh, sure, there'll be some laughter and jokes about you, but Gim, I'd say your secret's safe. Only thing, Maw Shoeman's is off limits to you in the future."

Gim exploded. "Off limits? Hell, Rango! I think I'm in love with Honey. I told her I'm gonna call her up for a date sometime. Thought I might take her home to meet Mama and Auntie Maw."

Daringly, I replied, "Sure, and maybe ya'll can try on clothes together."

For a long moment, there was silence, and I wondered if I still had a best friend. Before I could decide, Gim punched me as hard as he could in the arm. And staring straight ahead, with a wry smile he said, "Best birthday present I ever had."

The End

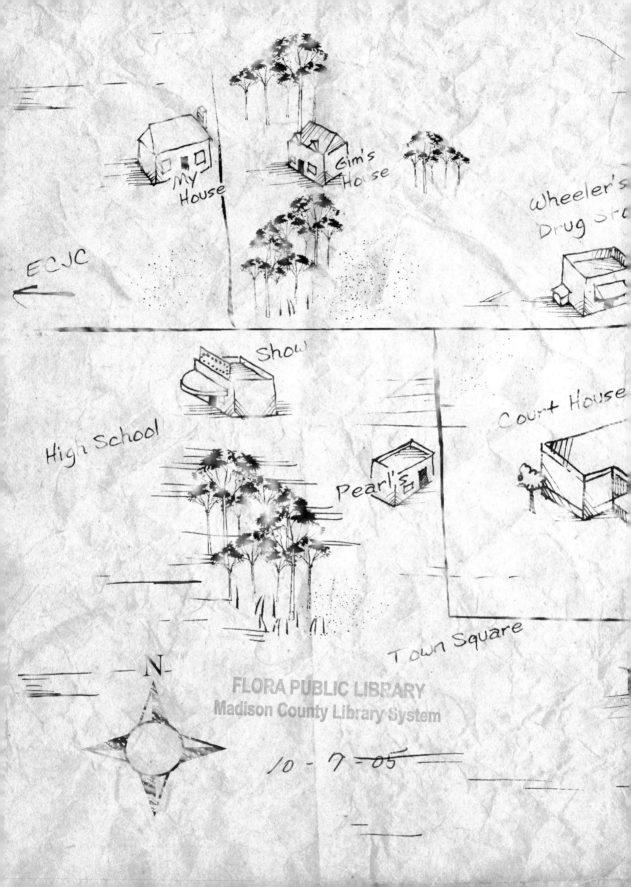

My House

Gim's House

Wheeler's Drug Sto

ECJC

Show

High School

Pearl's

Court House

Town Square

N

10 - 7 - 05